Christopher Fowler is an award-winning novelist, short story writer and scriptwriter best known for his dark urban fiction. He has written seventeen novels and well over 100 short stories in nine volumes. In addition to this new collection, Serpent's Tail have published three earlier volumes: *Personal Demons*, *The Devil in Me*, and *Demonized*.

His short stories have appeared in *The Time Out Book of London Short Stories*, *The Time Out Book of New York Stories* and *The New English Library Book of Internet Stories*, *Dark Terrors*, *Best New Horror*, *London Noir*, and many others.

He reviews for the *Independent on Sunday*, and has written articles and columns for a variety of magazines including *Time Out*, *Black Static*, *Smoke*, *Pure*, *Dazed And Confused*, *Big Issue*, as well as several broadcast dramas for the BBC.

Praise for Christopher Fowler's work

Personal Demons

'A reassuring wallow among wolves, ghost trains and the whole Judeo-Christian brat pack of predestination and sin' *Guardian*

'A writer of extraordinary imagination' *Sunday Express*

'Ghoulishly irresistible' *The Times*

'Compulsive – gruesome, gory and great fun' *Time Ou*

The Devil in Me

'Not merely beautiful writing. A hint of Promet *Kirkus Reviews*

'Sex toys, super models, serial killers and the cult of ce observations of society today. The wonderful stuff…

Demonized

'Fowler's strength lies in the way he unveils the darker side of the ordinary: *Demonized* is scary precisely because it's so familiar… fresh and thought-provoking… Elegant and playful prose' *Guardian*

'Placing his artistry somewhere between HG Wells, Iain Banks and Ian McEwan, Fowler manages to pull off a collision of black humour, thematic elegy, and dark, disturbing imagery through his elegant and energetic prose' *Big Issue in the North*

'Fowler proves time and time again that he can write short fiction like few other authors are able – confident and adept and readable. Certainly a must-buy' *Shivers*

'With a clear understanding of the legacy of the ghost and horror story, but a contemporary edge, Fowler explores the shady areas and the darkness before the dawn' *Bookmunch*

'Thrillingly taut, perverse and nasty imaginings' *Independent on Sunday*

'Fowler's powerful narratives are subtly affecting and make you think again about the way you look at the world around you' *Buzz*

old devil moon

Short stories by
Christopher Fowler

First published in 2007 by Serpent's Tail,
an imprint of Profile Books Ltd
3A Exmouth House
Pine Street
London ECIR OJH
website: www.serpentstail.com

ISBN 978 1 85242 925 6

Designed and typeset at Neuadd Bwll, Llanwrtyd Wells

Printed in the UK by CPI Bookmarque,
Croydon, CRO 4TD

10   9   8   7   6   5   4   3   2   1

contents

This collection is for Roger Gray, book liberator, book lover – and for the beautiful Izabella.

'One dark night, gonna fly right out my window, gonna fly so high in the night sky that the people below won't see me go.' —Jeffrey Comanor

foreward: the sinister life

This is my first new collection of dark fiction in nearly five years. Every story has a backdrop to its writing, and real events have a way of filtering down to inform even the most whimsical pieces. Over the course of creating these tales, all sorts of disturbing and unbelievable things were happening in the news. These are just a few I noted.

In Stockton-On-Tees, a poverty-stricken family succumbed to heroin use, and as her son died, the distraught mother went to bingo to try and win money for his gravestone. Ironically, George Bush chose her neighbourhood for a visit, and his security operation cost the British government a million pounds.

Pat Robertson, the US Christian evangelist, appeared on national television suggesting it would be a good idea for American hit squads to murder the president of Venezuela for his oil.

In London, a *Big Brother* house member simulated masturbation with a beer bottle on a channel subsidised for its contribution to quality television, and garnered more column inches in the national press than the US government's final refusal to cut CO_2 emissions.

In Japan, internet suicide groups were infiltrated by bogus suicidees planning to kill their fellow members for cash, which had the effect of making teenagers think twice about killing themselves in groups.

In Britain, an eleven-year-old girl was rushed to hospital suffering from a heroin overdose, while on the same day another announced she was pregnant and looking forward to being a pre-teen mum. It was revealed that half a million UK children belonged to street gangs.

In Plymouth, four mothers filmed themselves goading their toddlers into fighting each other. They did it, they said, to make their children hard and stop them from turning into 'faggots'.

In America, where an estimated 37 million citizens live below the poverty line, one Christian Right group decided to improve the world by financing trips to locate the remains of Noah's Ark, while another threatened to kill cinema owners for agreeing to book *Brokeback Mountain* into theatres.

The suicide business returned to normal in Japan, and the new year's death toll tripled.

Endemol, the makers of *Big Brother*, produced a season casting mentally ill contestants in the hopes that they would humiliate themselves and hurt each other on live television. With racism shown to be endemic on the programme, public opinion finally started mobilising against them, but the producers felt that its export market had been 'fantastically improved' by the sight of burning effigies in India. It emerged that the show was most popular with schoolchildren.

Hollywood turned the World Trade Center attacks into an upbeat action movie, and the director toured with the fireman pulled from the wreckage, thus rendering the film impervious to criticism. US presidential advisors announced that they would solve global warming by 'inventing something', even though they wouldn't directly acknowledge it was happening. Belize pressed the United Nations World Heritage Sites Committee to acknowledge that climate change was destroying its famous reef, but the US decided to reject the petition because it would 'damage harmonious relations with the committee'. Meanwhile, the Northern hemisphere posted the highest average temperatures in over 2,000 years.

Taxpayer-subsidised Channel 4 announced its latest adventure into the amelioration of the human spirit: 'Wank Week'.

Our language continued to change. 'Creationism' became 'Intelligent Design', and 'Liberalism' became 'Godlessness'. 'Post-9/11' has become shorthand for anything we should be wary of. 'Democracy' was rebranded as 'Free Market', and came to mean 'Something You Choose To Have Or We Will Bomb You'. Labour turned Tory, Tory turned Green, and caring was something you did before and after your career.

Surveys were published with some interesting data tucked inside them. Only 60 per cent of women in the UK were now sexually active. Over a million British schoolchildren were experiencing mental health problems. Over a million elderly people went an entire month without seeing someone they knew. London's most rapidly growing demographic group was deemed to be single people living in apartments full of gadgets.

Experimental drugs tested on six English volunteers placed them at death's door and inflated their heads 'like the Elephant Man'.

Chinese cockle pickers returned to Morecambe despite the fact that nineteen employees had drowned in one afternoon while digging for shellfish.

In County Durham, a giant inflatable sculpture designed to create a sense of harmonious calm took off with thirty people trapped inside it, killing two and injuring a dozen others.

A Russian spy died after being poisoned by a radioactive spray applied to his sushi. And the dead journalist Alistair Cooke had his legs sawn off and replaced with drainpipes by New Jersey-based Biomedical Tissue Services, a modern-day Burke & Hare company prosecuted for trafficking in body parts.

With CCTVs adopting face-recognition strategies and electronic tracers of every kind invading British society, Orwell's concept of a Big Brother state truly became a reality when a contestant on *Big Brother* admitted she had no idea what the title of the show meant.

At this point, I thought about abandoning the book altogether. How could I compete with real life, which was more fascinating and relevant than weird fiction?

You might legitimately ask why I haven't mentioned all the good things that happened, but the fact is that I'm drawn to the left side, a prevalent darkness. Dark fiction is still something I produce in my spare time, like building galleons out of balsa wood or repairing clocks. Friends are happier thinking of it as a hobby, my other job, an alternative to watching television. When you write for yourself, you don't think so hard about accumulating readers. That's the peculiar part of authorship – books are imaginary units sold like tins of biscuits, and the sweeter you make the biscuit taste, the more popular it becomes. But sometimes you need to invoke the bitter, because you'd get sick on a diet of chocolate.

The establishment pays scant attention to authors who write from the sinister side of life, but I think the fantastical can often hold the key to reality. I try to do my part in upholding a fine, if somewhat peculiar, literary tradition, one that paradoxically frees me to do whatever I want. Let the world change. Let the news make our jaws drop in disbelief. Let it inform our writing, even just a little, even though we just tell stories. The day we stop being amazed by everything that goes on around us, *that's* when life really becomes sinister.

Christopher Fowler
King's Cross, London, 2007

the threads

'I don't know how people can bring themselves to live like this.'

Verity studied her surroundings in clear discomfort. She had perfected a way of standing with her fist on her left hip, legs apart, her fawn skirt stretched across her thighs, in a manner that unsettled the Muslims who passed around her. Even when she was well covered, she had a way of appearing faintly indecent if she chose to. She wore heels, even though the earth floor was rutted and muddy. At this time of the morning the souk had yet to fill with tourists. Sunlight filtered through the overhead slats, casting matchstick stripes across the confluence of winding narrow alleyways. In front of each store sat a boy, usually aged between ten and sixteen. Too many kids with nothing to do, too many vendors selling the same things, shoes and bags and lamps, shopkeepers peering out of the shadows to collar passing trade. Outside the medina, the warm dry desert air was starting to rise. Here it was still cool.

'It's a less evolved society, but not much worse for that,' said her husband, Alan Markham. 'They've a tendency to retreat to the safety of religious dogma, which is rather touching but not especially harmful, except *in extremis*. And of course bribery is a recognised part of their culture. A service is performed and money changes hands, it's seen as completely normal here.' He leaned in to smell the cardamom seeds and cumin powder that lay in the great raked trays of a shop. A young man popped up in an opened panel among the spices, so that he appeared to be buried to his shoulders. All of the vendors stood like this, at the centre of their wares. 'You have to strike a bargain that's less than half the original price they suggest. It's all part of the game. Give them too much and they'll have no respect for you. They're like children.'

'Nothing looks very clean. Mind you, they have to wash five times a day, so I suppose that counts for something. The hotel has Moulton Brown shampoo in the bathroom, did you notice?' Verity tried not to be too judgemental, but always found it difficult.

Markham set off again, brushing aside the entreaties from the spice seller. Verity had difficulty keeping up. She had seen how most of the English tourists behaved, the wives clutching their husbands' arms as if expecting to be torn from their sides by madmen. The secret of enjoying North Africa, she felt, was not to be afraid of people simply because they were different. Somewhere far away from the medina were modern roads, shops and offices, although they were probably run with hopeless inefficiency. But here in the medina, this was how everyone wanted to imagine those yellow clay towns built on the edge of the Sahara, all back alleys and burkas, the call of the muezzin, the stench of the market.

She watched her husband waving away the vendors as he studied the storefronts with an anthropological eye. *One last chance to start again*, he had pleaded, *let's get out of London, just the two of us. Things will be better this time.* They needed to be; the money had all but dried up and she did not want to return to work, just to bail him out of another failed business. Truth be told, she no longer had much faith in him. These days, most of their conversations were really arguments that neither side could win.

Verity backed against a wall as a moped driven by a small boy hurtled past. Incredibly, he was holding fifteen cardboard trays filled with eggs between his body and the handlebars. On the way in from the airport they had passed a couple on motor scooters carrying a bed between them.

'In London you don't say a word when the restaurant bill comes to an absolute fortune, but here you'll haggle over a few pence just because they tell you to do it in the guidebook,' she admonished, stopping to look at a handful of sickly chameleons climbing over each other in bamboo cages.

A huge-eyed brown child smiled up at her from behind the cages. She and her husband had not chosen to have children. She had seen how other people's had grown up, spoiled, rude, lost. The children here were different. They helped their parents, and appeared to enjoy doing so. Families were involved in the great adventure of living. They weren't shut away from each other.

'I know what I'm doing. If you want to buy silks, you have to be patient and let me do the negotiating. It's my job, after all. You at least used to have some respect for that. It was what brought in the money.'

Alan Markham had cut away from the octagonal blue and white fountain that piddled feebly in the centre of the medina, where the men washed their hands and feet at prayer-call, and was heading into the manufacturing quarters. Here there were virtually no women to be found, only boys with blackened, poisoned nails, hammering at curlicued spiderwebs of metal, bed-heads and chandeliers, and men with ruined lungs, seated cross-legged in the dense, dust-filled air of their workshops, chipping away at delicate white triangles of plaster. Here, too, were the tanners and dyers, working beneath hanging pelts and skeins of crimson wool that were draped above them like the guts of great beasts.

'God, it stinks.' Verity held her handkerchief against her nose.

'This is where we have to go, away from the tourist traps. You said you wanted to visit somewhere different.' He shouted above the sound of blacksmiths hammering, backlit by sunsprays of sparks. It was as if they had stepped backstage, behind the artifice of tourist-friendly exotica, to where the real work was done. In one workshop a hundred crimson lanterns hung at different heights, bathing the walls blood red. Alan had bought and sold Anatolian and Kurdish silks for several years. He knew what was valuable, and what was rubbish. When he found the store he was looking for, he walked straight in, ignoring the sales pitch of the boy who had been left outside to hector passers-by.

As his eyes adjusted to the gloom, he examined the neatly folded stacks of rugs in burnt oranges and reds that had been piled from floor to ceiling around the narrow shop.

'Tell me what you are looking for,' said the middle-aged man with the gap in his white teeth, welcoming them. Markham's peppery hair and striped cuff shirt had marked him as an Englishman. The shopkeeper was always earnest, but especially serious when he recognised potential in a customer. Selling was an art he had carefully studied for nearly fifty years. The Englishman was more than a casual browser trying to keep his wife amused. There was something in the way he turned and regarded the towers of cloth. The shopkeeper's boy was unrolling silk scarves in razor-blue and sunset red, but only the wife was bothering to cast her eyes over them. She seemed less comfortable than he, which was unusual. It was the women who tended to lead the way into his shop. Markham accepted a dark plum from a brass tray and sucked at it as he browsed.

'Upstairs?' he asked, indicating the floor above, his index

finger raised. With a deferential nod, the storekeeper led the way up a narrow staircase lined with tablecloths. The room over the shop had no more than four square feet of space free at its centre. Every other inch was filled with silks, tapestries, scarves, runners, and cloths graded by shade and shape, endlessly refolded and arranged. The lathe-and-plaster ceiling bulged threateningly inwards, making the room even smaller.

A tiny filigree table had been set out for mint tea. The boy appeared and poured three glasses, not from a great height, as waiters did for tourists, but with the spout lowered.

Markham was looking for something in particular. The air was full of tiny iridescent carpet fibres that turned the shaft of sunlight angled from the single high window into a rainbow. Verity leaned back against the rolls of material, lifting the weight from her heels. It was December, a pleasant temperature, a good time to come here, but the heavy food exhausted her, and the arid air made her thirsty all the time. No wonder they valued their shade so much, designing their public buildings to capture and display the shadows in appealing arrangements. She eyed the glass of tea and decided not to risk the germs that might lie on the rim.

'This is for your wife,' said the shopkeeper, waiting for the boy to unroll more fabrics, each brighter than the last.

'Oh, I don't know.' Markham raised his leonine head and puffed out his cheeks, affecting an air of diffidence. 'Something heavier, in blue perhaps…something more special.'

The shopkeeper instructed the boy in Arabic, then followed him to find the cloth. Verity shot her husband a look, raising an eyebrow. He pursed his lips faintly. Code: *don't say anything.* He had seen something in the corner, and was moving towards it. He casually examined the material, pouting, pulling, rubbing.

'I like this one.' She pulled out an indigo silk square with a scarlet rose at the centre. Slender white tendrils snaked from its core to the outside edges.

'Put it down, it's tourist shit.' He could be most dismissive of her tastes. He suddenly stopped examining the object of his interest, dropping his hand as the shopkeeper returned. She had seen him do this before, but never with such studied nonchalance. He had to be very excited about something to appear this bored.

He glanced at the bolts the boy and the old man unfolded before him, but she knew he was barely seeing them, even though he launched into a half-hearted negotiation for two sparkling ocean-green tablecloths.

'I think I need to discuss this with my wife for a minute,' he told the shopkeeper in respectful French. The old man understood, nodded and withdrew downstairs.

Markham leaped back to the cloth he had seen and pulled it free, showing her, a slit tapestry of geometric designs in red, yellow and black. 'Look at this. It's a Shahsevan kilim from the Hastari area of north-western Persia, around 1900, they're normally about six by twelve but this one's a runner, a weft-substitution weave finished in cotton. God knows what it's doing here. There's a name in the corner. I've never seen anything of this shape and size in the catalogues, but it's quite authentic. It's worth a small fortune.'

She could see the sweat beading above his ears. He was already wondering if there were others. Markham wiped his fidgety wet hands on his jacket. This was the equivalent of finding a signed first edition of *Bleak House* in a roomful of Jeffrey Archers. He called to the shopkeeper and went to work.

She had to grant him some grudging respect. He played the game very cleverly, slipping the cloth between a range of similar but worthless panels, offering to buy some little thing for his wife – would there be a discount if he bought several, this one, this one, perhaps *this one*? Carelessly casting them aside as if he didn't much care one way or the other – *pour amuser la dame*.

But it was not to be. The shopkeeper smiled politely and

removed the one essential item, replacing it carefully on the stack, lapsing back into French with a wagging finger. 'Pas en vente, désolé.'

'But she likes it.' Markham indicated his weary wife. *Don't rope me into this*, she thought. He gave a little shrug. 'I think it's rather a nice little thing.' He could not help looking back at the runner. The implication: *Too bad it's not for sale; your loss*.

The old man seemed to consider for a moment, but a cloud passed over his eyes, and he became intractable. Markham offered what he considered to be a good sum, then a little more, but only because he knew that the tapestry was worth a hundred times that amount.

Two American girls bustled into the tiny attic and acted as if no one else was there, climbing over the bolts to pull down the surrounding stacks. To Verity's surprise, her husband suddenly clapped his hands and gave in with good grace. 'Never mind then, just these silks. The big shawl for my wife, and these two as a gift for my mother.'

The shopkeeper seemed relieved. He and the boy immediately started to prepare the purchase as Markham made way for his wife and another bundle toppled over behind them, cascading rainbows of satin down the staircase. Verity thought he would insist on bullying the price lower, but he did not. The boy was dealing with the American girls, and the old man was deftly tying ribbons over brown paper as Markham took another plum from the hospitality tray, leaving it in his mouth as he thumbed notes from his back pocket.

As they moved into the street outside, he took her elbow and guided her into the first turn-off. 'Slow down – my heels,' she said, but he kept up the pace. 'Why did you use plastic to pay? He'd have gone cheaper for cash.' She knew something was up, and realised what it was when she saw the tip of the fabric protruding from his jacket. 'You didn't steal it.'

'He had no idea of its value. It would have gone to waste up there, simply waiting to be attacked by weevils.'

The sun was high in the market square. Fortune tellers, street pharmacists, tumblers, acrobats, water bearers and snake charmers were out in force. Markham and his wife made for the post office behind the colonnade, and queued in the hard bright hall beneath slow-turning fans as Markham repacked the item, folding it tightly into the brown paper parcel. He seemed uncharacteristically indecisive, breaking out of line at the last moment.

'What's the matter with you?' she asked. 'If you're feeling guilty, take it back.'

'I was going to post it home, but I'm thinking about customs.' He tapped the package. 'This is extremely valuable. And I don't feel guilty. I don't approve of returning antiquities, not if they're only going to be stored in some filthy old museum with poor security, or worse still in a tradesman's shop.'

'Then let's go back to the rhiad and get some lunch. I'm hot and tired. I want a shower.'

He was leading her out of the post office when she heard a sharp crack. He had bitten down on the plum stone. 'Christ.' He clutched his jaw and winced. 'Jesus.' The pain was bad enough to make him stop dead.

'You're making a fuss. Show me.' It had sounded awful, like a cap exploding. She forced him to open his mouth. The stone had split an upper left molar clean in half. He shook her hand aside and spat blood on the ground. A piece of tooth came out with it. He let out a groan.

'How many times have I told you before? You had to go and—' She tried to keep her annoyance in check. 'You should get the rest of the tooth taken out. They'll be able to find someone at the rhiad.'

The girl at their hotel appeared unconcerned. 'There are many dentists,' she said.

'Well, where are they?' asked Verity with impatience, as if expecting one to walk through the curtained entrance to the reception office.

'In the square. I can arrange for a boy to take you—'

'In the square? No, no—' She had seen the ones in the square, seated cross-legged before pyramids of brown pulled teeth arranged on dirty squares of cloth. The higher the pile, the more successful they were considered to be. 'My husband has broken his tooth. He needs to have all of the pieces removed or there could be an infection.'

'Yes, yes, the square.' The girl was trying to provide her guests with the best solution, but they seemed to want something else. She watched blankly as they headed off to their room, arguing with each other.

After half an hour of reading brochures and making incomprehensible calls, Verity rose from the bed and went to change her shoes. 'Well, nobody else seems to be available, and if you're absolutely sure you can't wait until we get back to London, we'll have to do as she suggested,' she said. 'Come on, you won't be able to eat if we don't do something. Just have it cleaned up. You can get it replaced back in Harley Street.'

'A street dentist, are you mad? Their practices are two hundred years out of date. Do you have any painkillers on you?'

'Did you see anything remotely resembling a pharmacy near here? We can try to find one, but don't look at me – I took my last Valium yesterday.'

'All right, we'll go back to the square and I'll walk past, but I'm not going to use one if he's not clean.'

They returned to the square to find three dentists still sitting cross-legged in the winter sunshine, patiently waiting for custom. Markham regarded each in turn before settling on the third, who was at least the most senior. 'Might as well be this one,' he said. 'He's got the biggest pile of teeth in front of him.'

The dentist gestured at his triangular footstool. When he smiled, he revealed a row of white teeth too peppermint-perfect to be real. 'Don't be worried,' he said in perfect English. 'I have never lost a patient yet.'

Markham seated himself while the dentist rinsed his hands with bottled water. Verity eyed the antique instruments spread out on his sheet with suspicion. She watched while the dentist pushed Markham's head back and made his examination. He soaked a white cotton pad in something from a fluted amber bottle and rubbed it over her wincing husband's gum. 'To numb your mouth,' he explained.

'He's right,' Markham assured his wife, gape-mouthed. 'It's already working.'

'This is your wife?' asked the dentist chattily.

'Yes,' Verity confirmed, stepping nearer.

'Perhaps you should go away for a few minutes. It is better.'

'No, I'm perfectly fine. I don't get squeamish.'

'I mean it is better for me.'

'Oh.' The local women were never seen on the streets unless they were shopping. Feeling vaguely affronted, Verity turned away and looked at the distant shops edging the souk.

Selecting a fearsome instrument that looked as if it had been designed to pull up floorboard nails, the dentist began to extract the pieces of Markham's broken tooth.

A few minutes later, he came across the square to find her. She was seated in the faded first floor café of the Hotel de Paris. 'Fifty dirhams,' he said, pleased with himself. 'He wanted more but I didn't see why I should.' He drew out a seat and looked around for a waiter.

'Show me,' said Verity. 'Oh, he's put a cap in there.'

'Just a temporary replacement until I get back, to stop any germs from getting in. He got all the pieces out and cleaned up the wound, then dried it with some kind of herbal paste to stop infection. I daresay one could go to a homeopathy clinic in Mayfair and pay a fortune for the same thing.'

'Well, you've changed your tune,' she said with a rueful smile. 'Half an hour ago you were calling him a savage.'

'Then I'm prepared to admit I was wrong.'

'Do you think you should be drinking anything?'

'He said it would be fine. I'm not at all numb. It wasn't like one of those injections that turns your face into a piece of slack meat for three hours.' Still, he grimaced when he sipped a glass of chocolate.

They returned to the rhiad, read cheap paperbacks and lounged around until early evening, when they strolled out into the medina once more. Smoky stalls had been set up to serve evening meals of snail stew, lamb and pigeons pastry-baked in cinnamon and icing sugar, but most of the shops were still open, the same bored teens seated before stacks of slippers and leather handbags, stained-glass lanterns and mosaic vases. In clothing stores, sinister shop dummies cast from fifty-year-old moulds sported crooked dry wigs and faded fashion items.

Verity was bored. After a while, becoming lost in the backstreets of the medina was a very repetitive part of the exotic experience. She watched her husband tipping the guidebook into the shafts of dying sunlight, trying to find a particular restaurant that had signposted itself by being more expensive and harder to find than any of the rest, and wondered when their mutual affinity with one another had divided, leaving them with this marriage of inconvenience.

He found the place. They ate pastilla beneath a vast wrought-iron chandelier in a courtyard of topaz tiles, beside other Western couples who had run out of conversation. He was telling her about some colleague at work who was about to be fired when the food fell out of his mouth and he clutched the tablecloth so hard that their wineglasses shook to the floor, shattering. The waiters were solicitous, fearing the attack might be construed as food poisoning, and quickly helped him to his feet.

'What kind of pain is it?' she asked, trying to understand.

He was clutching his cheek on the side where the tooth had been removed. 'Let me see,' she pleaded, opening his mouth in the light of the restaurant foyer, but there was nothing beyond a little inflammation of the upper gum to indicate the source of the problem. Even so, she understood that it emanated from the replaced tooth. 'I'm taking you back to that dentist,' she insisted, knowing that the dentists had probably left their pitches for the night.

Back in the square, a pall of orange smoke hung over the great arena of food stalls. She was strong, and held him upright as they passed a row of lolling sheep heads laid out on a trestle table, their tongues protruding as if in mockery, their marbled eyes still and unflinching as flies danced across them. The area seemed less safe now. The colourfully costumed water bearers had been replaced by loitering rent-boys and matchstick-chewing men with watchful eyes. Drums played somewhere, badly amplified scratch beats aimed at luring Westerners into an empty bar.

'We should never have come here,' she said under her breath. 'We should have taken accident insurance.' He was growing heavy in her arms.

The dentists' pitches had been taken by hawkers selling cheap jewellery. A fight was breaking out nearby. She looked around. 'I don't know—'

The teenaged boy was slouching at the counter of a small café, flicking nuts into his mouth, watching the world pass. He wore a dust-stained burnous and fez. When he spotted Verity he stood up and stepped forward.

'You are looking for the dentist. I see you today. Your husband.' He mimicked a painful tooth.

'Yes, my husband—' she began gratefully, allowing him to slip from her arm to a chair. 'He is in terrible pain. We must see the dentist at once.'

'He has gone to my uncle for dinner, but I can take you there.' He reached down and placed Markham's arm around his waist, pulling him up. 'It is not far.'

They headed back into the souk, Verity following with her husband's panama hat gripped between her hands. The stores were lit with lanterns now. Fast-food chefs were turning pungent chunks of fried meat on skillets, decanting them into folds of bread. There were more women around. They hurried through alleys filled with beetling dark yashmaks, keeping close to the walls in order to avoid being run down by mopeds. Verity had a vague idea that they were near the tanneries once more, but every street looked the same.

'Here, here.' The boy led them into a store, then through the back into a second saleroom where the dentist sat drinking tea with his uncle.

'We meet again,' said the uncle, a rotund man with a gap in his teeth, rising to give them room. Verity struggled to place his face and failed. 'I sold you some silks. The dentist is my nephew, and this is his boy. We have been waiting for you.'

She felt suddenly fearful, but Markham appeared not to understand. They had been deliberately returned here, she was sure, as part of some cruel plot. She wanted to be home, to be done with all this – *foreignness*. The dentist was nodding and smiling inanely, as if to confirm her worst thoughts.

'Come, let us show you the source of the trouble,' said the shopkeeper, leading her husband to a stool. He pushed gently down on Markham's shoulders, manoeuvring him into position so that the dentist could get a better look, then wedged his hand into Markham's mouth. His fingers tasted of old carpets. Markham tried not to gag.

'Good, good.' The dentist smiled and nodded at his uncle. He reached into Markham's mouth and worked the cap loose, pulling it off and examining the inside. Her husband's groan of pain subsided into a whimper.

'Come, look.' The dentist beckoned her, tipping the cap so that she could see. Unnerved, Verity found it difficult to approach him. Something inside the tooth appeared to be moving. When she saw them, her hand flew to her mouth.

'I want my tapestry back,' said the shopkeeper. 'All you have to do is return it to me.'

'What is it?' asked Markham miserably. 'What's wrong?'

'I don't know what they are,' said his wife, unable to tear her eyes from the writhing crystalline threads that remained in the sticky blackness of the tooth cap. They looked like elvers, but finer, longer, like strands of living silk. With mounting dread she peered inside his mouth. The tiny worms had burrowed deep into the bloody, swollen cavity where his tooth had been, creating small mushroom-white boils. Silvery threads wriggled and vanished into livid flesh as the light from the overhead lanterns hit them. Markham released a terrible, rising howl of agony.

'We kill a sheep and grow them inside, they are parasites, very good for breaking down meat and making it tender. Too painful in someone who is still alive.'

She saw now how the security system worked, how they were all connected, the girl in the hotel, the dentist, the boy at the bar, how they all knew and protected each other, guiding tourists from place to place, manipulating them. She saw how they punished transgressions. 'For Christ's sake, Alan, will you explain to these people?'

Markham studied the shopkeeper with contempt. 'I don't know what you're talking about,' he persisted. She knew he would not admit to being wrong – he never did. He would not lose face, whatever the consequences.

'There is something you can take to kill them, and the pain will stop. It is very easy, and takes no more than a few minutes. If you don't they will continue to breed – and to eat.'

Markham tried to speak, but spluttered droplets of blood on to his chin.

'The tapestry,' the shopkeeper repeated. The dentist and the boy stood beside him in solidarity.

'How dare you accuse me of something I haven't done,' said Markham, his sense of outrage glinting through winces of agony. 'I'm British, I don't steal from people.'

'Please, sir, this can easily be resolved. We are all civilised human beings.'

'Civilised!' He spat the word back at them. 'Is that what you call yourselves? You hide away your women while you sell us your trash at inflated prices, and we buy from you because we pity you. You think we want to take home this sort of crap?' He threw his arm wide at the display of dazzling silks, almost falling. 'You force your children to weave your rugs and we buy them out of pity. Don't tell me you're civilised. You're nothing more than desert nomads who've been given calculators. You pray to Allah but you're working for the white man. Pigs and monkeys can be raised to do that.'

The shopkeeper climbed to his feet, indicating that the dentist and the boy should do the same. They gently ushered Markham and his wife back out of the shop, speaking across each other in Arabic. As soon as the couple were off the premises, they dropped the steel shutter with a slam.

The street was emptier now, and looked different. Verity supported him through the alleyways, but could not find the right route back. They moved deeper into the medina, where the streets were hardly lit at all, and the muddy path became almost impassable in places. She lost track of the time. Markham was slowing down, his breath growing shallower.

She could no longer hold him upright. She let him rest, studying his face in the lamplight. His right eye was bloodshot and swollen. Tiny threads of red and white had traced themselves across the shimmering cornea. His slick skin had yellowed, as the worms drew their vitality from within, leaving dead cells behind as they burrowed.

A tiny woman in a billowing chador hurried past. Verity held up her hand to indicate that she needed help but the woman darted out of the way, disappearing down a side alley.

Her skirt was stained with mud. She pulled the big shawl they had bought around her husband, wrapping his head tightly in it, and tied the other half around herself. Exhausted, they rested in the doorway of a derelict mosque, beneath the only street light, sliding slowly down into the shadows until they were sitting on their haunches. Markham was shaking hard now. He could no longer speak.

'Someone will come for us,' she assured him, whispering gently. 'There's nothing to be afraid of. Someone will come for us.'

He rested his head on her shoulder and fell into a stupor. The overhead light went out. In the sharpness of the African night, they looked for all the world like any of the other Muslim beggars in the market.

the lady downstairs

What annoys me most is that he doesn't notice.

There are so few females in his life, and the ones that he does meet are usually in distress or hiding something. They're titled, or troubled, or – well, one wouldn't use the word in polite company, but it also begins with a T, and may be preceded by the word 'Bakewell'. I see them all, because I see all of his clients. I open the door to them, I send them away or ask them to wait, or show them up the seventeen stairs to his room. You don't let a stranger into your house without noticing something about them, and there's usually something to notice. The ladies may have red-rimmed eyes and damp handkerchiefs, or may adopt a disdainful air to make me think they are the mistresses of their situations. The gentlemen are more obvious still, their rage barely concealed as they hop from one foot to the other, their eagerness to see my lodger brushing aside the most common courtesies. Sometimes our visitors are fearful, and search the street to make sure they have not been followed. These ones rush inside as if they have been scalded, and once my door is safely closed behind them, apologise for their behaviour, wringing their caps and glancing to the top of the stairs, half-expecting him to pop out of his rooms and solve their problems right in the hallway, as if I would allow such a thing.

'I've no objection to you conducting your business in private,' I warn him, 'but I will not have these types unburdening their woes in my thoroughfares, no matter how heart-wrenching they may be.' He finds my attitude hard to comprehend; I know he would see anyone anywhere if their circumstances fired his imagination, just as a doctor might attend a patient if certain symptoms aroused professional curiosity.

I tell you this so that you understand; I miss little of what goes on in this house. I keep a respectable establishment by making sure that those within it behave respectably. But Mr Holmes does not notice. The doctor is kindlier, but in his own way is just as bad. He remembers to wipe his feet, and thoughtfully enquires after my health, but his main concern is the one patient whose symptoms he will never fully understand, the patient with whom he spends more time than with Mary, his own wife.

I shouldn't complain, for a landlady's life is rarely interesting, and the comings and goings are a small price to pay for housing such a famous London figure. There are annoyances, of course: the infernal scratching of that violin, the muffled explosions from unstable compounds in the laboratory he has rigged up in my back room (without my permission), the immovable stains that appear on the carpets, the ghastly burning-cat smells that waft down from the landing, invariably at teatime when I am about to tuck into a kipper, the unsocial hours kept by a man who finds sleep a stranger. Yet I am fond of him because his enthusiasm leaves him so unprotected. He knows the doctor is concerned for his well-being. But he never notices me.

Of course, he is the Great Detective, and I am only the landlady. To hear him pronounce judgement you would think no one else was born with a pair of eyes. We don't all have to shout about it from the rooftops. But my job is to notice everything, though I get little thanks.

Allow me to present you with an example. Only last week, on a drizzling Tuesday night at half past ten, as I was readying myself for sleep, there came a knock at the door. The girl had gone up to bed, and I was left to greet the caller, a frantic lady of some forty summers, in a dripping fur hat, clutching a wet fox-collar about her throat.

'Is this the house of Mr Sherlock Holmes?' she asked, without so much as a good evening.

'Why yes,' I replied, 'and I am his landlady, Mrs Hudson, but Mr Holmes has left strict instructions not to be disturbed.'

'I must see him,' said the lady. 'It is a matter of the utmost urgency.' I say lady, for I assumed her to be one though she was not wearing gloves, and the wetness of her clothes suggested that she had not alighted from her own carriage, or even a Hackney. She had a bearing, though, and a way of looking that I have seen too often when ladies look at landladies.

'If you'd care to wait in the front room I'll see what can be done,' I told her, and trotted off upstairs. I am nervous of no one in my own house, but sometimes Mr Holmes can be alarming. On this night he spoke to me rudely through the door, and finally opened it a crack to see what was amiss. As I explained that a lady waited downstairs, I could see my lodger hastily rolling down the sleeve of his shirt, tidying something away and complaining that it really was too bad he should be disturbed in such a manner. Knowing him, I took this to be an agreement that he would see her.

'Is she in need of medical attention?' he asked briskly. 'Dr Watson is still away.'

'No,' I replied, 'but she is quite distraught, for she has run here in the rain without stopping to dress for visiting.' And I showed her up. As she passed me, I smelled essence of violets on her clothes, and something else I recognised but could not place, a nursery smell.

I stood on the landing, listening. She introduced herself as Lady Cecily Templeford, but then the door closed and I heard no more. Still, it was enough. I read the women's weeklies, so I knew that Lady Templeford's son recently married beneath him. It was quite the scandal among the leisured classes, which I am not part of, but I make it my business to read about their small sufferings, who is engaged to whom, and why they should not be.

I went to the parlour and searched through the periodicals in the fire bucket. I soon came to the story. The Honourable Archibald Templeford married Miss Rose Nichols after a brief engagement. His mother refused to attend the wedding nuptials on account of Miss Nichols' former profession, namely performing as a songstress in the twice-nightlies, where she was known as 'The Deptford Nightingale'. Miss Nichols subsequently gave birth to a baby boy named Godwin. I was still reading this item when the door to Mr Holmes' apartment slammed open.

'If you do not help me, I do not know what I shall do,' she said loudly enough to wake up the serving girl on the top floor. 'I have no one else to whom I can turn, and need not tell you what this would do to our family should the news be made public.' And with that she swept past me once more, almost knocking me flat, her grand exit marred only by her struggle with the front door latch.

'Allow me,' I offered, squeezing past to shove the lock, for the wood swells in wet weather, but for this help I received a look that could freeze a pond in midsummer.

'The poor lady seemed very distressed,' I ventured, wary of my lodger's reluctance to discuss his clients. 'I do hope you can help her.'

'That remains to be seen,' said Mr Holmes, 'but it is nothing you should concern yourself with, dear lady,' and with that he shut his door in my face. This does not bother me, for I am used to his ways, and I am just the landlady. I open the doors and close them. People pass me by. I stick to my duty, and they to theirs.

The next morning Mr Holmes went out, and did not return until five. He appeared haggard, in low spirits, and I gathered from his mood that the investigation he had undertaken was not going well. I knew he had visited the home of the Honourable Archibald Templeford because I heard him giving the cab driver the address, which was published in my weekly along with a fetching painting of the drive and grounds in Upper Richmond.

'How was your day, Mr Holmes?' I asked, taking his soaking greatcoat to hang in the hall.

'Somewhat less productive than I had hoped, Mrs Hudson,' he replied, 'though I venture to surmise not entirely without purpose.' He often speaks like this, saying much but revealing nothing. Most times, I have little interest in my lodger's cases. He does not vouchsafe their details, and wishes to discuss them with no one but the doctor. But sometimes I glean a sense of their shape and purpose, although I see them through the wrong end of a telescope, as it were, the clients coming and going, the snatches of hurried conversation, the urgent departures late at night, the visits from policemen like Inspector Lestrade, full of cajoling and flattery, and when those tactics fail, threats and warnings. It is like being backstage at some great opera, where one only glimpses the actors and hears snatches of arias, and the setting is all round the wrong way, and one is left to piece together the plot. Like any stagehand I am invisible and unheard, but a necessary requirement in the smooth running of the performance.

My lodger spent the next morning locked in his rooms, banging about, the ceiling above my dining room creaking like a ship in a tempest. Resolving to see what caused his agitation, and knowing he had not eaten, I took him some beef broth, and was gratified when he accepted it, bidding me enter.

'I worry you are letting this business with Lady Templeford tire you,' I ventured, only to have him fix me with a wild stare.

'What on earth do you mean, Mrs Hudson?' he snapped, sipping at the broth before setting it aside with a grimace.

'I noticed that because she arrived here in such agitation, you were compelled to deal with her case, despite being busy with other work.'

To my surprise he raised his long head and gave a great bark of laughter. 'Well Mrs Hudson, you will surprise us all yet,' he said. 'First Watson, and now you. I shall start to wonder if my investigative technique is catching. So tell me, what do you discern about the lady in question?'

'It's not my business to voice an opinion,' I said, wary of incurring his displeasure.

'Let's say for a moment that it is your business. It would be intriguing to know the female point of view.'

'I know she is upset by the marriage of her youngest son to a girl she considers to be of low morals,' I replied, 'and is shocked by the early arrival of a child. More than that I cannot tell.'

'But you have said much, perhaps without even realising it.' He inclined his head, as if seeing me through new eyes. 'The night before last, Lady Templeford's new grandchild was snatched from his cradle, and no one has seen him since. What do you make of that?'

'Its poor mother must be quite mad with grief,' I said, remembering the picture of Rose Nichols in my paper. Then I considered the enmity that existed between the bride and her mother-in-law, and how the son must be caught between them.

Mr Holmes was clearly thinking the same thing. 'Then take pity on Archibald, trapped between them, Scylla and Charybdis.

At six o'clock his wife Rose enters the nursery to wake and feed her son, and there where the child should be is only rumpled bedding. They search the house until half past six, when Archibald returns from the city, and are still searching when Lady Templeford arrives to dine with them.'

'There will be a dreadful scandal if you do not find it,' I said excitedly. 'Lady Templeford would naturally suspect her daughter-in-law, for a woman who sets a son against his mother will always be blamed, especially when there is a child involved.'

'Do you really think so?' Mr Holmes' eyes hooded as I continued.

'Mrs Drake, the lady who keeps house at number 115, informs me that Rose Nichols had a long-time suitor in the Haymarket, and there is talk that the child might be his.' I realised I had gone too far, offering more of an opinion than was wanted on the subject. 'Well, I must get on with my dusting,' I said, embarrassed. 'The parlour maid is off today and the coalman has trod dirt into the passage.'

He showed me his back with a grunt of disapproval before I had even turned to close the door.

I know my place. Landladies always do. I cannot help but form an opinion when I see so much going on around me. And, dare I say it, Mr Holmes is so convinced of his abilities he sometimes takes the long route to solve a simple puzzle. The disguises, for instance. I have seen him enter this house as a tramp, a blind man, a war veteran, on sticks, with a funny walk, first hopping, then dragging, in hats, in beards, in rags and on one occasion with a wooden leg, and frankly I have seen better impersonations at the Alhambra. I wonder that his suspects are not put off by laughing too hard. What is wrong with simply keeping out of sight? It is what a woman would do, because women know the ways of men.

But Mr Holmes does not know the ways of women. Oh, he

acts superior around them, opening the door in his smoking jacket, listening to their stories with his elbow on his knee and his hand at his chin, appearing the man of the world. Why, then, does he become flustered when Elsie offers to clean his rooms? Why does he watch her from the turn on the landing as she smoothes beeswax into the banisters? I shall tell you: it is because he sees the female form from afar, and puts women on a pedestal, because they have never been close enough to disappoint him, and he will not let them nearer.

But I am speaking out of turn again, for which you must blame a Scottish temperament. Let me describe the conclusion in the case of Lady Templeford.

The morning after I had spoken out of turn with Mr Holmes, Inspector Lestrade turned up on my doorstep. I took his coat and requested he wait in the parlour, for I do not want the police trampling mud upstairs. Mr Holmes came down presently. As my offer of tea was accepted, I stayed outside the door while I waited for the kettle to boil.

'Well, this is a fine business, Mr Holmes,' I heard the inspector complain. 'A baby kidnapped from its cot and no ransom note! It has been more than two days now, and I cannot hold off my men any longer for your shenanigans.'

'Your men will destroy any chance we have of uncovering the crime,' my lodger replied with ill-concealed temper. 'The answer lies in Rose Nichols' house, and I cannot have the scene damaged until I have ended my investigations.'

'But what have you uncovered? Precisely nothing, sir!'

'Not true, Inspector. Rose Nichols' nursery is situated at the back of the ground floor. Its door was shut with keys belonging only to the master of the house, and the rear of the building is surrounded by flower beds. You will recall that rain has fallen constantly for the last few days, and the garden earth is soft. Yet not so much as a single shoe or bootprint has been left beneath any of the windows. Nor was any latch or lock on either the door or windows forced. I must conclude, therefore, that Lady Templeford has indeed been right in her suspicions, and that the crime occurred at home. It is now a matter of proving the wretched girl's guilt before she brings further disgrace to her new family.'

Well, when I heard this I nearly scalded myself. Entering with the tray, I set to providing some hospitality in that chilly room. 'Hot tea, Inspector, and for you, Mr Holmes.'

As soon as I entered, my lodger ceased to speak. He was waiting for me to leave.

'Will there be anything else?' I asked.

'No, Mrs Hudson, we must not detain you. Go about your duties.' His long hands waved me aside impatiently. Unable to find a reason to stay in the room, I took my leave. Now, as if suspicious of my whereabouts, Mr Holmes rose and firmly shut the door behind me, so that I could hear no more.

But I had heard enough. The 'wretched girl' was obviously a reference to Rose Nichols. Lady Templeford was accusing her of maternal neglect at best and murder at worst, suggesting she was solely responsible for the abduction of the child. I may know nothing of the criminal mind, but I understand a mother's nature.

I thought of Rose, low-born and swept off her feet by a noble suitor. Soon she finds herself surrounded by new relatives who frown upon her profession and status in life, who doubtless try to prevent the marriage and stay away from the wedding, causing Rose great embarrassment. She is installed in a grand mansion, overseeing servants she has never before commanded. She is cut off from the theatre, forbidden to see friends from her old life. A child arrives with unseemly haste; the family cast aspersions on her honour – but what if the Honourable Archie Templeford has been forced to marry hastily to avoid a scandal?

Even he would now be against her. No longer a star of the stage, admired by friends and suitors, Rose finds herself a prisoner in her strange new abode. Then calamity strikes. Perhaps she discovers poor Godwin smothered in his cot, and has hidden the body from shame – friendless and alone, she will be condemned by all those around her, including Mr Sherlock Holmes, who is himself in thrall to those of nobler demeanour, and believes all he has heard about women of Rose's class.

When I passed my lodger on the stairs a little later, I found myself speaking out again. 'I see the story of the missing baby has reached the noon papers, Mr Holmes. I heard the boy calling it out from the corner. I wonder if you have visited Lady Templeford in town,' I asked. 'Her husband is reported to be—'

'It is common knowledge that Viscount Templeford is in poor health, Mrs Hudson, and does not welcome the attentions of strangers at his Devon estate. Her ladyship is presently staying in Mount Row. Perhaps—' He turns and fixes me with an irritated look. 'Perhaps it is best for us both to stick to our respective professions. On my part, I promise not to attempt to polish the silverware, nor wax the banisters.'

He was right to scold me. I had allowed myself to assume a role I was unfit for. I returned to the tasks of the day, preparing the luncheon menu and arranging payment for the tradesmen.

Still, I could not rid my mind of the suspicion that there was more to the case than Mr Holmes assumed. As I fulfilled the morning's duties I thought the matter through most carefully. I myself am born of low parents, and have – to my shame – behaved poorly with women whom I regard as lower than myself. However, a mother's bond is strong enough to cut through any ties of class, and I could not believe that Rose Nichols took the life of her first-born child in order to spite her husband's family.

That afternoon, Elsie overturned a milk-can in the scullery, and we were forced to move the furniture to clear the mess before it curdled, so I missed hearing Mr Holmes' return from what I assumed to be a further trip to Richmond. That evening, at the more respectable hour of seven, Lady Templeford called again, and I was on hand to usher her in. She removed a brown corded top-coat, and finding it too hot in the front parlour, unbuttoned a matching jacket, which I took from her and hung in the hall.

Her manner had changed. The almost theatrical panic in her eyes had given way to a steely composure. She was determined to see Mr Holmes, and would accept no refusal. Deciding to forego the rigmarole of ascending, awaiting a reply, then returning to the parlour, I sent Lady Templeford directly to the first floor.

But I stayed on the stairs, watching and listening.

This is what I heard. A creak of floorboards. Mr Holmes pacing back and forth. A stern, high voice. 'How you could allow the press to be informed…breach of confidence…this brazen woman paid her fancy man to take the child…public knowledge…drag my family name into the mud…cannot stay at Mount Row a minute longer.'

This is what I saw. The polished toecaps of my lodger's shoes, twisting past the gap in the door. The glint of his grey eyes. The swish of Lady Templeford's dress as she rose and turned, her buttoned boots matching the detective's pace. Her pale hand brushing at a mark on her blouse. Suddenly I had an inkling of the truth.

I hurried back downstairs as the door to Mr Holmes' apartment opened. There was barely time to find what I was looking for; Lady Templeford was already on the top stair, about to descend. I went to the cloak stand and removed her jacket, hastily searching the pockets. I knew she would see me with my hand upon her personal belongings and my reputation would be ruined, but was determined to prove my theory correct.

Thank heaven Mr Holmes called to her from the landing at

that moment. 'Lady Templeford, I have decided to accede to your wishes and search the premises of this mountebank, if you truly believe him to be the mastermind of such a deception. I shall accompany you.' Clearly the finger of guilt now pointed to Rose's former suitor. But I had found what I sought, and knew the truth. It suggested one solution. I turned to speak, but Mr Holmes gathered the coats from the stand and helped his client into them before springing to the front door. Then the pair were gone in their haste to reach the Haymarket premises of Rose Nichols' supposed lover, leaving me alone in the hall.

Once more, I was the landlady, made invisible by my sex and my station, a mere commissioner at the threshold of a more adventurous world. With a sigh, I returned to my kitchen. The potatoes would not peel themselves, and Elsie could not manage alone.

I heard the rest from the newspaper boy outside Baker Street station. The evening papers were full of the story. The missing baby had been found unharmed on the premises of one Mr Arthur Pilkington of the Haymarket, formerly of Clerkenwell. Neighbours heard the baby boy crying on the step of his lodging house. The former suitor of the Deptford Nightingale had been taken into custody at Bow Street, though he denied any knowledge of the infant. He was to be charged with kidnap. It was alleged that Rose remained in love with her former paramour. The police were hoping to discover whether the mother colluded in the abduction of her child. Mr Sherlock Holmes was to be congratulated for the part he played in restoring the infant to its father, the Hon. Archibald Templeford.

I pursed my lips as Mr Holmes passed to his room that night, unable to congratulate him. He failed to notice the withheld compliment, but I managed to hold my peace. He had reminded me of my place often enough for one week.

The case was called to mind just once more, when Lady

Templeford came again, this time at ten in the morning. Her mood was one of jubilation. 'I must speak with Mr Holmes at once!' she cried, as if announcing her intention to the street, and pushed past me on her way upstairs, as though I were a ghost and she had intended to pass right through me. She met him on the floor above. 'Happy news indeed! They have arraigned the blackguard and his mistress, and my son is preparing to commence divorce proceedings. None of this could have happened without your help.'

At the foot of the stairs, I trembled for what I was about to say. My sense of justice was strong, but so was the conviction that I would be going against generations of wealth and class. A woman of my position cannot afford to make mistakes.

'Mr Holmes,' I called out. 'I must speak to you plainly.'

'Mrs Hudson.' My lodger was taken aback. 'You must see that I am entertaining a most distinguished visitor.'

'What I have to say concerns her too,' I ventured, standing my ground, although there was a quaver in my voice. 'I fear you have been deceived.'

'What is this imposition?' Straight-backed and frowning, Lady Templeford drew herself up to her full imposing height and faced me upon the stair. I took an involuntary step back.

'On the night Lady Templeford arrived in distress, a smell clung to her fox-fur coat, something a mother would recognise. It was the smell of a baby. But there was something else, a chemical stronger than that secreted by an infant. When she returned, the second smell still emanated from her pocket. While this lady was in your rooms, I glimpsed something in the jacket she gave me.'

'Really, this is too much!' Lady Templeford protested. 'Mr Holmes, why do you allow your staff to behave in this unseemly fashion?'

'Laudanum, Madam,' I cried, forgetting the correct form

of address. 'Every woman of the working class recognises its smell, a drink cheaper than gin and sadly in just as much use. An opium-based painkiller prescribed for everything from a headache to tuberculosis, fed to infants by their nursemaids in order to keep them quiet – often with fatal results. I hear the drug has found popularity among even the grandest ladies now. You cannot deny it – the bottle was in your pocket.' I had seen the octagonal brown glass and smelled its contents. 'It is my conjecture you paid one of your son's servants to remove the baby from its cradle and deliver it to your lodgings in Mount Row. But there are many apartments around you whose occupants might hear an infant cry, so you silenced the poor mite with laudanum. Shame upon you!'

'The woman is mad!' cried her ladyship. 'I shall not countenance such an accusation.'

'Then this will do it for you,' I told her, raising the bottle so that Mr Holmes could see it. 'Your name is written upon the label. Your doctor will verify the prescription, I am sure.'

The look upon her face revealed the truth to my lodger. In that moment, she lost her most powerful ally.

No man can survive without the influence of women. But we live in a world that belongs to men. Even our own dear queen has withdrawn completely from British life, her strength brought low by the memory of her husband. What hope can there be for other women without her?

The truth did indeed come to light, although I do not know whether justice will be done. It is not my business to know. Certainly, Mr Holmes was not best pleased. How could he be in his position? Still, I look up to him. And he must look down upon me.

To him, I will always be the lady downstairs.

the luxury of harm

When I was eleven, I was warned to stay away from a new classmate with freckles and an insolent tie, so naturally we became inseparable partners in disruption, reducing our educators to tears of frustration.

For the next eight years our friendship proved mystifying to all. Simon horrified our teachers by illegally racing his Easy Rider motorbike across the football field. We took the deputy headmaster's car to pieces, laying it out in the school car park as neatly as a stemmed Airfix kit. We produced a libellous school magazine with jokes filched from TV programmes, and created radio shows mocking everyone we knew. When you find yourself bullied, it's best to team up with someone frightening. Simon perverted me from learning, and I made his soul appear salvageable whenever he superglued the school cat or made prank phone calls. I fretted that we would get into trouble, and he worked out how we could burn down the school without being caught.

Boys never tire of bad behaviour. Through the principles of economics and the theory of gravity, the Wars of the Roses and Shakespeare's symbolism, we cut open golf balls and tied pupils up in the elastic, carved rocketships into desks and forged each other's parental signatures on sick notes.

During puberty, Simon bought a mean leather jacket. I opted for an orange nylon polo-neck shirt with velcro fastenings. He looked like James Dean. I looked like Simon Dee. In order to meet girls, we signed up for the school opera. Simon met a blue-eyed blonde backstage while I appeared as a dancing villager in a shrill, off-key production of *The Bartered Bride*. We double dated. I got the blonde's best friend, who had legs like a bentwood chair and a complexion like woodchip wallpaper, but her father owned a sweet shop so we got free chocolate. I rang Simon's girlfriends for him because he was inarticulate, and hung around his house so much that his mother thought I'd been orphaned. Our friendship survived because he gave me visibility, confidence and a filtered charisma that reached me like secondary smoking. He stopped me believing there was no one in the world who understood me. And there he remained in my mind and heart, comfortable and constant, throughout the years, like Peter Pan's shadow, ready to be reattached if ever I needed it, long after his wasteful, tragic death.

But before that end came, we shared a special moment. By the time this happened, we had gone our separate ways; he became the conformist, with a country home and family, and I turned into the strange one, living alone in town. Recontacting Simon, I persuaded him to come to a horror convention with me, in a tiny Somerset town called Silburton, where the narrow streets were steeped in mist that settled across the river estuary, and fishing boats lay on their sides in the mud like discarded toys. The place reeked of dead fish, tar and rotting shells, and the locals were so taciturn it seemed that conversation had been bred out of them.

The hotel, a modern brick block that looked like a caravan site outhouse, had no record of our booking, and was full because of the convention. In search of a guest-house, we found a Bed & Breakfast place down beside the river ramps and lugged bags up three flights through narrow corridors, watched by the landlady in case we scratched her Indian-restaurant wallpaper. The beds felt wet and smelled of seaweed.

By the time we returned to the convention hotel, the opening night party was in full swing. A yellow-furred alien was hovering uncertainly in the reception area, struggling to hold a pint mug in his rubber claws, and a pair of local Goth girls clung to the counter, continually looking around as though they were afraid that their parents might wander in and spot them, raising their arms to point and scream like characters from *Invasion Of The Body Snatchers*.

Every year the convention had a theme, and this year it was 'Murderers on Page and Screen', so there were a few Hannibal Lecters standing around, including a grinning lad with the top of his head sawn off. The bar staff took turns to stare at him through the serving hatch.

'Is this really what you do for fun?' Simon asked me, amazed that I could take pleasure from hanging out with guys dressed as Jason and Freddie, films no one even watched any more. 'Who comes to these things?'

'Book people, bored people,' I said simply, gesturing at the filling room. 'Give it a chance,' I told him. 'There's no attitude here, and it gets to be fun around midnight, when everyone's drunk. Come on, you said your life was very straight. This is something new.'

Simon looked unsure; he hardly ever read, so the dealer rooms, the panels and the literary conversation held no interest for him. He talked about his kids a lot, which was boring. I wanted him to be the kid I'd admired at school. He could relate to drinking, though, and relaxed after a couple of powerful local beers that swirled like dark sandstorms in their glasses. Simon could drink for England. 'So,' he asked, 'are they all writers looking for tips?'

'In a way. Take this year's theme. We're intrigued by motivation, method, character development. How do you create a realistic murderer? Who would make a good victim?' I tried to think of a way of involving Simon in my world. 'Take the pair of us, for example. I'm on my home turf here. People know me. If I went missing, there would be questions asked. For once, you're the outsider. You were the tough guy, the bike-riding loner nobody knew, and you're unknown here. That would make you the perfect victim.'

'Why?' Simon wasn't the sort to let something beat him. His interest was piqued, and he wanted to understand.

'Because taking you out would be easy. It would still require an act of bravery, and be a show of strength. Killers seek notoriety to cover their inadequacies. But they also enjoy the remorse of loss.'

Simon snorted. 'How the hell does that work?'

'There's a strange pleasure to be taken in melancholy matters, don't you think? A kind of tainted sweetness. Look at the Goths and their fascination with death and decay.'

'Okay, that's the victim sorted, so who's the killer?'

'Look around. Who would you choose?'

Simon scoped out the bar area. 'Not the Jason or Freddy lookalikes. They're geeks who would pass out at the sight of a paper cut. They'd be happy to watch, but they wouldn't act.'

'Good, keep going.'

'And the Goths couldn't kill, even though they're professional mourners. They look tough but play gentle.'

'Excellent.'

'But him, over there.' He tapped his forefinger against the palm of his hand, indicating behind him. 'He looks like he's here to buy books about guys who kill their mothers. It wouldn't be such a big step to committing a murder.'

'Yeah, we get a few of those at conventions. They sit in the front row at the Q&As, and are always the first to raise their hands with a question. There's one guy, a retired doctor, who even gives me the creeps. Over there.' I pointed out the cadaverous Mr Henry, with his greasy comb-over and skin like the pages of a book left in the sun. He never missed a convention, even though he wasn't a writer or publisher, or even a reader. 'He once told me he owns one of the country's largest collections of car crash photographs, and collects pictures of skin diseases.'

'That's gross. I knew there would be freaks here.'

'Relax, he's too obvious. If there's one trick to serial killer stories, it's making sure that the murderer is never someone you suspect. Have you noticed there are some very cute girls hanging around the bar?'

'You're right about that,' Simon grudgingly admitted, watching two of them over the top of his glass.

'You should go and make their acquaintance,' I suggested. 'I'll just be here talking weird books with old friends, or the other way around.'

I got into a long discussion/argument about the merits of *Psycho 2* and *3*, about Thomas M. Disch and William Hope Hodgson and what makes a good story, and lost all track of the time. I only checked my watch when the waiter started pulling shutters over the bar. Bidding farewell to my fellow conventioneers, I staggered off through the damp river air toward the guest-house.

Somehow I managed to overshoot the path, and ended up on the seaweed-slick ramp to the harbour. The only sounds were the lapping of the water and the tinging of masts. The tide was coming in, and the boats were being raised from their graves like reanimating corpses. Drunk and happy and suddenly tired, I sat down on the wet brown sand and allowed the sea-mist to slowly reveal its secrets. It formed a visible circle around me, like the kind of fog in a video game that always stays the same distance no matter how hard you run. A discarded shovel someone had used to dig for lugworms stood propped against the harbour wall. Orange nylon fishing nets, covered with stinking algae, were strung out like sirens' shawls.

And through the mist I gradually discerned a slender figure, his head lolling slightly to one side, one arm lower than the other, like the skeleton in the Aurora 'Forgotten Prisoner' model kit, the one that features on the cover of the *Seventh Book of Pan Horror Stories*. It was standing so still that it seemed to be more like the unearthed figurehead of a boat than a man.

There was a strong smell of ozone and rotting fish. The figure raised a ragged, dripping sleeve to its skull, rubbing skin to bone. It seemed as though it had ascended from the black bed of the sea.

'I fell off the fucking dock and tore my jacket. I am so incredibly slaughtered,' said Simon, before tipping over and landing on his back in the sand with a thump.

The next morning, screaming seagulls hovered so close to my bedroom window that I could see inside their mouths. Shafts of ocean sunlight bounced through the window, punching holes in my brain. My tongue tasted of old duvet. I needed air.

I knocked on Simon's door, but there was no answer. Breakfast had finished, and the landlady had gone. The Easy Rider motorbike still stood in the car park behind the guest-house.

The tide was out and the mist had blown away, leaving the foreshore covered in silvery razor-clams and arabesques of green weed. On the stone walkway above the harbour, an elderly lady in a teacosy hat marched past with a shopping bag. There was no one else about. The gulls shrieked and wheeled.

Carefully, I walked across the beach to the spot where Simon had fallen, and knelt down. It took a moment to locate the exact place. Rubbing gently at a patch of soft sand, I revealed his sand-filled mouth, his blocked nostrils, one open shell-scratched eye that stared bloodily up into the sky. I rose and stood hard on his face, rocking back and forth until I had forced his head deeper into the beach. I carefully covered him over with more sand, smoothing it flat and adding some curlicues of seaweed and a couple of cockle shells for effect. Finally I threw the shovel I had used on his neck as far as I could into the gelid, stagnant water of the harbour.

cupped hands

There are places in the world where you can have a showdown with your soul, he thought. *Places where you have nothing to fall back on but your own steel.* This place, it turned out, was one of them.

He was in an area the world charities had forgotten. They were busy laying electrical cables and digging freshwater wells for underdeveloped African states, but they stayed away from this miserable, war-damaged patch of rock. There was nothing here but black sandflies that raised crimson welts the size of marbles on your arms. Nothing here but sandstorms and dust and stones, the unburied ruins of cinderblock houses, strands of blue plastic shredded from makeshift housing that had blown hundreds of miles and would never degrade. He had read plenty of journalists' articles on the ennobling heritage of Africa, had even helped to write a few, but there was no sign of it here. After a century of tribal wars, everything had been smashed to grit. History leaked from the pores of most Western cities; they couldn't help revealing the past to everyone who passed through them. *Try seeing the past here,* he thought, *it only goes back as far as the last tinpot potentate arming a bunch of teenaged boys with reconditioned AK40s and telling them to wipe out anyone who disagrees with state policy. One fucking kleptocracy strutting through after another before stripping the curtains from the consulate and hightailing it out of the region.* Three hundred miles of sun-seared wasteland, with nothing more than the odd scorpion or beetle to keep you company.

It came as a shock to stumble across Grand-Assour, not that anyone ever did. The town wasn't exactly an oasis, although it had been once. No trees survived now, hardly any plants even, except the hardy spine-covered tongues of agave cactus that grew in the cracks between rocky slabs, but there were still over four hundred people living here, making it the oldest and largest town in the desert. Actually, it had become the only town. The biggest houses were shabby but attractively proportioned and made of concrete, not lime-smeared rubble and corrugated iron. There was even a town square with a rusted wrought-iron pergola, not that anyone could sit out in a high season heat of 140°F. The people of Grand-Assour stayed indoors during the day, hidden behind interior walls of stone and clay. There was no arable land to till, and hardly anything to buy or sell. So why, Neil Chapman wondered, did they stay?

He had thought about that long and hard when he first arrived. He'd wanted to know the town's history, but its collective memory had desiccated in the heat, and the half-recalled tales of grandparents' lives were blurry with lurid fables. Grand-Assour had once been part of a much larger settlement, that much was remembered. The French were here, the Dutch and the English. There were once green fields, and the lake had been filled with fat brown fish. But then there was the war, a low-level conflict with a neighbouring tribe that was now entering its sixth decade. People had learned to live with small outrages.

After one particularly heated and bloody skirmish in the mid-sixties, the lake disappeared overnight. The ground beneath it developed a fault and split wide, draining the town and transforming it into a silted desert. People thought God was punishing them for fighting, so at least the fighting stopped, but the lake became a crusted pit, the white buildings yellowed in sandstorms, the plants shrivelled and died, and all the colours of life were sucked away. Still, people stayed. Where could they go? Stranded in the dead centre of an African state nobody wanted to know, overseen by a president who cared only for his power-games with the West, nothing for three hundred miles in any direction, they relied on a meagre government subsidy, and something even more important...

Neil came to Grand-Assour because he thought it would be the making of him. He came because of a woman. He had dropped out of Cambridge in his second year because he was failing, and because he was in love with Ellen. She was as pale as glass but strong as sunlight, and could not speak the truth to him. After he came down in disgrace to meet her at her parents' home in Windlesham, she told him she had changed her mind about their future. Seated in the cool green garden, she had seen something in him that she could not admire, and this phantom fault had nagged at her until she could no longer bear the idea of being together. Neil was so shocked that he grabbed her face in a pinch, which he should not have done. He had never hurt a woman in his life. She remained rigid as he left, frightened of him, watching him pull away with a cool stare that told him her fears had been confirmed. When he looked back, the sight of her almost made him turn around and beg forgiveness. Almost.

Ironically, Ellen's refusal brought this latent flaw in his nature to the surface, although he could not see it then. All Neil knew was that he needed to get far away from the woman who had seen his soul. He had been studying geological faults in North Africa to determine whether they were caused by man or nature. Now he took a private commission to investigate seismic disturbances in drought regions, and the last town on his tour was Grand-Assour.

The company thought he would be able to help them pinpoint future areas of drought, so that appropriate actions could be taken in advance. Their aim was not as altruistic as it sounded; they wanted to sell predictive technology to corrupt governments. Some hope around here, where even essential grain imports went missing under the bribe-blinded eyes of local officials. So the company pulled out and he stayed on with Najja, a slender jet-skinned girl with an absurdly large smile and a name meaning 'Second Born'. He taught her a handful of English songs and she taught him some muscular sexual tricks which nearly wrecked his lower back. He slipped her into his hotel room and smelled her flesh as he stripped the veils of her dress away from her long thighs. Her body was as hard as a man's, her buttocks high and tight, as round as the moon. Only her pubis was soft to the touch. She lay back and watched him, smiling silently as he awkwardly lowered himself between her legs. Najja made him feel inadequate and exposed. Her skin was suited to the sun; his was red and forever peeling. Her body did not yield as he thrust into her. He barely managed to leave an impression. She took a delight in making love despite the fact that he would have been thrown out of the town if her family discovered she was no longer a virgin. She was fifteen, and expected to bear children soon, so her father had lined up a neighbour who had known her since birth, and she was still stringing him along while Neil tried to come up with a plan to get them both out of town in one piece.

Adan, which was the Spanish equivalent of Adam but also an African term for a large bat, was becoming impatient to set a wedding date with her, and things were starting to get tricky, especially as Neil was running low on cash. Adan looked like his animal namesake, only meaner and with a lot more teeth. He owned the only real store in town, and was considered a fine catch. Najja's father had presented her to her future husband in traditional courting dress, and had received signs of approval from him. Accordingly, the families had set the date for the end of the month. Which was another problem for Neil, because Najja was now pregnant, and her belly was already beginning to swell.

That was when he met Jack Whittaker, who came up with the idea that would bail both of them out of trouble. Whittaker was the son of a failed British politician, the family black sheep who had been packed off to the Foreign Office, only to cause so much trouble that they had posted him to the farthest corner of Africa that anyone could think of, and that corner was Grand-Assour. He said he'd been a freelance journalist, a businessman, and a 'soldier of fortune'. Neil soon learned it was best not to ask questions about the scrapes his compatriot had got into over the past six years. He kept to himself, and spent most evenings in the courtyard of the town's sole hotel, *L'Auberge du Soleil*, a crumbling concrete box with six baking rooms, fans that didn't turn and a flyblown lobby coated in cracked yellow plaster.

Whittaker kept a stack of newspapers, and although they were always at least three weeks old, he shared them with Neil because Neil had the gin, not the sickly local liquor they boiled in gourds out by the town's main highway, but the real thing, juniper-sharp with a hint of licorice, clean and fresh in the mouth. He'd traded a crateful for a nasty favour, and now the supply was running low. Sensing that Whittaker might prove to be his only route of escape, he kept him oiled and happy through the evenings. Whittaker needed to move on too, for reasons he wouldn't disclose, although he encouraged Neil to believe it had something to do with a mysterious Chinese shipment rumoured to be passing through town a few weeks before he showed up.

Meanwhile, the pair sat in the courtyard smoking stale Turkish cigarettes and drinking warm gin, reading about cold climates and faraway events while they watched the dust-tornadoes skitter across the horizon and waited for something to come along.

Although Neil was at pains not to show it, the situation was getting desperate. In two weeks' time, Najja would undergo a virginity ceremony that would reveal her condition and show up her intended husband as a cuckold. Turning the most important single man in town into a laughing stock wasn't a good idea, as he had supposedly once cut off a rival's head and stuck it in his yard with a sapling planted in its mouth, just because the man had said something sarcastic about his negotiating skills. Disrespect was counted a crime in Grand-Assour, and taking revenge was not only permissible but demanded. Neil could imagine which part Adan would hack off and plant from a man caught fooling around with his fiancée.

It was Whittaker who had spotted the article.

'How badly do you want to get out of here, Neil?' he asked, jetting a streak of blue smoke from his sunburned lips and running his hand across a heat-dried page of newsprint.

'It's not a matter of choice,' Neil told him. 'I've got two weeks to jump a ride, and not enough money to pay someone for the petrol.' He couldn't pay his back-rent at the hotel either, but decided not to mention that detail. Problem was, very few vehicles crossed the three hundred miles of scorched-white nothing between Grand-Assour and the next town, and the few that did wanted a small fortune to take a passenger. Although she thought she was coming along for the ride, he was planning to leave without Najja. The last thing he needed was a pregnant schoolgirl hanging around his neck. There was a good chance they would torture her once they discovered the truth about her condition, but Neil barely knew how to save his own skin, let alone hers.

'According to this,' Whittaker grunted, checking the date of the paper, 'the government's cutting the water truck budget again. They're going down to one man.'

'Show me,' Neil demanded, turning the paper around. 'How old is this thing? Damn, they've already started.'

Towns like Grand-Assour no longer had freshwater supplies of their own – the few artesian wells that had been dug here had been fed from the lake, and now that was covered in a cracquelure of flaked mud – so once a week the government paid a water truck to come in and deliver around 1,500 gallons, which was traded like currency around the place until the average citizen received about a gallon and a half apiece, which they saved in tin canisters in their houses.

Neil saw what was passing unspoken between them. *When you've got a lifeline like the water truck running as regularly as a French train to a town that gets no other visitors, you'd better make sure it's well protected, or some unscrupulous son-of-a-bitch is going to try and hijack it.* He knew that was why they always travelled with two men up, one driving, one riding shotgun to keep an eye out for marauders. But the truck was also protected by the fact that it carried nothing but its great tank, and around here they didn't know how to parlay water into hard cash without bringing down a firestorm of trouble from the local government troops.

Still, reducing the truck's budget meant dropping to a single driver, and that meant two men with a plan would stand a chance of getting themselves a set of wheels and a tank full of diesel. That was the idea; he just wanted a ride out across limbo territory to a hotel with running water and a decently stocked bar. When mistakes started tying him down, he had a habit of running away, but this self-knowledge didn't prevent him from doing it again.

He thought carefully. The paper hadn't published the schedule, but everyone in town knew that the water truck usually arrived around five on a Thursday afternoon. The drivers often stayed over and headed back early the following morning, but the truck was locked up and guarded by armed local kids until they left. The town's margin for error was perilously small; many families ran out of water by Thursday morning, but the truck was a prioritised necessity in an area where nothing could be relied upon.

'No use waiting until they get all the way here,' said Whittaker, his cigarette stub crackling as he sucked at the dry tobacco. 'Way I see it, we've got three options. First, we could take the truck at around three in the morning, which means bribing maybe half a dozen kids, and you know how risky that could get. All you need is for one to get away and raise the alarm.' The children would sell their services to the highest bidder, and the truckers had government bounty cash on offer. 'Two, we could move in as they head back at around 5:00 am. Friday morning, but the driver will be rested and alert by then. Three, we could head out into the desert a way on Thursday and catch him before he arrives in town. It's the last thing he'd be expecting. Then we turn the truck around, take him further out on to the route and release him. By the time he reaches town on foot, we'll already be at the border.'

He had indeed made up his mind, and at some point in the hazy warmth of the evening Neil agreed to go along with him. He knew Whittaker wanted him to think he'd once been a mercenary with a price on his head, caught flogging black-market landmines to the North Koreans before fetching up in this dump. He was cagey enough about his past to keep a lid on any questions about his personal life. But Neil was sure the truth would be more mundane than that. No doubt like himself, Whittaker had been escaping past entanglements with a woman determined to pin him down, and had probably left the Foreign Office owing his ex-public schoolfriends money. In a town like Grand-Assour, you could reinvent yourself in the image of whoever you wanted to be, but Whittaker's tipped-back straw hat and artfully stubbled chin were a little too nuanced to be convincing.

Melded together by a taste for cheap gin and new pastures, they stayed talking until Tuesday clicked over into Wednesday. Rising unsteadily to his feet and bidding Whittaker goodnight, Neil arranged to meet him in the morning to finalise the details.

The sun was already high and hard when he crawled from his bedstead with a jackhammer hangover. *If you're planning to head into the African desert,* he thought, studying his face in the spotted bathroom mirror, *it's not a good idea to have a raging thirst and a tongue like a dried-out hamster.* The town symbol, painted on sun-split wood above the entrance to the main square, was a sturdy young woman with a sheaf of corn on her head. The symbol should have been a thirsty, ragged kid with his cupped hands outstretched, an innocent child dependent on the most basic requirement for life. There was nothing left here for anyone now, least of all a Westerner with abandoned ideals.

It was too late to start developing a conscience, so he spent the morning getting ready to clear out. Skipping the hotel wouldn't be hard; the proprietor slept in the shade of the courtyard all afternoon, and Neil's belongings fitted into a small nylon backpack. It was easy enough to slip past him. Outside, the sun was so strong that it felt like someone had heated a golf club and laid it across the back of his neck. He had promised to meet Whittaker at the flyblown café in the empty main square, but didn't expect to run into Najja, walking towards him in a faded grey dress that flapped about her bare brown legs, watched by a pair of rotund town gossips.

'I need to speak to you,' she said too loudly, grabbing at the white tail of his shirt as he walked away from the hotel compound. 'My father is very suspicious. He has asked my grandmother to examine me tomorrow. You know.' She cast her gold-flecked eyes coyly to the patch of cloth between her long thighs. 'She says it is part of the ceremony. You promised we could leave this town. Why are you avoiding me?'

'I have some business to figure out,' he told her. 'You shouldn't be talking to me right here in the street. If any of your girlfriends see you, they'll guess what's been going on, then we'll both be in trouble.' There were stories of girls being stoned to death for losing their maidenhood before wedlock. This was a place that thought a man still bore the right to have his daughters circumcised.

She laid a broad hand on his chest. 'You are bored with me, Neil.' She pronounced his name as if it had two syllables. *Nee-all.* 'The light has gone from your eyes. I am not a fool.' Then she noticed the backpack. Her luminous eyes widened. 'Where are you going?'

'I told you I couldn't talk to you about my work,' he said, stealing a line from Whittaker. 'I have a meeting.'

'Will you come to me after you finish your work? We must talk. I cannot stay here. They will kill me if they find out.'

'Sure, baby, after I've finished I'll come and find you,' he lied. 'I may be quite a while. Why don't you wait at the old schoolhouse for me?'

She stood, confused by his attitude, and he walked on. But this time, he did not look back. She had sensed a change in him as surely as a bird grew wary of a shifting shadow.

Whittaker was leaning against the wall of the café, smoking. When he saw Neil, he ground out his cigarette and hoisted his battered leather satchel on to his back. 'I was beginning to think you'd chickened out,' he said. 'I've got the bike.' He owned a rusty old Triumph which he'd been attempting to repair without the right parts ever since they'd met.

'That piece of shit hasn't got more than twenty miles in it,' Neil said, alarmed by the idea of riding such a junkpile into the desert.

'Twenty miles will do it. The truck arrives at five. If we set off now, I reckon we should intercept it around fifteen or twenty kilometres outside of town.'

By three, most of the town was asleep and the children were in the schoolroom learning 'The Lord Is My Shepherd'. Neil could hear their sing-song voices reciting the psalm the town's alcohol-addled missionary kept pushing on to them, and knew they had no clue as to what the words meant. The Triumph had a habit of backfiring, so they wheeled it to the main gate and out on to the stone highway before kick-starting it. Nobody even saw them leave, but they would find out soon enough.

The road was so bad that they were forced to travel more slowly than Whittaker had anticipated. The low yellow walls of the town receded, and then there was nothing, just the dried-up bed of the old lake, sand and rock like the surface of the moon, and a few bleached dead absinthe bushes. Neil was just beginning to get nervous when they spotted a sand-tail in the distance. 'It's coming,' he said. 'How are we going to stop it?' He'd been giving the matter some thought on the back of the motorbike and had not come up with anything.

'How do you think we're going to stop it?' Whittaker snapped back, never taking his eyes from the swirl of kicked-up dust. 'We're going to flag it down. We're white men. The driver won't be expecting any trouble from us.'

Soon they could hear a distant rumble. Whittaker dropped the bike across the road, allowing it to appear as if it had broken down. The truck was an ancient grey flatbed, converted to hold a vast steel cylinder on the back, held in position with riveted girders. As they walked forward up the middle of the road, raising their hands, Neil tried to see who was driving, but the windows were covered in sand. He thought the truck wasn't going to stop, but at the last moment it crashed gears and slowed, coasting to the side of the road. The driver rolled down his window and watched them impassively.

'Our bike broke down,' said Whittaker, as if dealing with a small child. 'Engine no good. We need a ride, just to Grand-

Assour. Can we ride with you?' He saw now that the driver was barely out of his teens. After a low moment of deliberation while the driver regarded them with thoughtful, hooded eyes, he leaned across and pushed open the passenger door. Neil's fear that he would not let them on board faded, to be replaced by a fresh apprehension about how Whittaker would kick the driver out of his vehicle. He began to wonder if he needed the ride this badly, then thought of Najja's impending ceremony and decided that anything was better than going back.

Whittaker pushed himself into the truck's cab and sprawled into the centre of the bench seat. He introduced himself to the driver, whose name was Sefu, and they set off. Africa was all about getting around by hitching rides, but Neil could see that the driver was wary of them.

'Why you leave bike beside road?' asked Sefu with suspicion.

'I'll come back for it later,' Whittaker told him. They should have asked if they could load it on to the back of the truck, behind the water tank, thought Neil.

Whittaker offered the boy his bottle of water, but Sefu merely gave a shrug over his shoulder at the great tank. He was joking, but, typical to the ways of these people, treated the jest with great seriousness. They drove in silence along the rutted white road, and Neil wondered how long it would be before Whittaker decided to act. If the truck got too close to town, there was a danger that someone might come out to meet it.

Outside, the great pitted plain hardly seemed to move. There was nothing to provide any measure of distance, only the bare white sky, the theatrical-flat horizon, a few distant dust clouds whipped by whorls of hot air. The land offered no clue to its design or purpose, a realm beyond good or evil, as dead as space, harsh and harmful and free of conscience. Neil stared at it in wonder.

Whittaker was saying something to the driver in a low voice, and Sefu was nodding faintly, never removing his hands from the wheel or his eyes from the road. The boy was young, fit, alert. He had been entrusted with this most responsible of tasks, and was clearly determined to let nothing distract him. Neil could see that the driver-side door was locked. He tried to attract Whittaker's attention but was ignored. Whittaker continued talking softly to Sefu, who was starting to shift uncomfortably in his seat.

Time divided and slowed, and the cabin was hot. Neil felt his eyelids closing. They were getting near town, because pieces of trash glittered at the roadside. His eyes shut, but just as they did there was an explosion of movement, and Whittaker was suddenly making his move, grappling with the boy, who kicked down on the brake pedal, slewing the truck in its tracks.

Sefu was strong, and fought back. His arm crossed Whittaker's and a bone cracked with the sound of someone stamping on a dry plank. Neil twisted in his seat, pressing his back to the door in horror as Whittaker dug the blade of his pocket knife hard into the driver's throat. The drama unfolded in virtual silence. Sefu's limbs thrashed and his head snapped back, the wide pink slit in his long neck opening to release a jetted mist of scarlet across the windscreen. Neil shouted out, shoving at the spastically lashing arms as Whittaker released the driver-door and kicked at Sefu, tumbling him from the rig.

The boy landed face down on the road, clutching at his severed windpipe as blood pumped into the dry dirt. Whittaker dragged on his partner's wrist, pulling them both out of the cabin.

'Christ, what have you done?' Neil heard himself saying. 'He could die!'

'He's already dead, you fucking idiot,' Whittaker gasped, clutching his right arm, and now he could see that it was broken above the elbow. A dark patch was blossoming through his shirt sleeve. 'Help me get him off the road.'

Neil pushed at Sefu's body with his boot, rolling him into the rock-strewn ditch that lined the highway. 'You didn't have to kill him,' he said angrily, 'he was just doing his job.'

'You don't leave witnesses,' Whittaker replied. 'We never did in Zimbabwe.' And at that moment Neil realised his misjudgement. This was no ex-public schoolboy with an exhausted trust fund and a string of dodgy property deals behind him.

'You were one of Mugabe's men, weren't you?' he asked, remembering the distantly heard gossip. 'One of his mercenaries, sent to burn down farmhouses and wipe out the local troublemakers during the elections.'

'You're pretty fucking slow for a kid who's supposed to be well educated,' said Whittaker, dropping down to the truck's running board and tearing open the sleeve of his shirt to survey the damage. 'What the hell did you think I was doing in Grand-Assour, sticking around for my health?'

'You already knew about the truck,' Neil muttered dumbly.

'I figured you could come along for the ride. Just as well, seeing as I've busted my arm. You can keep me company while I wait.'

'Wait? For what?'

'For the town to pay my ransom, after they run out of water.'

'They have an emergency reservoir, they'll be able to keep going until someone gets here.' He thought of the plastic tank of brackish, filthy water on the roof of the derelict bus station off the main square.

'There's nothing in it.' Whittaker watched him as he withdrew a Turkish cigarette from the pack with his lips. 'I unscrewed the pipe and emptied it into the ground right after I left you. They're already shitting themselves.'

'Then they'll send for another truck.'

'How?' He grimaced as he lit his Sultan and flicked away the match. 'You know as well as I do that they have no phones, nothing but a telegraph office only one guy knows how to use.

By now they'll have got the letter. They could send someone out here first thing tomorrow to meet my demands, and get their water back, but instead they'll call a bunch of meetings with the town elders and sit around deciding fuck-all until the first of their babies starts to dehydrate. All we have to do is sit tight and wait them out.'

Neil held Whittaker's gaze. 'You're really expecting them to bring you money?'

'At this minor public school you attended, did you study any courses about African politics?' he asked quietly, turning away to watch the horizon, where the red sun was sinking behind a layer of brown dust. Of course he was bargaining for cash; men like Whittaker smuggled contraband and salted it away in private banks. Neil was only now beginning to understand the kind of man he was dealing with. He realised that he had been chosen from the evening they had first met. He had supplied the alcohol and banter while Whittaker checked out his background, seeing if there was anything he could use.

'How much have you asked them to bring in return for the water, Jack?' Neil thought of the dried-out town square and the run-down council building grandly titled 'Headquarters For Financial Investment' in letters that had already rotted and fallen away. 'How much does a town like that have?' He tried to avoid looking at Sefu's partially covered body, which was alive with dancing blackflies.

'My old man only ever gave me one piece of advice. He said always have a plan. He needed plenty of them, because he was usually in trouble. He was a liar and a thief, but I always listened to him.' Whittaker seemed to be in a fugue state, disconnected from the reality of their situation.

'They'll telegraph the water depot and get the local troopers out,' Neil warned. 'What will you do then?'

'You've got to learn to calm down,' Whittaker said, finally

looking up. 'You're too young to have a heart attack. When the fighting starts, a lot of men hyperventilate and panic. Their bodies betray them. You don't want that to happen. The telegraph got smashed up last night. They'll never fix it. They'll have to do the unthinkable and rely on themselves.' He flicked his cigarette butt into the ditch. The red point spiralled and bounced on the driver's body, scattering flies. 'They're like lost children. They can't last until the next truck arrives, not in this heat.'

'But what happens when Sefu fails to return with the water truck? Someone will come looking for him.'

Whittaker let out a long, weary sigh. 'No, they won't. Because he wasn't returning to the depot this trip. He was heading on to the coast. Once a month he makes a drop.'

'How do you know all this? You didn't just read the article in the paper, did you?'

'You may have had a decent education, sonny, but you're as dumb as a fucking stick. Didn't you wonder how the guy whose future wife you deflowered got to be the town's big cheese? He's the bank's only customer. Before the lake dried out he made a fortune smuggling emeralds for the Chinese. They paid him in cash but he also took his cut of the stones. Now he probably wants to plant your nuts in his garden. Trust me, I did you a favour getting you out of there.'

He climbed to his feet and pulled his leather satchel from the bloodstained cabin. 'We have enough food for five days and all the water we can drink. By tonight the whole town will be thirsty, and any remaining water they can find will be going bad. They're stubborn people, but they'll come round to my way of thinking by tomorrow, even with all their town meetings. They'll have to use their vegetable cart to reach us, but they'll get here.'

'You honestly think they're going to empty their vault into a bag and wave it off into the sunset? You're crazy.'

'Adan will come because of his family, and he'll come alone.

He hasn't got anyone else to carry his emeralds out here. He'll trust me to hand over the truck.'

'You need me around,' Neil told him. 'You can't drive three hundred miles with a broken arm.'

Whittaker tore open a pack of dried beef and threw him a stick. 'Chew it slowly,' he said. 'You're on strict rations for the next few days.'

The sun vanished behind the water truck, and twenty minutes later the land turned blood-red. A deep star-ranged darkness dropped with the falling temperature. They had both packed mylar travel blankets, because they were light and folded up small. Huddled in the cab, unable to sleep, Neil tried to think of a plan that would get him out. He hadn't been thinking clearly; now he remembered the abandoned motorbike. It was clapped out but the tank had been full, and there was a slim chance that it might make most of the journey to the next town.

Whittaker appeared to be sleeping deeply as he slipped the bike's ignition key from the mercenary's jacket. He shifted position but continued to snore as Neil quietly opened the cabin door and dropped down on to the road.

He knew that the Triumph lay a fair few kilometres back along the route out of town, but figured he would be able to make it before sunrise. There would be no chance of going on once that searing fireball rose above the arid landscape once more. *At least,* he thought, *I have an arrow-straight dirt track to guide me back.* As he walked, a deepening sense of dislocation settled over him. He was utterly alone, tramping across an inhuman landscape, the only sentient creature in a land where even snakes had a hard time surviving. When he passed the only landmark they had sighted from the road – a fat brown slab of rock pushed up from the earth in some ancient past – he knew he would never get there before daybreak. Checking his watch, he made some hasty calculations. In three hours he had walked less than halfway towards the bike. Whittaker's delay in acting now became explicable. He had wanted to leave the only other vehicle beyond reach of either of them. Reluctantly, Neil turned in his tracks and headed back towards the water truck.

'Know what they say about this part of Africa?' said Whittaker, opening one eye and examining his companion's dust-caked clothes. 'If you come here trying to get away from yourself, all you find is yourself. There's nothing here that isn't already inside you.' He rose and scratched, then dropped to the side of the road for a piss. He knew where Neil had been, and knew why he had returned.

'Fuck you, Jack, I'm not part of your plans. It's a lousy way to make a living, waiting for a bunch of kids to die of thirst.' His voice was little more than a croak. He squeaked open one of the brass taps on the water tank and shoved his head beneath it, blasting the white dust from his face, allowing the cool liquid to cascade down his throat.

'So now you have a conscience?' Whittaker asked, intrigued. 'It didn't seem to trouble you when you got the girl pregnant. Don't tell me she knew what she was getting into. The fact that you didn't force her to fuck you doesn't make it right. You were ready to leave her to die.'

'I know, and I'm ashamed of it now,' he admitted. Something about being trapped here in the desert with this utterly amoral man was forcing him to rethink his own culpability.

'English schoolboys.' Whittaker spat at the dry ground. 'Your food, your women, you just never grow up. It makes you so easy to use.' The sun climbed, and the shadow of the truck shrank beneath itself. The horizon bleached into a harsh dead glare until the ground shimmered, replacing itself with sky. Neil had only travelled across this landscape before, never become a part of it. The absence of life created an absolute that demanded a response. Whittaker's was to become the kind of cold-blooded creature that survived in extremity. Perhaps there was no other way to prosper here. But then Neil thought of the people of Grand-Assour. A child with outstretched arms and cupped hands, implicitly trusting an adult to sustain him with life.

With nothing to do but wait, time lazily stretched and yawned. He crawled beneath the truck and fell asleep, waking only with the falling temperature of night. His last conscious image was of a dust-stained face, youthful and guileless.

The fierce morning sun burned his bare ankles. His legs had protruded from beneath the truck. Whittaker made breakfast, such as it was; another strip of dried meat and water from the truck's tank, cooled by the night air. They remained together in edgy symbiosis now, barely speaking to each other.

Neil removed a shovel from the truck and tried to bury the driver's body as best he could, but the ground proved too difficult to break. He looked up from the shallow pit he had created and wiped his forehead. 'If this guy is so smart, he's not going to turn up here unprepared. He'll protect himself. And if he's used to dealing with the Chinese, he won't be too worried about taking you out.'

Whittaker pushed back his hat and watched him work from the cabin of the truck. 'I've allowed for that.'

'What do you mean?'

'If he tries anything, the town loses its water. You have to understand something about places like Grand-Assour. Most of the people who are born there stay on, no matter what happens. Adan's entire family surrounds him. He's not going to put them or anyone in the town at risk. It's his weak spot.'

But he's not going to give up his wealth, I thought.

The day passed on feet of molten lead as the blue of the sky bleached through to an eyeball-drying whiteness. Nothing stirred. Every breath Neil took seared his mouth. He wondered how long the town could hold out. Whittaker was confident that Adan would arrive with the ransom today, but as the hours passed, their hopes faded. There were only two places to be; in the truck, which was stifling, or underneath it. Flies clustered around the tank's spigot, sensing the only moisture for miles. The lowering sun brought a welcome drop in temperature. The mercenary would not be drawn into conversation, as though he was afraid he might have to admit defeat, and sat angrily smoking in the cab, oblivious to the heat.

Neil passed a second uncomfortable night beneath the truck. By now a colony of ants had discovered his hiding place, and had taken to leaving inflamed crimson lumps on his ankles and wrists that he was unable to resist scratching. The next morning he dragged himself out and massaged his aching neck muscles as a hallucinogenic red sun loomed large on the horizon once more. The natural cycle mockingly operated *in extremis*.

Whittaker was more talkative after dousing himself with water from the tank. 'The bastard has to be here today. His kids will be close to dying by now.' Neil felt sure something bad had already happened in the town. Why else had no one come? Behind the truck, the dirt had blown from Sefu's face in the night, and his gaping mouth was filled with writhing iridescent flies laying thousands of tiny white eggs. Just a few days ago, Neil's world had been calm and ordered. He saw that he had liked life in the town more than he had realised. Now, he was living in a nightmarish limbo where everything was dependent on outside forces. He could do nothing until someone came to help.

Suddenly, it seemed that he had switched places with the people of Grand-Assour, who spent their lives locked in a stasis of waiting for something better that would never come.

He checked his watch, but it appeared to have stopped

functioning. The hands had stilled on either side of midnight. He felt disarranged by heat and hunger. Whittaker was retreating into his own private world, and only occasionally glanced up to glower at him from the truck cabin.

It had passed noon when they saw the wavering brown shape walking towards them through ripples of rising heat. Whittaker scrambled to his feet and climbed down from the truck. 'Stay close to me,' he hissed at Neil. 'You move, and I'll kill you.' He opened his jacket to reveal a small army handgun. As the figure came close, they saw that it was not Adan, but Najja. She wore a plain brown shift and sandals, a hide water bottle on her hip. Her hair was tied back from her face. Used to the glare of the sun, she kept her eyes wide, but Neil could see she was exhausted. She had walked all the way from the town. She stopped some metres before them, careful to keep her distance.

'Where's Adan?' asked Whittaker. 'What happened?'

She ignored him, looking anxiously at Neil. 'I warned you. They gave me the test. My grandmother told Adan I am no longer a virgin. She begged him not to kill me, so he sent me out to this place. He does not want me now, because I am impure, and he knows that you do not want me either. This is my punishment.'

'But he gave you something for me, didn't he?' Whittaker insisted. 'Where's the bag?'

She dug into the pocket of her shift and pulled out a crumpled brown paper packet.

'Throw it over to me.' He gestured back. 'Neil, get behind the wheel of the truck.'

'You can't leave her here,' Neil shouted. 'She's dead on her feet. You'll be damning the entire town.'

Whittaker had had enough. Pulling out the gun, he aimed it at Najja's face. Terrified, she threw the packet over to his feet. As Neil helplessly watched the transaction, he wondered how many more times such a thing would happen in this land. He reluctantly climbed on to the running board of the truck and heaved himself inside, turning the key in the ignition as Whittaker tore open the packet.

A handful of gem-sized pebbles dropped from the paper and fell to the road, rolling apart from each other. Africa is a land destroyed by lies and pride. There were no emeralds. All the ground could offer up here was stones, for setting walls, for grinding into plaster. Whittaker had underestimated his opponent's anger. Releasing a howl of rage, he fired as Neil slammed down on his arm. The sound of the explosion was muted in this dizzying open plain. The bullet punctured the tank, precious water spouting on to the road, blackening the dirt.

Whittaker grabbed at the truck's riding handle to hoist himself up, and without thinking, Neil stamped on the accelerator. The mercenary was caught by surprise and fell back into the road, bellowing as Neil drove over his right foot. He heard only the roar of the engine as he turned the steering wheel and continued over the prone body, feeling the truck lift and buck as the great tyre beneath him crushed the bones in Whittaker's leg, then smashed his hip. The screaming climbed high above the engine noise as the tanker rolled on, shattering the thorax trapped between rubber and stone, forcing bloody ribs through the cotton of Whittaker's checked shirt. The truck dropped as it flattened the mercenary's chest cavity, then popped his head like a thumb pressing down hard on the thorax of a beetle.

Najja held out her arms to Neil as he passed, and in that split second, darkened in relief by the sun, she was reborn in the image of the thirsting child he held in his head. His boot rose from the accelerator and switched to the brake. Reaching down his own hand, he pulled her on board, on to the bench-seat beside him.

They stopped to seal the leak in the tank with Whittaker's old straw hat, shredded and mixed with earth. As they worked silently together, he knew he would have to take his chances back in town.

He began to turn the truck around, to bring water to the people of Grand-Assour.

the night museum

Welcome To The Night Museum

The Museum is located between Arches 4 and 6 of London Bridge Ferryboy's Vaults (formerly the Sir Joshua Pimm Home For Seamen's Personal Diseases)

Admission is free

Opening hours: 12:00 am–4:00 am Mon–Fri
12:30 am-4:30 am Sat

CLOSED Sun for private functions
(exc. Walpurgisnacht)

Please do not touch the exhibits

WINTER SEASON INFORMATION

The Night Museum houses the Dagenham
Fawcett Collection of Unique Artefacts

The building comprises six sections:
The Lady Augusta Lavinia Travernum Hall of Antiquities
The Lord Pettigrew Stanivlas Plunkett Chamber of Damnation
The Countess Dorothea Spang Vestibule of English Cruelties
The Very Reverend Trebuthnot Skank-Damply Rotunda
The Councillor McTriffid Blaster Memorial Corridor
The Ron Git Wing (Recent Acquisitions)

Chief Night Museum Custodian: Olivanda Drainboil

A Few Words From The Curator

Dear friends, welcome, one and all, to the Night Museum. After all the other museums have closed during the hours of darkness, we prepare to open our doors to discerning members of the public. Our museum is underlit and pocketed with gloomy corners that strain the eye. It smells of mildew and lavender polish, of too few people and too much damp, dark wood.

Welcome, gentle visitors, to a repository of the unexpected. We hope you enjoy your visit. Please do not use the toilets on the second floor as they are intermittently dangerous, and may cause physical harm during blowback periods. The third floor has a large number of gaps, and is not to be trusted. We accept no responsibility for visitors becoming irretrievably lost or mortally wounded during the tour. The cafeteria stocks an interesting selection of commemorative sandwiches from British military history, but combinations created before 1880 may induce vomiting among those with unsuited stomachs. All sandwiches come with free carbolic wipes. This month's special: 'Crimean Horse With Mustard Seeds On A Wholemeal Bap'.

The Night Museum Shop has currently requested a product recall on all eyeballs purchased from the Burke & Hare Bequest, as these items have been found to contain parasites which may prove harmful to anyone with an A-T-T-C-A DNA strand. Please also be aware that although the Ming Tannis papyruses purchased in the shop are reproductions, several still carry potentially fatal curses. Please be careful when using Lady Mona Dracona souvenir hatpins, as they are tipped with curare. We hope you enjoy your visit.

Dagenham Fawcett (1843–1899)

In the fine tradition of great Victorian explorers, Dagenham Fawcett was unique, in that he failed to discover anything of the remotest use to the British Empire. He did, however, return from his Mongolian travels with a rare form of bubonic bacillus that accidentally killed the King of Norway after being released into the ornamental pond at Buckingham Palace.

Passing through Turkey, Siberia, South America and Africa, he amassed the vast collection of artefacts, mostly stolen or purchased with beads and handfuls of grit, that comprise the unique collection housed here. His self-published treatise, 'The Treatment of Supernatural Infestations Of The Urinary Tract', became a standard work in parts of the Nile's Upper Delta. Fawcett patented his mechanical device for removing trapped wind from bilious natives, and tested a working model on the impoverished children of London's East End, causing the tragic 'human barrage balloon' accident of 1882. The original device is still in operation, and can be tried out on the third floor of the museum.

Fawcett refused a knighthood for services rendered to the female patients of the Trans-Slovenian National Clinic of Fertility, but accepted a Légion d'honneur medal on behalf of Oodles, his much operated-upon pet chihuahua. A subsequent legal action brought by his patients resulted in a painful public flogging, scorning and involuntary vasectomy in the town square. Humiliated and ridiculed, Fawcett married Lady Augusta Lavinia Travernum (née Mountebank) in 1893, and later succumbed during an attack of blood sterility in the East. The mysterious circumstances of his death remain unexplained to this day.

◆

Please note that the Night Museum's famous exhibit
The Vessel Of All Counted Sorrows is currently
closed for examination by experts after being stolen
by brigands and returned in cloned form.

◆

The Lady Augusta Lavinia Travernum Hall of Antiquities
now houses the Travernum Bequest of Curious Sanitary
Equipment, including the Rain-Flushing Drainage Pit of the
Sampito Archipelago Indians, Dr Nathaniel Scowling's Self-
Mulching Portable Zinc Cistern and the Great Toilet of Stern
(formerly the Great Pot of Stern). All devices may be tested
upon production of a doctor's certificate and driving licence.

◆

Due to a technical fault, the *Valide* Dowager Sultana
Seyfeddin Mehmet II's Looking Glass of Restored Youth
is currently only working in the opposite direction.
This item appears by kind permission of Mr Cliff Richard.

◆

Headsets rented for the tour of the Conservatory
of Tropical Illnesses and Mummified Scabs must
be returned within one hour to be disinfected.

❖

Due to the unfortunate events befalling diners at the museum's annual Hallowe'en memorial dinner, ceremonies for the revival of the dead are no longer allowed in the restaurant.

❖

A Note On The Collection From Custodian Olivanda Drainboil

First, would the persons who removed the knees of the Emperor Augustus Satan III from the glass case on the lower ground floor and replaced them with soup spoons kindly return them before dawn on June 21st as they are needed for the Solstice Ceremony.

Dr Nathaniel Scowling, Md Pna will be giving a lecture on Hungarian Erotic Bathchairs in the deconsecrated chapel at midnight on Thursday. (NB This lecture will be delivered in Welsh, with mimed actions for the hard of hearing.)

Deconsecration Night

This annual event, in which disreputable gods have their idolatrous status ceremonially removed, takes place on Midsummer Eve, and attracted a lot of publicity in certain secular quarters last year after the museum's resident religious-status removal officer, Pastor Walter Bleen, failed to deconsecrate the Cillit Bang, Volcano god of its namesake Indonesian cargo cult. His lack of success created an urgent need for placatory sacrifices from attendees chosen from the audience. If you do not wish to be selected for sacrifice, kindly do not sit in the front three rows of the chamber.

Arrival of a New Exhibit in the Ron Git Wing

This acquisition, recently discovered in a sealed-up sewer by members of the Deptford Creek Potholing Society, is now known to be the Gethsemane Relic Box upon which the fabled Arbingham Clam was modelled. Inscribed with the legend *Non Sum Pisces*, or 'I Am Not A Fish', the box is carved from alabaster and wormwood, and appears to have been struck by lightning on at least three separate occasions.

The items once contained inside were said to have curative powers, according to the Night Museum's resident antiques expert Dropsy Mower, but are now missing, along with the two potholers who made the discovery. The box's unusual smell is said to stem from deposits left in the box by lung weevils.

The Great Pot of Stern

This enormous ceramic bucket was knocked from its stand by drunk Spanish sailors in 1908, and was repaired by the late Sir Archie F'Arcy with the aid of a scalding tube and Brewer's Elastic Cement. Unfortunately, Sir Archie went mad in the process of tabulating the 209,000 separate identical pieces of china making up the Great Pot of Stern, and rebuilt the pot inside out; hence the strange patination in the glaze, which was caused during the pot's latter use as a pagan defecation receptacle.

The Sacrilegious Fungus of Spangly-Po

This patch of ancient tree fungus caused the West African War of Seven Thousand Cuts after tribal members noticed that it resembled Cilla Black.

St Agnetha, Our Lady of Patient Reward and Redemption

This saint is no longer in use and is not accepting prayers.

◈

Please note that the witches on the fourth floor are undergoing restoration and are currently out of bounds.

◈

The Siberian Gulag Razor-Chair beside the entrance to the third floor gallery is a prisoners' torture device, and not for sitting on. Weary visitors are advised to keep moving at all times on this floor, as hesitations in motion attract deadly brain fleas breeding in the walls. It is unlucky to touch The Penis of Prince Alfalfa, or even to stand within eight inches of the display.

◈

Exhibits Of Special Interest

Moraturu, God of Unnatural Practices

This ancient sacrificial altar depicts many interesting adult acts performed by Moraturu and his young acolytes, and is currently being recreated for us by the ladies of the Cheltenham Spa Water Ballet Team in the basement of the museum. The altar is currently closed for cleaning following an unsanctioned sacrificial act carried out by a member of the public during one of the museum's periodic blackouts.

The Hell Hound of Gash

Black Shag, the flame-eyed screaming Norfolk Hell Hound, no longer haunts flat foggy marshlands around the village of Gash, where his owner was brutally slaughtered in a threshing machine, and is now the official mascot of the Night Museum. He can be found in the cage on the ground floor and loves having his tummy rubbed, but before petting him, please check with the custodian to make sure that he has been decanted.

The Germs of the Archangel

These effervescent vials of fluid are encased in a jewelled retort stand in the Lord Pettigrew Stanivlas Plunkett Chamber of Damnation, and register a grade seven level of toxicity, which means that only lead walls and holy water can prevent their escape if inadvertently tipped over. They were extracted from the lower intestine of the Archangel Gabriel, and their power has yet to be fully understood, but we do know that they can bend radio waves and alter the fabric of time during thunderstorms.

Samarkand Tree Bores

The darkened glass cases beside the entrance to the second floor hold a number of nocturnal tree-dwelling creatures that do not readily reveal their presence. They can be seen by pressing your face against the glass and remaining immobile for fifteen minutes, after which time they will fly from their branches and attempt to attach themselves to your face with a banshee scream.

They were first discovered by Lord Pettigrew Stanivlas Plunkett in 1922, in the tragic Saharan camel accident that claimed the life of his third wife Spongella, their son Dwightly, their aunt Immeldra, their twin cousins Carrie and Blasphetimine, their vicar the Very Reverend Svetlana Dongle, his children, their grandchildren, their concubine Fatima of the Lash, their butler Putney, their native bearers Ongo and Bopso Ngfa, their Yorkshire terrier Chortles and seventeen junior members of the Dagenham Girl Pipers.

The Erotic Frieze of Montefiore

This eighteen-hundred-year-old tableau was discovered in an Egyptian railway siding by Dagenham Fawcett in 1892, and consists of nude alabaster figures performing 'The Seven Hundred Positions of Aroused Frenzy'. Dagenham Fawcett spent three years cataloguing the positions before testing them out on his new wife, Lady Augusta, over the course of a rainy weekend in Cardiff. Lady Augusta subsequently undertook holy orders at Our Lady of Suffering and Periodic Discomfort (Orkney Branch). Dagenham Fawcett lost the use of his legs as a direct result of his experiment, and concluded that the Erotic Frieze is to be viewed for entertainment purposes, and not intended as an instruction manual.

The Great Royal Secret

Carefully restored by a remote sect of Orkney nuns in 1888, the Great Royal Secret has been kept in a golden casket lined with Balmoral velvet since 1900. The box has two double-twist spandrel keys, one of which is held by the Head of Endpapers in the Royal Library at Sandringham, the other of which is kept around the neck of Durnley, the corpse of Queen Victoria's beloved King Charles spaniel, buried at an unmarked location on the Isle of Wight.

The casket was only opened twice in the twentieth century, just before each of the world wars. Only the reigning monarch may be permitted to view the Great Royal Secret, and then for just two minutes and thirty seconds before incurring the Great Royal Wrath. The Chief Privy Seal was caught glancing at it over King Edward's shoulder, and had his eyes put out for his troubles. As the only two people to use the Secret are both dead, the contents of this casket remain a mystery. (The Orkney nuns were first sworn to secrecy, and then interred alive as an added precaution.)

The Topaz Dagger of Ormond

This graceful golden blade is encrusted with semi-precious gems and etched with the figures of those victims ritually killed in the Great Purge of Kandepoor (1785). It is currently under investigation by the City of London police following its connection with the Pentacle Murders of Whitechapel (2007), after being borrowed by Councillor McTriffid Blaster to open a tea caddy during a late-night parliamentary session.

Countess Dorothea Spang's Predictive Wheel of Death

Once thought to be a simple carnival novelty produced by dustbowl sharecroppers in the American Midwest in 1929, this exhibit has been reassessed by experts, and is now known to have belonged to the Tongue-Tearing Winsi Cult of Kathmandu. The colourful spiked wooden wheel is attached to a series of pulleys and springs that tell the fortune of the user, with predictions ranging from 'A Long & Fecund Life' to 'The Agony of Eternal Grimacing Torment'. It is possible to influence the outcome of the future by pressing Lever 'B' while holding in buttons 'L' through 'Q'.

The Pleading Monkey of Sumavera-Sum

This wretched creature was once the pet of the Princess Arthur of Connaught, and is in the habit of rolling its large tearful eyes and begging children to open its cage. However, if allowed to escape, it will bite its way through everything from living tissue to concrete. As its saliva contains an incurable form of Black Pansy Death, this is not desirable. The Pleading Monkey is scheduled to be put down on December 28th, and again on January 4th.

The Al-Q'Ha-Himm D'Whaa Sand Homunculus

This wind-dried skeleton belongs to an ancient demon with the power to indiscriminately send fiery comets raining upon one's enemies (and friends) but is harmless providing the demonic entity is not reconstituted by water of any kind, including the perspiration from human palms. (Please mind the rain bucket next to the exhibit – roof guttering above the case is currently awaiting repair.)

Dr Phileas Bose-Trunkly's Book of Wonders

This tome was allegedly written on the buttocks of female midgets and smuggled out of Aflenistan (formerly the People's Republic of Wong). The catalogue, bound in human flesh, was designed to record the Eleven Plagues of Aflenistan, which befell the people of that benighted principality after they disobeyed the orders of their leader, the Exulted Grand High Emperor of the Sacred Heavens above Wong. The recorded plagues include the Great Fall of Mud, the Embittered Mockery of Legs, and Death by a Thousand Hats.

Lady Simplistia Clittering's Book of Nocturnal Garden Verse

It is no longer possible to flick through this wonderful anthology due to accidents of a botanical nature that leave sufferers feeling vague and sexually unfulfilled.

The Tin Nose of the Very Reverend Trebuthnot Skank-Damply

This mortal remainder of the celebrated Anglican is all that survived following his attempts to convert the native tribes of Angora to Christianity. His death would not have occurred had he not mistranslated their cry of 'Not Today, Thank You' as 'We Are Proud Heathens'.

Please be aware that the wall tiles in the Very Reverend Trebuthnot Skank-Damply Rotunda are capable of firing poison darts if leaned upon. Also, please remember that the razor-spined glass fish in the aquarium have the power to leap from their water and blind the unwary with their whip-stings. Stroking of the stuffed lizards currently on loan from Princess Michael of Kent may cause immediate inflammation of the bowel.

The Precious Tableau of Lady Sumptua

This delicately fretted porcelain diorama depicted the rise and fall of the Mayan civilisation in over seven thousand individual scenes carved over a period of four hundred years by blind nuns, until it was dropped last month.

Suggested Tour of the Museum

Start in the trellis lift at the rear of the ground floor vestibule (the hardy may take the Penryth Escalator, but please be aware that this does not always lead to the required destination). Tipping the liftman is suggested, as for a few pennies he will supply visitors with safety hints not covered in this leaflet. Upon disembarkation in the basement, it is best to don galoshes and protective gloves if visiting the toilets or snack bar. Torches may be rented for the exploration of the crypt mummy cases – these are recommended in order to avoid the large hole to the rear of the basement, which leads directly to the Well of Walled-Up Children.

Many visitors ask why the eyes of the painting of Viscount Rochdale of Sporley appear to follow the viewer around the room and sometimes out into the corridor. This is because the painting was modelled on – and indeed contains – the eyes of the Viscount's imbecile cousin, Bungo.

Passing this painting, you will find yourself opposite a passage leading to a case containing the Chattering Skeleton of Kettering Parva, which was discovered in the destroyed remains of Kettering Parva House, with its teeth still sunken into Lord Kettering's thigh. The skeleton is believed to be that of Lady Swarfega Kettering. The smaller skeleton to its right may be Lady Swarfega as a child.

At the top of the stairs leading to the first floor, a hyacinthine urn contains the Nasal Contents of the Antichrist of Bengalore, and is highly flammable, therefore not to be used for the disposal of cigarettes.

Passing by several cases displaying the rubber trouser-masks of the Ulu Sect, we come to the Gift Shop, where you may purchase items such as T-shirts bearing the legends *My parents went to the Night Museum and came home crawling with lice* and *That's not dinner on my shirt it's ectoplasmic mucus.* We currently have brain-fever leeches in stock, and a plentiful supply of dung produced by the Hell Hound of Gash, which is ideal for fertilising strawberry beds. Please note there is a product recall on our Lavenham Iron Witch Bridles, which, once closed about the head, cannot be opened.

Many of our visitors find it safer to break their tour at this point and seek help from our on-site medical advisors, especially those who have ventured too close to the Spitting Ant display without goggles.

The Night Museum contains over 3,000 items of dubious provenance, which are constantly being reassessed. For example, the inlaid gold Devil's Tongue Cup formerly attributed to the private collection of the Duke of Edinburgh has now been reattributed to the collection of Attila the Hun.

One unmissable exhibit remains at the top of the building, where the Great God Pan is himself displayed in a variety of poses suitable for viewing by over-21s only. Be careful what you wish for while standing within three feet of this imposing figure, as Pan has the power to monitor thoughts and act according to instructions. We hope to have rounded up most of the missing schoolgirl party from Durham's Lady of Suffering Catholic Comprehensive in the next few nights, and wish them a speedy return to human form.

❖

It is not possible to take photographs of the exhibits, as the building is filled with magnetic clouds that tend to fog film and cause cameras to malfunction. Visitors with artificial limbs or heart transplants are not permitted to lick the third floor Strontium Processor, despite notices insisting that all visitors should do so.

❖

The curators would ask you to fill out the Visitor Comment Form (pp. 103–672 only) so that we may continue to improve our museum for your mental purification. Completion of this form entitles you to enter the national lottery to find the Isle of Man's annual ritual sacrifice victim.

❖

You may wish to make a thankful donation as you leave, and will find a receptacle for such a purpose in the main hall. This is not to be confused with the Mull Anglican Spittoon, which is a similar size and shape. Please note we no longer accept payment in Spangerian Centimes, despite their continued validity on the Commonwealth Islands of Dengit Pu-Yana and in parts of the Upper Umboko. All monies will go towards the provision of new dousing hoses in the Sir Joshua Pimm Home For Mentally Diseased Gentlefolk.

We wish you an enlightening, safe and informative visit,

Signed
Dagenham Fawcett (currently deceased)

starless

It was not until Professor Hugh Banks saw himself dead that he began to understand who he was. By then, though, the wheel of time had turned another revolution, and his old self was irretrievably lost. The creased and faded photograph of the physics professor had been taped to the railings, and smiled vaguely back at him, inviting mockery. He was appalled to find himself there among the legitimate deceased, and was ashamed of his cowardice. In the three days that followed, it was as though he glimpsed himself glimmering faintly within a vast field of stars, drifting away through the murk of the city's night sky, his features growing ever more distant and indistinct, until he could do nothing except continue gazing into the black dome of night, hoping to catch a glimpse of himself.

Stars expand as they start to die. Their centres devour all remaining helium and hydrogen, shrinking while their surfaces stretch and grow cold, their light dying. How long each one lasts depends on its original mass, but die it must, to finally collapse and detonate, shimmering into dense darkness.

The largest, brightest stars have the shortest lives. They cannot sustain themselves, because the amount of nuclear fuel they burn is too immense. Stars far brighter than the Sun survive for only a few million years. Our Sun can survive for 10 billion years, but even this time is short in the great scheme of existence. Mass decides all. It will choose the fate of a star at the end of its life, making it a black dwarf, a neutron star or a black hole. In its own scale, the universe changes as quickly as people change. People are made of stars.

The change had begun on a Tuesday morning in the last week of September, when the dying heat of summer had risen from the city's misted parks in a final breath, and Hugh's wife had glanced away from the television mounted on the kitchen counter to briefly study him before returning her attention to the bickering housemates of *Big Brother*. 'You're late for work again,' she warned. 'You'll be—' She stopped, but he thought she was going to say *late for your own funeral.*

He checked his watch. 'Fifteen minutes, Carol. My class won't miss me for that long. None of them would miss me at all. I'm covering the life cycles of stars. Do you honestly think any of them is remotely interested? It's a required part of the course. How do you create passion in someone who's busy text-messaging through lectures?'

'Complaining is all you seem to do these days.' Her tone was not accusing, but her eyes did not leave the screen.

He shrugged on his jacket and headed for the door, collecting his briefcase and wallet as he did so. What had made his fingers hover over his car keys before leaving them behind on the table? Looking back on the moment, he had no idea.

He boarded the packed Northern Line train at Finchley Central station, heading towards the University of London. As he stepped through the tube doors, he checked his watch and saw that it was 8:50 am, a quarter of an hour later than the time he usually set off. The carriage passengers were too exhausted to extend either grace or space, so his *Daily Telegraph* remained unfolded, and he stood with the sway of the rails, steeped in the disappointments of his life, the impassive glances of his wife, the indifference of his children, colleagues, students. Having satisfied this masochistic urge, he absorbed the murmur of conversation around him and willed himself into dreamless limbo.

The rocking of the carriage shifted him through the passing of years, and the fading of dreams. It seemed impossible to imagine that his world had desiccated into such a state of aridity that a peaceful night and a perfect end would now seem more appealing than another season spent in the universe of his own making. Looking around at the other self-hypnotised commuters, he wondered if they experienced any sentience at all, or whether it had become so deeply buried that only an apocalypse could cause it to resurface.

And an apocalypse was what Professor Hugh Banks got; just outside Euston Station the train slammed to a stop and all the lights went out. There were some yelps of surprise, but nobody screamed. After a few moments the carriage began to grow warmer, the breathing heavier, and small enquiring voices were raised. There was a driver announcement, so electronically displaced that only a handful of words could be picked out amongst the random scatter, but the meaning was clear enough. An 'incident' had occurred at King's Cross Station, just ahead. There was something about calmly making your way to the back of the train and disembarking via the last set of doors to the platform at Euston. Pale yellow emergency lighting stuttered on, and the passengers, a more cosmopolitan mix than which was unimaginable, became infected with a curious Englishness that encouraged them to leave their seats in an orderly file, as if vacating a ditched aeroplane or a sinking liner.

The brown air outside was thick with burnt dust, and then, he noticed, the smell of caramelising rubber. Only now were the talons of panic beginning to dig in. The pace of the crowd quickened; there was pushing from behind. They were swept along the darkened platform and up the escalator with increasing speed. Bursting into the cleaner atmosphere of the street, he saw the pulse of blue ambulance lights strewn across Euston Road and heard emergency sirens sawing the air. He wanted to ask what was happening, but his reticence was born from a life of invisibility, and instead he removed his jacket, placing it neatly over his arm, and slipped away into the grey back streets.

He had planned to walk the rest of the way to the college. The morning was cool and, apart from the chaotic disruption around King's Cross, pleasant enough for a stroll. He would be able to blame the trains for his late arrival. As he passed the window of an electronics shop in Gray's Inn Road, he saw the television coverage. An explosion at King's Cross Station, a scene of terrified devastation, woozily captured on mobile phones in a smouldering carriage. An unconfirmed link to a known terrorist group, reporters in confusion, sooty-faced businessmen clutching their heads with scarlet handkerchiefs as they were led away towards the pristine tower of University College Hospital. Behind the reporters, palisades of commuters shuffled on to their offices, careful to leave space between each other in the dimly remembered pedantry of civilised behaviour.

Tearful tourists were attempting to assemble their fractured memories for intrusive microphones, and an early estimate ran across the screen in red: thirty feared dead, a hundred injured. No one below was likely to have been left alive. A sudden devastating impact; the way of the world, the way of the universe.

Stars are like people; they evolve. They burn fuel, unleashing shards of light across their fields. They are born, produce, then age and die. As a star starts to lose mass from its surface, gas spurts from the outer layer, creating powerful stellar winds. The older it gets, the more of these fiery, unpredictable gales it produces, and the less stable it becomes.

Suddenly he felt nauseous, and was unable to proceed towards his scheduled lecture at the University of London. Instead, he found an empty back-street coffee shop and sat quietly at the metal table, collecting his thoughts, his heart pounding in his chest. When the coffee was gone he stayed on, unable to rise from the chair. It was hard to say why, exactly, but there was no possibility of going to work now. His mobile rang, startling him from reverie, but he silenced the disrespectful beep. Outside, he removed its battery to free himself from temptation, and dropped it down the nearest grating. This small gesture was enough to lighten his mood and firm an unvoiced resolve. His step grew more confident, his stride longer. Without consciously considering his actions, he turned about and carried on walking, all the way up to Hampstead village.

After a strange, disconnected day passed in the parklands of North London, he took another leisurely stroll, stopping to watch the news reports in a Camden Town café. The Metropolitan Police had mounted Operation Theseus, named for the god who had found his way through the Minotaur's labyrinth. Thirty-two bodies had been removed, but another fourteen were still missing. The emergency services acted with metronomic efficiency, ordinary men and women moved to acts of great determination. Terrorists had claimed responsibility, their targets ill-defined, their intentions unfathomable. A screen-flash unfolded: another two victims had been uncovered and identified, like the addition of new species or the naming of heavenly bodies. In a King's Cross Bed & Breakfast within sight of the rescue operations, he sat on the end of his single bed, looking out at the van-clogged street, and waited to be added to the list.

He knew he could live without his mobile phone, or ever going home again, but only late that day had it dawned on him that he would not be able to use his credit cards. Visa and Amex and Nokia and the Halifax Building Society would all be engaged in tracking him down, even if the police were not. He was carrying £167.40 in cash, and would not be able to generate more than that. A considerable sum was hidden inside his grandfather's box in the garage at home, but obtaining it would be risky. He realised now that the moment he saw the first news report, he had determined to leave his old life behind. But to become truly invisible, he needed to go back.

Outside the station the next morning, a makeshift garden of remembrance had silted with plastic-wrapped bouquets, and he was shocked to see the photocopied picture of himself – frowning in sunlight, almost unidentifiable – taped to the railing under the headline 'MISSING', as if his family had mislaid a pet. Feeling suddenly conspicuous, he tore the paper free and screwed it into his pocket. He brushed his hair differently and donned his reading glasses, which made signs and pavements indistinct, before threading his way out of the crowd, but no one was looking at him. Instead, they milled about examining the floral tributes, as though attending a flower show. Or perhaps they were expecting something supernatural to happen in a time of stress, the fanfared arrival of the Angel of Victory. With head lowered and jacket raised, he made his way home by bus.

When a dying star develops the immense mass of a black hole, its gravity affects everything around it. Gravity is so incredibly strong near the collapsing star that even light can be trapped inside, creating an anti-world of utter blackness. Other planets feel the changing pull, and are adversely affected. The star, in dying, may have more effect than it ever had in life.

When Arjun came in at half past eleven, Meera knew she was in for trouble. Her husband had been drinking with colleagues in a Goodge Street bar since six, and he stank of lager and cigarettes. He followed her around the kitchen, invading her space, poking at her with an accusing forefinger; his sentences began 'The trouble with you…'

She knew that it would not be enough to remain silent and let him win the fight. Recently this strategy had begun to fail, as he sought new ways to goad her into response. Half-cut, he remained stubbornly unoriginal: sexual jibes at her expense, complaints about her need for order and control. He patted her face jokingly, but there was a slap building behind his open palm. Arjun was thin, small, high-voiced, and his office pals had clearly fuelled him with a need to assert his power. When the slap came it was coupled with a plea for understanding, the revelation of hypocrisy entirely overlooked.

He wandered away from her as if crossing the deck of a ship, and opened the coffin-like AEG refrigerator, placing his hands on his knees, thrusting his head inside to find something worth eating. She felt like running at the door and slamming it hard, sending him face down into the salad crisper. The fridge door would slowly swing open to reveal a grisly display; a cracked skull, dark fluid draining from his nose and mouth. But committing any act of violence was beyond her. Becoming like him would be an admission of defeat, and running away seemed a better solution than confrontation. So running away was what she prepared to do.

'Toothbrushes. Underwear. Shoes. Passports. Oh God, what have I forgotten?' Her whisper was rising in alarm, crossing over her unnerved daughter's questions. Maya was sliding across the wood-floored landing behind her with clothes hanging from the side of her overnight bag, caught up in her mother's panic. Meera threw out her hands, trying to calm them both. 'Wait, wait – take it slowly. We can't do it like this. I have to think for a minute. We can't just leave.'

'We have to, Mother,' Maya rasped back. 'He's out cold on the lounge sofa, dead to the world, when else are we going to get the chance? Your face is bruising up, just like last time. You should have left him long ago.'

'Well, I didn't. I thought he would change but he just gets more volatile.'

Maya shovelled underwear back into the bag. 'We could push him downstairs and say it was an accident, and people would believe us. Everyone knows what he's like. They all hate him, and they think you're an idiot for staying.'

'Nothing was ever achieved in the heat of the moment,' Meera decided. 'If we leave now, someone might see. We'll stay here and decide what to do in the morning.'

'I don't want to spend another night in this house with him.'

'He's downstairs, he won't hurt either of us. In the morning he'll be apologetic, and will creep off to work with a flaming hangover. We'll stay tonight.' Her decision was final; part of her remained a loyal Indian wife, even though she was English, even though they had never loved one another. Meera and her daughter returned to their bedrooms and passed sleepless hours until dawn.

Falling into late, uneasy sleep, they finally arose to find that Arjun had left for work, and turned on the television to see news of the King's Cross Station bomb.

The most massive stars have the shortest lives. Stars that are forty times the size of the Sun may live for only a few million years. The less substantial a star is, the longer its lifespan. The faintest, most invisble ones that burn the slowest will last the longest. The ones that burn bright die fast. Stars are people written large. That is why they are so interesting.

Outside the bay-windowed stucco house where he had lived for the past eleven years, Hugh Banks watched as his wife and sons piled into their car – his ancient Volvo Estate – and backed out of the drive. The boys were smiling about something, and seemed more animated than usual. Neither of them appeared to be concerned for their father, missing since the previous morning. Waiting until they had turned the corner, he slipped out his keys and entered the house, only to find that they had already changed the alarm code. He was barely able to get away before the siren started to whoop, the line connecting through to the local constabulary. It was a shock to realise that his family subconsciously hoped he had been on the train. His suspicions confirmed, he ran without ever looking back.

His remaining cash was being scoured away; London was an expensive town in which to survive without credit, but he had no way of reaching his savings. The King's Cross Bed & Breakfast was more like a hostel, for it took in asylum-seeking families with cheap suitcases and wary eyes. The room's strict rulebook deposited him on the street at nine o'clock each morning, to sit in cold parks and cafés for a large part of the day. Whenever he could, he monitored rolling news programmes for developments. On Thursday morning, he was surprised to see Carol in the background of a press conference, presumably waiting to speak about the last time she had seen him. She was one of a group of partners and children who had lost someone, but the news item ended before her turn came. He unfolded the crumpled photograph in his pocket, and his bogus death was suddenly real. The old Hugh Banks was dead. He had no new identity. To his family and friends and in the eyes of the state, he was officially missing, presumed blasted apart. The dissipation of his identity had unnamed him, his loose particles scattering into the fabric of the city, and yet the freedom he so desired had somehow bypassed him. He returned to the café and measured the day in cups of stale coffee.

He felt entirely constrained by the collapse of his financial status, but confronting his wife merely to talk about money was unthinkable. Vanishing was supposed to bring freedom, not destroy it. He recalled the tragedy of the bombing and wondered if he was the only one in this extraordinary position. Throughout history men and women had evaporated, some never to be heard of again. He thought of the writer Ambrose Bierce, who had headed to Mexico in 1913 after the suicides of his wife and son, and who had disappeared without trace. Disappearance was as much the province of cowards as heroes. He remembered the feeble-minded murderer Lord Lucan, whose friends had smuggled him away. The idea was repellent, almost unthinkable, but how many had used the destruction of the World Trade Center in order to vanish?

Others had carefully prepared, but his decision had been taken on the spur of the moment, and it had stranded him without an exit plan. He was too old and well-padded to survive for long without money, and the thought of taking a menial job filled him with the dull ache of dread. He had imagined that the bomb would blast apart his cage doors, but instead it was providing him with an even smaller prison.

What had driven him to seek fresh happiness? People were trying to create a new sensation that never existed before. In the past, what pleasure did people have? They worked themselves to death, living in a state of fear that they would not have enough to eat the next day. He saw himself returning to that primitive state, and the idea truly terrified him.

To the human eye, stars appear to be stable, but some reveal variations in brightness. A few show huge changes that appear to be the result of cataclysmic events. Others burst into dazzling luminescence for a few fleeting seconds. When the core is unable to continue the process of fusion, there is nothing to balance gravity, and the centre collapses. The core's implosion releases such an enormous amount of energy that it blasts the exterior of the star apart in a supernova.

Countering the volatile instability of the universe requires continuous acts of creation.

Maya sat on the threadbare lounge sofa, worrying a nail between her teeth, her toast untouched, while her mother paced back and forth before the fireplace.

'He always caught the Northern Line,' Meera reminded her. 'There are people down there they'll never be able to identify. What a terrible way to die, trapped in a tunnel. We need to tell the police that he left the house and never came home. I wouldn't have the strength to identify his remains.'

'But you wanted him gone, and now he has. You need to see the body.'

They called the hotline printed in red at the foot of the rolling news screen, and were connected to an officer whose sympathetic tone masked the fact that she was discreetly checking her call to screen out potential time-wasters. A face-to-face interview followed that lunchtime. Photographs and documents were exchanged. The machinery of identification was set in motion. There was no way to put it delicately, the officer apologised, but an estimate of body parts indicated that there were at least twelve unclaimed bodies in the wreckage of the railway carriage. The intensity of the blaze had even rendered dental records useless. Mother and daughter returned home to wait.

It was during the long afternoon spent in front of the television that Meera began to face the reality of life without her husband, and realised that she would miss even an abusive drunk like Arjun. Not because she loved him – that faint sensation had been scorched from her heart long ago – but because she was now being processed through a legal system that would strand her without money, status or mobility. She had a teenaged daughter to feed and clothe, bills to pay, rent to find. She had prayed for Arjun to disappear, and now that he had, she was suddenly afraid. Her life had existed in manageable stasis for so long that any notion of change felt dangerous and undesirable. It was fashionable to roam abroad seeking freedom, but what she most wanted was a reason to stay behind.

Money, and the lack of it, had loomed over their lives for so long that further deprivation seemed little more than an inevitability. Arjun ran a profitable mail-order software company, but shared nothing with his family. Now that he was gone, her freedom felt like a gravitational pull that would keep her tethered in the familiar wearying orbit of her life.

During most of a star's life, it remains in a self-regulating state known as thermal equilibrium. If more energy is released from the star's centre than can be radiated away at its surface, its temperature rises and the star expands. If less energy is produced, the star shrinks and heats up, which stops further contraction. Thus, the star remains in balance. All things lose and gain energy in this way, creating equilibrium.

The residents of King's Cross survived in a state of permanent flux, arcing between pains and pleasures; life there had never been stable, all remained in motion. Hugh Banks stepped over luggage, wandering between commuters and backpackers, students and pensioners, trying to understand where he fitted. His clothes were already becoming shabby. The sole of his right shoe had separated in the rain. He had seven pounds left in his pocket, and could not face another café.

The scuffed brown-painted public house in the parade of shops opposite had been run down to the point of invisibility. The smoke-wreathed drinkers hunched in sepia shadows were near-derelicts, and showed fewer signs of life than the fruit machines. The room's lawless limbo made him reckless, and he ordered a strong beer, drinking most of it in a single draught.

During his second pint, he made his way to a gloomy corner table and found himself falling into conversation with a paralytic, argumentative tramp, who, upon second sight, was not a tramp at all but some kind of unshaven young businessman down on his luck.

'You might as well get smashed,' the other drinker slurred. 'We could all be dead tomorrow. I nearly died on Tuesday. The bomb at the station – I should have been on that train. Ran for it and missed it, had to take the one behind. So shaken up I went to stay with my girlfriend. I'd never stayed all night before. My wife doesn't know where I am, and I'm never going to tell her.' He flicked open his wallet and displayed her photograph, as if somehow needing to validate his story.

'Why would you do that?' asked Hugh, amazed that anyone would walk out on someone with such a kindly face.

'She's too English,' Arjun replied, as if the nationality was enough to damn her in the eyes of others. 'I met this young girl from Thailand, half my age. They really know how to look after a man, dirty in the bedroom, clean in the kitchen, that's the way it should be. I'm going back to Bangkok with her. I'm still young. I'm finished with all this domesticity.'

Hugh could not bring himself to admit that he had almost boarded the same train, but needed to speak. 'I thought about those people groping blindly in the dark,' he said softly. 'The air thick with soot, the cries of the dying. Is it such sacrilege for those left above the ground to admit that they might somehow be feeling the same way?'

The drunk man's watery eyes drifted from him in incomprehension. He shook the contents of his wallet on to the table, scattering coins, scooping folded photographs into the ashtray. 'Don't need all this. Terrorists and crazies everywhere, life is short, who needs responsibilities? This stuff just pins you down to earth. They don't even know who's down there. When you're born, you think you can reach the heavens, but you just end up underground.' He lurched to his feet and staggered off to the toilet. By the time he returned, Hugh had left.

The liaison officer called Meera to say they had reached a body that might belong to her husband. 'An Asian male around thirty years old, although it will be hard for you to make an accurate identification.' She paused awkwardly. 'He has no facial features.'

They showed her pictures of his blackened body, the seared remains of an expensive grey suit, an appendix scar across his stomach. She knew it wasn't Arjun, but surprised herself by telling the police it was. She desperately wanted to believe the lie.

Hugh arrived at the little terraced house not knowing what to expect. When Meera opened the door, he held his wallet open to display the pictures of herself and her daughter that he had retrieved from the pub ashtray. He thought she was going to faint, and quickly stepped inside, closing the door quietly behind him. Her reaction required his action.

Stars are formed in immense molecular clouds of hydrogen and dust. The densest parts of these clouds undergo gravitational collapse and compress to form spinning globes of gas, forming new stars from the ashes of the old. Star-factories can be found in the arms of spiral galaxies.

Young stars emit powerful blasts of radiation that heat the surrounding matter until it glows brightly. Such jets can be trillions of miles long and travel at 500,000 miles per hour. Once this point is reached, the new star will have a life of 10 billion years, and its sparkling light can be seen right across the universe.

Hugh and Meera studied each other at arm's length.

Something had fallen into place between them, something so fast and fleeting that they barely registered it. The shadows of their unloved partners brushed and released them. It was as if they said: this is what people do, collapse and grow, transforming to spark better lives from the darkest moments, because this is all there is, a limited series of chances to put things right, to make things better, to create, to produce positive energy. The heart is an organ that can repair itself. It releases light that can be seen by others attuned to the same radiation.

They watched each other's eyes for a long time before they finally, tentatively touched, looking for secrets to which they already knew the answers.

The bomb that dispersed so many in King's Cross Station on that terrible Tuesday morning in September created two bright new forms; they could be seen in fiery prisms that glistered across the universe, but only if you knew where to look.

take it all out,
put it all back

Late one night, Lukas Forrest stumbled out of the Royal Oak public house on to the grey wet cobbles of Columbia Road to swear at the heavens. He had leaned his backpack against the bar to play on a gambling machine, and while he had been intently losing fifteen pounds to the board of pulsing yellow lights, someone had walked off with his belongings.

'Just once I'd like to come out on top – or just equal,' he yelled drunkenly into the sky. 'Is that asking too much?' Not being especially religious, he addressed himself to Zeus, figuring that one god was as good as another when it came to outraged invocation. Besides, Zeus had at least created order from chaos, and therefore knew something about the structure of the universe.

It would sound harsh to call Lukas a loser, but any statistician would do the maths and discreetly step away. Things went wrong around him, and who was to say it was simply due to bad decision-making? He had come to expect the worst from life, and adjusted his hopes and fears accordingly.

A week later, when he was walking Sparky, his Jack Russell,

across the muddy winter fields of Victoria Park, a football hit him hard on the back of the head. The force knocked his glasses from his nose to the pathway, cracking one of the lenses. They were new, and he could ill afford to buy another pair. He turned to protest, but the boys playing football were tensed and looking for trouble, and he was a mild man. So he picked up his cracked spectacles and placed them in his pocket, called the dog to heel and began to make his way home.

He had just reached the bridge on Mare Street, and was worrying about how he was going to survive the week and pay the optician's bill, when he saw the wallet lying on the dirt-crusted pavement. Inside were credit cards and some cash; seven twenty-pound notes and a tenner. He knew he should return it untouched, but the downturn in his luck persuaded him to pocket the cash and drop the wallet in the nearest pillar box, where it would hopefully be sent back to the owner.

Lukas had always thought of himself as a man undesired by luck's mistress, but for the first time he had come out even. An odd thought began to form in the back of his mind, and coalesced two days on, when he was making breakfast in his little third-floor Hackney flat, not concentrating on what he was doing. The opaque sunlight flared through the dirty windows, blinding him as he sawed away at the loaf, and he slipped, slicing open the skin between his thumb and his palm. The board stained dark as he cursed his stupidity, squeezing together the parted flesh. There were no plasters, so he was forced to hold the skin tight until the blood coagulated.

He heard the flap of the letterbox clap, and, still gripping his bloody hand, went to check the mail. In one of the envelopes he found a cheque for fifty pounds. Lukas entered a lot of competitions, but had never won anything. This time, though, he had submitted the winning entry to a puzzle set by the local pharmacist. He had also won a free allergy test and a year's supply of verruca treatment.

Lukas had always believed that on some fundamental level the world, indeed the universe, operated on a relatively fair system of balance; perform a good deed and ultimately you'll be rewarded, harm the planet and it will fight back, a yin–yang of cause and effect that prevented everything from spiralling out of control. Some mean twist of fate had excluded him from this balancing act, though, for every spin of the wheel had brought the pointer around to LOSE, and every decision in his life had proven a wrong one. Debts stacked, injuries accumulated, slights were perceived, kindnesses backfired.

But now, for the first time, Lukas sensed that he was on to something. Twice in succession, a misfortune had been quickly followed by a reversal of fate. For years he had felt excluded from the governing grace of the cosmos, watching enviously as others had leapfrogged past him into good careers and satisfying partnerships. What if it was finally his time to join the fortunate ones? He needed to find a way of testing the system.

That afternoon, he took a bus down to the river and drifted through calming drizzle on the Embankment, hoping to find a way of bringing bad fortune upon himself. Then, stepping from the kerb as he attempted to cross the busy junction on the south side of Blackfriars Bridge, he was knocked from his feet by a cursing cyclist. A small accident, no harm done, but the tumble put a rip in his only jacket. As he wiped himself down he realised he was quite upset, the only silver lining to his spill being the faint hope that something good would happen to balance his misfortune.

He did not have long to wait, for within the hour a red umbrella tipped back to reveal a heart-crushing girl, who stopped him to ask for directions to the nearest tube station. His offer to accompany her accepted, he passed a pleasant twenty minutes walking by her side, feeling the envious glances of those he passed. Although they parted with hardly a word, her simple acceptance of him hung around like a long summer day.

More importantly, it proved to Lukas that the system of balance worked. Since his birth it had been out of alignment, but something had happened on the night he had challenged the gods, some small fracture had occurred to knock him back on track. He saw doomed, penurious people all around him, complaining bitterly in dole queues, tearing up slips in betting shop doorways, lurching drunkenly along night streets muttering to themselves, and now he was no longer one of them. It was a wonderful feeling.

A minor traffic skirmish had resulted in a confidence boost with the opposite sex. Perhaps a riskier accident would get him a proper date. He headed back to the traffic island and promptly stepped off in front of a speeding motor scooter. The pizza delivery bike hit his right hip, spinning him on to the wet tarmac. Even better, when the furious rider scrambled to his feet, he punched Lukas in the chest.

Lukas hobbled home, but this time no pretty girl came to him for help. He examined the blue bruise that had appeared on his chest like the shadow of his heart, and wondered if he had been over-hasty in assuming his luck had altered. Logically, how could it have? After all, that competition letter would have to have been posted the day before he had cut himself. Hearing a bump on the stairs, he went to his front door and found a young woman dragging a suitcase along the landing. He had not seen Karine for several months. 'You're back,' he said in surprise.

'Yeah, I had a great time in New Zealand, but my folks really started getting on my nerves, and I was missing London.' She was more slender, more tanned than before, but he could tell that something else had changed. Karine lingered in the hall, leaning on the banister. 'So, are you going to put the kettle on and welcome me home?' she smiled. She had been pleasant enough once, but faintly dismissive. Now she seemed to be noticing him for the first time.

'Right, yeah, come in.' Lukas held the door open, marvelling as she passed him. They sat at the kitchen table and talked of her adventures on the far side of the world. She asked if he had missed her, and cocked her head to one side, smiling oddly. The rain stopped suddenly and sun appeared behind the council blocks, splitting prismatic colours through the speckled glass of the balconies, shining on her auburn hair. She needed conditioner.

'It's good to come home and find a friend here,' she said, laying her hand flat on the table, as if tempting him to cover it with his own. 'I wasn't a very good neighbour, was I? You offered to help me when I first moved in, and I virtually slammed the door in your face.'

'I understood,' said Lukas, amazed by her change of attitude. 'I figured you wanted your privacy.'

'I left my boyfriend because he wanted to let his mates fuck me,' she explained. 'I was understandably off men for a while. But now I'm not.' She had been offered a job in the loss adjustment department of an insurance company in town, and had accepted. She was starving hungry, and wondered if he would want to get something to eat with her?

The only place they could find open was an all-you-can-eat Indian buffet bar, which gave him the shits, but at least he got to spend time with her. *My luck really has changed*, he told himself, voiding himself on the toilet throughout the night. *But how? Why? Can it be trained and honed like a skill?* He needed to conduct further tests. More than that, he needed...

'I need a plan, Gabriel.'

'What are you talking about?' asked Gabriel, his oldest friend, who presented Lukas with an image of what he would be like if he really let himself go. There was nothing about Gabriel that suggested an angel. He was a games designer who made money he never took time off to spend. In appearance he was a living parody of a tech-head, luminously pale, out of shape, skin like greaseproof paper. He conducted nearly all the solitary functions of life at his desk, eating, sleeping and having sex there. If the Mac store started selling iCommodes, he would never have to leave his workroom again. As such, he was a bad person to take advice from, but a good one to bounce ideas off.

'For the plan to work, it will be necessary to visit bad luck upon myself in order to make a gain, and of course if this is merely a system of equal balance there would be no point, but what if I find there really is some universal principle of cosmic payback at work here?'

'Everything has a system,' Gabriel offered, thinking more of Unix than a celestial blueprint. 'But you could really hurt yourself.' He drained his pint and rose. 'Another one?'

Lukas followed his friend to the bar. 'There are different types of bad luck, Gabe. What looks like bad luck to others might actually not be so bad to me. Look at those ambulance-chasing compensation companies. They set out to make accidents appealing, for Christ's sake. They encourage people to fall over broken pavements and under fork-lift trucks for money.'

'You're telling me that if you injure yourself, something good will happen to you?'

'Works every time,' said Lukas. 'Watch this.' He placed his left hand over the empty pint glass on the bar and gently squeezed. The glass cracked, then burst, leaving three shards embedded in his flesh. With a grimace of pain, he pulled the pieces free. A rivulet of blood pooled in his palm and ran along his wrist. The barmaid looked up at him in alarm.

'Jesus, Lukas, are you nuts?' Gabriel snatched up a bar-towel and wrapped it around his hand. 'You're going to need stitches in that.'

'All the better.' Lukas checked under the towel as flowers of blood blossomed in his hand. He made his own way to the Accident & Emergency department of University College Hospital, and watched with interest while the nurse placed suture-plasters across the cleaned cuts. Then he went home to await results.

He didn't have to wait very long.

'You poor thing,' said Karine, wincing as she touched his hand. 'You could have severed an artery.' He'd told her there had been an accident with a pane of glass in the loading bay at work. 'I can see I'll have to look after you,' she said, and did. She stayed over in his single bed, and spent most of the night vigorously wriggling down on his member. In the morning, he looked across at her tousled hair on the pillow, her arm carelessly thrown across a pale breast, her impossibly flat stomach, and could not believe his – *don't say it*. A thunderhead of apprehension clouded his mind when he realised that he would have to work to keep his good fortune.

'It starts to slip when I'm not watching,' Lukas explained when they next went to the pub.

'What do you mean?' Gabriel dipped a crisp in his beer and sucked it pensively.

'My luck. It needs monitoring all the time. They're trying to downgrade my job to a Category 3. The flat is too small for me and Karine to spend any time in it. She gave me crabs. I'm not making enough money to take her out. The dog is sick and may have to be put down. The post office keeps losing all my mail. Everything was fine for a while, but then it starts slipping away from me if I don't keep on top of it.'

'That's 'cause most people's lives are never in balance,' said Gabriel. 'Everyone gets more bad luck than good.'

'Just my point. I've been given the power to change my life. I just have to make sure that the kind of bad luck I choose to inflict on myself doesn't cause any lasting damage. Then the good luck I get in return will outweigh it.'

'I think you're taking this all a bit too seriously,' said Gabriel. 'You're making up the rules to suit yourself. Have you ever thought that it might just be coincidence? We shape our own destinies. Our mettle is forged in the searing heat of experience.'

'Your marketing team came up with that slogan and put that on your games packaging, didn't they?'

'Yeah, but that doesn't invalidate it.'

'I'm wasting my time talking to you. I should be out there creating more good times for myself.'

'What are you going to do?'

Lukas removed a can of lighter fluid from his pocket. 'Come with me,' he said with a reassuring smile.

The pub where they had been drinking was in the middle of nowhere, a semi-derelict industrial estate built between a confluence of railway lines. At the end of its car park was a single denuded, tortured beech tree. Lukas climbed into his little blue Renault and rolled down the window.

'All you have to do is stay there and keep an eye on me,' he told Gabriel as he started the engine. Turning the car around, he lined it up with the beech, then got out and opened the bonnet. 'I need to make sure it goes up,' he explained, squirting lighter fluid over the engine. 'If anything goes wrong you have to come and pull me out, OK?'

'I don't know,' said Gabriel dubiously. 'This is your gig. I'm not putting myself on the line just because you've decided to behave like a total fruit.'

'Stand back then. I'll handle this myself. I worked it all out, I know exactly where to hit.' Lukas threw the can into the bushes and climbed back inside the car. After strapping himself in, he revved the engine and released the brake, fishtailing forward across the tarmac with a rubbery screech. The Renault smacked against the bole of the beech and the bonnet crumpled, but nothing caught fire. Lukas peered through the windscreen in disappointment, then backed up.

'Maybe I need to hit the tank,' he explained as he shot past. The dented front wheel arch scraped against its tyre as he reversed and roared backwards, slamming into the tree with a sizeable clang of metal. This time a spray of petrol shot from the side of the vehicle as Lukas struggled with his seatbelt. He kicked open the door and fell out, slipping in the puddle of fuel. 'Have you got a lighter?'

'Fuck off! I'm not going to be an accessory. Come away from there, you could be killed.'

'Stop worrying, Gabriel, this is the science of the universe.'

'Bollocks, it's about the girl, isn't it? It's not about luck or getting your fair share of life at all, it's all about the girl.'

Lukas ignored him, and dug for matches in his jacket, flicking one beneath the car. This time, there was a soft *whump* of yellow flame as it caught. Laughing, Lukas started walking away, and was surprised by the explosion that resulted moments later from the split fuel tank. He was thrown to the ground as pieces of burning plastic fell about him. Once Gabriel had stopped cowering, he ran over and threw his jacket across Lukas' burning hair. 'You're a bloody madman, you know that?' He unwrapped Lukas and pulled him to his feet. 'Christ, look at you. Something's cut a lump out of your neck. You'd better get something to stop the bleeding.'

Karine sat at the kitchen table, studying him thoughtfully, her chin resting in her hand. 'You seem to have a lot of accidents down at the depot,' she said finally. 'What was it this time?'

'A fire,' said Lukas. 'I managed to put it out. My boss said I was very brave.'

'Shouldn't you talk to your union about having to work in such dangerous conditions?' she asked. 'There are laws against things like this.'

'We don't have a union. I'm fine, really. It was no big deal.' He played it down, but she refused to take her eyes from him, and he noticed her worried glances throughout the rest of the evening.

The next morning he arrived at work to find the rest of the loading bay staff standing around. 'What's happened?' he asked.

'Didn't you hear?' said Said, one of the packers. 'Jamal caught his wife with another man yesterday afternoon. He packed up his stuff and walked out on her, just came in a few minutes ago to tender his resignation. It shouldn't worry you, though. He's recommended you to take over his position.' Jamal was Lukas' boss, and the promotion would carry considerably more responsibility, plus a higher salary.

'You don't look surprised,' Said remarked.

'I'm not.' Lukas smiled to himself as he made his way to the foreman's office.

The next few weeks went well. Without a word of discussion, he and Karine started looking for a larger flat. They found one in Kilburn, two light and airy rooms with a balcony, in an Edwardian corner building that faced the morning sun. Lukas found his job demanding but enjoyable. His hours grew longer, but the overtime came in handy. A few petty annoyances occurred, the usual soul-drag of urban life, but nothing he felt could not be overcome. He stopped hanging out with his best friend because Gabriel was a loser. Lukas felt protected, as though the impartial figure of fate had decided to balance her scales in his favour, wrapping him in her warm safe shadow. If things went badly at work and he got fired, he had the means to redress the balance. He explained his feelings to Said at the depot, who patted him on the back and laughed.

'What's so funny?' asked Lukas.

'My friend, I think you are beginning to understand the nature of Islam. Allah protects us all now. You will have a long and happy life, with many children, if He should will it so. The Qur'ān says there are eight gates to Paradise, and everyone shall be admitted but the man who has a grudge against his brother.' He smiled with a strange, penetrating stare, then walked away laughing.

It should have ended there, but of course it did not.

Lukas remained in favour with benign fate, the power of Allah, call it what you will, but without attention the balance slipped incrementally, imperceptibly away. Winter set in with a bad-tempered display of burst pipes, jammed boilers and leaking eaves. Work got tougher. The dog got sicker. Karine was released from her job as her company went into liquidation. Lukas' father was diagnosed with lung cancer. The bad luck, he realised with a falling heart, was rippling out to those around him now. It was as though he had somehow freed himself from the chain of life's misfortunes, only to spread them to those he cared most about. He had spent all his time worrying about his own life-trajectory, and could not see how selfish his own existence had become.

When Karine announced that she was pregnant, Lukas seriously began to fear for their future. They were united, and surely anything that happened to one would happen to the other. It was time to take steps that would ensure their protection, at least until the safe deliverance of their baby. He knew that he would have to do something more lastingly harmful to himself, so he called Gabriel once more. They met in Gabe's grandfather's musty old shed, at the end of a dew-soaked allotment backing on to a shabby city park.

'I'm going to need your help for this,' said Lukas, producing a thick red elastic band and tying it around his left hand. 'There's going to be quite a bit of blood.'

'I don't understand,' Gabriel complained. 'Why not your foot? You wouldn't miss a tiny toe, would you?'

'Maybe not, but I'd have trouble walking and would probably have to take time off work. The little finger of my left hand is best. It's a permanent mutilation, the kind of injury you'd describe to others as a piece of bad luck, don't you think?'

'Yeah, but your *finger*.'

'I don't need it, and it shouldn't upset Karine too much once she gets over the shock.' He handed Gabriel the gleaming new axe he had purchased at the local hardware shop. 'You've got to bring it down exactly where I indicate, OK? And if I pass out, or can't manage to cauterise it myself, you have to do that part too.' He pointed to the blade of the army knife that was heating up in the stove flame beside the work-bench.

'You think you've proven that your system works,' said Gabriel, 'but this is serious stuff now. I'm not sure I can handle blood and bone.'

'You design games where characters slaughter aliens by strangling them with their own guts,' said Lukas. 'This should be a piece of cake.'

'That's different, it's not real. You're flesh and blood. What if it goes wrong or you don't get good luck, or you just change your mind? Am I going to get into trouble for causing you injury?'

'I'll make sure nobody knows about our deal,' assured Lukas. He had promised Gabriel ten per cent of anything he made through the intervention of fate, although how they would work out the value of his forthcoming luck had yet to be decided. Gabriel's gaming company was faring poorly and he needed the money.

Lukas drew a line across the back of his pinkie with a blue felt-tip pen, then tightened the rubber band around its base. 'Here's the mark you have to hit. Think you can do that?'

'I guess.' Gabriel accepted the axe and felt its weight in his hands. 'You'll have to keep really, really still.'

Lukas flexed his fingers and splayed his hand palm-down on the wooden work-bench. He checked that the cotton swabs and disinfectant were within reachable distance. 'Don't worry about hurting me. I've taken enough Valium to kill a horse. You could saw the top of my head off without me feeling a thing. Think you're ready for this?'

'I guess so.' Gabriel needed the money. He slowly raised the axe.

'Get ready to slam it as hard as you can.'

Everything would have been fine if Gabriel had not closed his eyes before swinging the blade with all his might. It arced down and embedded itself into Lukas' wrist, severing veins and sinew and bone, spraying arterial blood across the shed with such power that it splattered the opposite wall. Lukas' eyes bulged in shock as he fell.

'Oh Christ!' Soaked, Gabriel looked at the partially severed hand dangling from his friend's arm. 'Oh Jesus Christ!'

'You fucking idiot,' Lukas gasped. 'You'll have to finish it. Pull the whole thing off.' The fingers of his left hand were still flinching as his nerve endings went haywire. 'Not the axe – use the Stanley knife.'

'I can't, oh God,' whimpered Gabriel.

'You have to. Hurry up, I'm losing too much blood.' Lukas had started to turn deathly white. Hardly daring to look through screwed-up eyes, Gabriel hacked at the stump with the sterilised blade of the Stanley knife Lukas had provided in case of emergency. With a tooth-grinding grimace he grabbed at the blood-slick hand, sawed and pulled. The fingers reacted like crab-legs, closing around his own. Tendons stretched and snapped, and the hand came free, falling to the floor like a muscular white spider.

'For God's sake, cauterise the end of my wrist.' Lukas' eyes had rolled up in his head, and he was pouring sweat. As he tried to control his trembling, Gabriel picked up the army knife and pressed the heat-blackened blade against the ragged exposed flesh of the stump. Lukas screamed, a terrible smell of burning meat thickening the air in the shed. Gabriel kicked open the door and violently threw up on the grass.

'It's still bleeding, pack the hand in a bucket of ice and get me to a hospital,' said Lukas before he fell to the ground.

The doctors insisted on sewing the hand back on, probably just to show off their surgery skills, so Lukas got what he wanted: incredibly bad fortune with a relative minimum of loss. Gabriel tried to negotiate a twenty per cent share of Lukas' good luck from the removal of his hand, but he backed down when Lukas threatened him with exposure, then with a cricket bat.

Karine was horrified by what had happened, but tended to him through the recovery. He told everyone that a terrible accident had occurred while he had been operating a lathe, but given the number of accidents he had endured in the last year, people now looked at him with confusion and mistrust in their eyes. Arteries and nerves were reattached, anti-inflammatory drugs were administered and the hand healed well, although the scarring around his wrist prompted him to read Mary Shelley with fresh eyes. He was soon able to start moving his fingers again, although he never regained much feeling in them.

As usual, it only took a day for the balance of fortune to reassert itself. An uncle Lukas had not seen since he was seven years old died suddenly, leaving him a beautiful farmhouse and several acres of land in the heart of the Hertfordshire countryside. Not only was the house a perfect place to raise children, but he and Karine were able to find good local work at only a slightly lower salary rate than London. The pregnancy progressed smoothly, and Karine gave birth to a squalling, healthy boy. They named the child Nathan, and Lukas renovated the farmhouse, building a nursery. Sparky, their Jack Russell, made a miraculous recovery and spent his days chasing rabbits in the fields behind the house.

After his falling-out with Gabriel, Lukas ceased to see any of his old friends and instead concentrated all his efforts on building a new life for himself and his beautiful wife.

When Nathan was one year old, the happy couple finally married and spent a month in New Zealand's South Island on their honeymoon, where Karine's overjoyed parents presented them with gifts.

Everything was going so well. But sometimes Lukas would glance across the pillow and catch his wife watching him as she lay awake. He had never been able to tell her the truth about his system for ensuring their happiness. He was worried that she might think him insane, that the smile in her eyes would die, that she would gradually withdraw her affections. Instead, he chose to carry the burden of his secret alone.

He found it hard to sleep at night. He had been raised in London, where there was very little wind or sky, but here in the countryside the elements seemed determined to ruin his sleep. After his wife and child were bedded down, he weather-watched from the window, trying to understand what had brought him to this strange understanding of the world. The conundrum gnawed at him, stealing energy, forcing him to question everything he had taken for granted.

His mother had suffered a life of drudgery before succumbing to bone cancer; where had the balance been for her? She had always told him that her greatest joy had been her only child, but he had failed to help her when she needed it most. Somewhere out there in the sparkling blue-black heavens lay the answer: a governing justice that provided the lucky few with the power to right themselves when everything seemed wrong. Ultimately, fate gave back as much as it took. It was as impersonal and implacable as the tide and the moon, as random as the patterns of the wind on the wheatfields. Good fortune was a cruel mistress who always demanded a sacrifice. No wonder they called her Lady Luck.

'Come back to bed,' murmured Karine, turning over and burying herself within the meringue-folds of the duvet. Lukas watched her sleep, untroubled by the precarious path of destiny.

One day Gabriel rang, out of the blue. After a few pleasantries he became serious. 'My business has collapsed,' he said. 'I'm being thrown out of my apartment.'

'I'm sorry to hear that.' Lukas was suspicious.

'Yeah. Things haven't been going so well for me lately. To be honest, I don't know what I'm going to do. Listen, I wondered…' There was a pause on the line. 'I wondered if I could do what you did. Change the balance of my life.'

'I don't know,' Lukas answered truthfully. 'I'm not sure how it works. I guess you could try.'

It was the last time they spoke. A month later he heard that Gabriel had killed himself. He went to the funeral but there was hardly anyone in attendance, and no one seemed to know the circumstances of his death, although it was rumoured that Gabriel had wrecked his beloved computers and hanged himself on the door of his workroom. Clearly, the system of balance did not work for everyone. Perhaps he had not believed enough.

Lukas reconciled himself to the realisation that he would never understand the workings of fate. People who refused to question their existence were usually happier. He watched his staff at the centre carry on through accidents, illnesses and random acts of cruelty without complaint or puzzlement, and resolved to be more like them. But he was bothered by the feeling that he had missed some fundamental insight about the strange turn his life had taken.

He finally experienced a revelation on the morning of his son's second birthday, when he visited the local newsagent on his way to work. He had continued to enter competitions and buy lottery tickets, even though he now had everything he'd ever wished for. Lukas checked the numbers, as he did every week, and realised that he'd won £16,000,000 in the rollover jackpot. Karine nearly deafened him with her scream when he rang and told her.

He went into work to tender his resignation. He wanted to tell the lads in the loading bay that he was leaving them all some money. As he walked through the hangar, he felt as though he had truly bested fate.

'Lukas, you are the luckiest man alive, mate!' called one of his employees.

Then he heard the warning shouts, the clang of scaffolding poles and clattering chains, and looked up to see the great wall of stacked washing machines keeling over towards him.

Lukas experienced his final revelation.

In the moment before he was obliterated beneath two hundred tons of kitchen appliances, before sinks and taps and cooker hobs fashioned in steel and glass and chrome slashed through his scarred skin to shatter his bones and burst his skull like a child stamping on a melon, he realised that the cosmic system of equilibrium was more intricate than he had imagined. That parched desert worlds were equally weighed against planets of glittering fecundity. That every penny you were allowed to take out had to go back in. And that ultimately, everything in the universe strove to find its level.

After all the things Lukas had seen in his life, the final image that gained access to his soul was the steel corner of an induction hob manufactured in Bielefeld, Germany, as it swung toward his eyes.

And the last thing he knew was that the balance of fortune following misfortune worked perfectly well in the opposite direction.

All things being equal, it really was a rotten life.

the twilight express

The funfair blew in one hot, windy night in late September, while everyone's doors and windows were sealed against the invading desert dust. Billy Fleet knew it was coming when he heard the distorted sound of a calliope drifting faintly on the breeze, but he didn't think then that it might hold the answer to his problem.

He leaned on his bedroom sill, watching the faint amber light move across the horizon of trees, beneath a velvet night filled with winking stars. The country dark was flushing with their arrival. On another night he might have climbed the trellis in his peejays and sat on the green grit of the tarpaper roof to watch the carnival procession, but tonight he had too much on his mind. The fair had travelled from Illinois to Arizona, and somehow made the detour here. There were a few dates yet that weren't played out, small towns with bored kids and fathers jingling chump change, but soon the carnies would be looking to put down roots as the dying summer cooled the hot sidewalks and families grew more concerned with laying in stores for winter than wasting good money on gimcrack sideshows and freak tents.

Billy turned restlessly under his sheets, wondering what it would take to clear his troubles, and the more he thought, the more desperate he became. His mother would cry, his father would beat him, and then a subtler meanness would settle over his life as friends and teachers pulled away, shamed by his inability to do what was right. It was a town that put great store by self-discipline.

But it wasn't cowardice that would prevent him from pleasing them, it was preservation. He wasn't about to throw his life away just because Susannah's period was late. No matter how hard she pushed, he wouldn't marry her. Hell, he wasn't sure he even liked her much, and would never have gone up to Scouts' Point if she hadn't complained that all the other girls had been taken there. The entire bluff was crowded with creaking cars, and though the scent of rampant sex excited him, it all felt so tawdry, so predictably small town. He had no intention of staying in Cooper Creek for a day longer than he had to, for each passing moment brought him closer to stopping for ever, just as his father had done, and boy, the family had never heard the end of that.

He couldn't just up and leave without money, qualifications, some place to go, and with just three weeks left before his graduation, it was a matter of pride to stay. He imagined the door to a good out-of-state college swinging open, taking him to a bright new future. But by the time summer break was over Susannah's belly would be round as a basketball, and the trap would have closed about him. He knew how the girls in the coffee shop talked, as if finding the right boy and pinning him down was the only thing that mattered. Mr Sanders, his biology teacher, had told him that after babies were born, the male stopped developing because his role in the procreation cycle was over. It wasn't right that a girl who came from such a dirt-dumb family as Susannah's should be able to offer him a little dip in the honey-pot and then chain him here through the best years of his life, in some edge-of-town clapboard house with a baby-room, where the smell of damp diapers would cling to his clothes and his loveless nights would be filled with dreams of what might have been.

There had to be another solution, but it didn't present itself until he went out to the field where the Elysium funfair was pitching up in the pale gold mist of the autumn morning, and watched as the roustabouts raised their rides, bolting together boards and pounding struts into the cool earth. There was a shop-soiled air about the Elysium, of too many tours without fresh paint, of waived safety permits and back-pocket accounting. The shills and barkers had not yet arrived, but Billy could tell that they, too, would be fighting for one more season before calling it a day and splitting up to go their separate ways. Funfairs rarely stopped at Cooper Creek; there wasn't enough fast money to be made here, and although the local folks were kind enough to passing strangers, they didn't care to mix together.

Billy sat on the back of the bench and watched as the gears and tracks were laid behind the flats. He saw missing teeth and caked oil, mended brake-bars and makeshift canopies, iron rods bound with wire over rope, and wondered how many accidents had forced the Elysium to skip town in the dead of night. That was the moment he realised he would be able to kill Susannah's baby.

He saw the question as simply one of survival. He had something to offer the world, and the only obstacle that waited in his path was a wide-eyed schoolgirl. As the yellowing leaves tumbled above his head, Billy felt the first chill decision of adulthood.

The funfair ran its cycle beyond Labor Day, but only passed by Cooper Creek for a week. He felt sure that convincing Susannah to come with him would be easy, but before that evening he needed to find a way inside the ghost train. He had watched the canvas flats of hellfire and damnation being put together to form a righteous journey, devil snakes and playing cards lining the tunnel through which the cars would roll. Now he needed to befriend the woman who was helping her old man set up the ticket booth, the one the roustabouts called Molly. He knew how to use seventeen years of healthy boyhood on a thirty-five-year-old overweight woman. Girls flirt with attractive men, but boys flirt with anyone.

When he approached her, she was bending over a broken step, and all he could see was the wide field of blue cornflowers that covered her dress. He stood politely until she rose, hands on hips, a vast acreage of sun-weather cleavage smiling at him. Her small grey eyes no longer trusted anything they saw, but softened on his face.

'Help you, boy?'

'Ma'am, my name's Billy Fleet, and I'm raising money for my college education by trying to find summer work. I know how to fix electrics, and it seems to me you need someone to work the ghost train, 'cause you got some shorts sparking out in there, and I ain't seen no one go in to repair 'em.'

'What are you, town watchdog? Got nothing better to do than spy on folks trying to earn a decent living?' Molly's bead-eyes shrank further.

'No, ma'am. I meant no disrespect, I just see you setting up from my bedroom window and know you're shy a man or two. This town's real particular about health and safety, and I figure I can save you a heap of trouble for a few bucks.'

The woman folded fat arms across her considerable bosom and rocked back to study him. 'I don't take kindly to blackmail, Billy boy.' Her eyes were as old as Cleopatra's, and studied him without judgement. 'Fairs don't take on college boys. It don't pay to be too smart around here.'

'Maybe so, but in this town a fair is a place where a guy gets a rosette for keeping a pig. This is a real carnival. It's special.'

'Ain't no big secret to it. You take a little, give a little back, that's all.' She saw the need in his eyes and was silent for a moment. 'Hell, if the town is so dog-dead you got to watch us set up from your bedroom at nights maybe we can work something out. Let me go talk to Papa Jack.'

That was how Billy got the job on the Twilight Express.

The night the fair opened, white lights punched holes into the blue air, and the smell of sage and dust was replaced with the tang of rolling hotdogs. Susannah had planned to go with her girlfriends, to shriek and flirt on the opalescent Tilt-A-Whirl, holding down their skirts and tossing back their hair with arms straightened to the bar, bucking and spinning across the night. She agreed with just a nod when Billy insisted on taking her, and he wondered whether she would really be fussed if he just took off, but he couldn't do that. He couldn't bear the thought of people bad-mouthing him, even though he wouldn't be there to hear it. So he took Susannah to the fair.

He couldn't bring himself to place his arm around her waist, because the baby might sense his presence and somehow make him change his mind. Babies did that; they turned tough men into dishrags, and he wasn't about to let that happen. She wore a red dress covered in yellow daisies like tiny bursts of sunlight, and laughed at everything. He couldn't see what was funny. She was happily robbing him of his life and didn't even notice, pointing to the fat lady and the stilt-walkers, feeding her glossy red mouth with pink floss as if she was eating sunset clouds.

He thought she would want to talk about the baby and what it meant to them, but she seemed happy to take the subject for granted, as if she couldn't care whether there was something growing inside her or not.

At the entrance of the ghost train, Molly watched impassively as he passed her without acknowledgement. Susannah baulked and tried to turn aside when she reached the steps to the car.

'No, Billy, don't make me go. It's dark in there. Let's take the rope-walk instead.'

'Don't make a big deal of it, Susannah, the ghost train's a few devils and skeletons is all.' He had stood inside the ride beside the flickering tissue-inferno, breathing in the coppery electric air, watching the cars bump over soldered tracks that should have been scrapped years ago, lines that could throw a rider like a bronco.

She saw the pressure in his eyes and gave in meekly, took her ticket and bowed her head as she passed through the turnstile, as if she was entering church. The car was tight for two adults; he was forced to place his arm around her shoulder. Her hair tickled his forearm. She smelled as fresh-cut as a harvest field. With a sudden lurch, the car sparked into life and a siren sounded as they banged through the doors into musty darkness.

He knew what was coming. After a few cheap scares of drifting knotted string and jiggling rubber spiders, the car would switch back on itself and tilt down a swirling red tunnel marked Damnation Alley, but just before it dropped into the fires of hell it would swing again, away to the safer sights of comically dancing wooden skeletons. The track was bad at the switch; a person could tip out on the line as easy as pie. The next car would be right behind, and those suckers were heavy. Papa Jack had fallen into a bourbon bottle a couple of nights back, and told him about a boy who had bust his neck when the cars had stalled in Riverton Fields, Wichita, a few seasons back. The Elysium had hightailed it out of town before their sheriff could return from his fishing trip, had even changed its name for a couple of years. A second accident would get folks nodding and clucking about how they suspected trouble from the carnie folk all along. He would make sure Susannah didn't get bruised up, he wouldn't want that, but she had to take a spill, and land good and hard on her stomach.

As the car hit its first horseshoe she gripped his knee, and he sensed her looking up at him. He caught the glisten of her eyes in the flashbulbs, big blue pupils, daybreak innocent. They tilted into the spiralling tunnel and she squeaked in alarm, gripping tighter, as close now as when they had loved. The moment arrived as they reached the switch. The car lurched and juddered. All he had to do was push, but she was still holding tightly on to him. In an effort to break her grip, he stood up sharply.

'Billy…what—'

The car twisted and he tipped out, landing on his back in the revolving tunnel. Susannah's hands reached out towards him, her fingers splayed wide, then her car rounded a black-painted peak and was gone. The cylinder turned him over once, twice, dropping him down into the uplit paper fires of damnation, scuffing his elbows and knees on the greased tracks.

And then there was nothing beneath his limbs.

When he opened his eyes again, he found himself in the fierce green fields behind the house. Judging by the smell of fresh grass in the morning air, it was late spring, but he was wearing the same clothes. The sun was hot on his face, his bare arms. The voice spoke softly behind him. He could only just hear it over the sound of the crickets and the rustling grass.

'Oh Billy, what a beautiful day. If only it was always like this. I remember, I remember…' She was lying in the tall grass near the tree, running a curving green stem across her throat, her lips. Her print dress had hiked around her bare pale thighs. She stared into the cloudless sky as though seeing beyond into space.

'What have you done with the baby, Susannah?'

'I don't know,' she replied slowly. 'It must be around here somewhere. Look how clear the sky is. It feels like you could see for ever.'

The day was so alive that it shook with the beat of his heart, the air taut and trembling with sunlit energy. It was hard to concentrate on anything else. 'We have to find the baby,' he told her, fighting to develop the thought. 'We went to all that trouble.'

He looked up at the sun and allowed the dazzling yellow light to fill his vision. When he closed his eyes, tiny translucent creatures wriggled across the pink lids, as mindless and driven as spermatozoa.

'I forget what I did with it, Billy. You know how I forget things. Will you make me a daisy chain? Nobody ever made me a daisy chain. Nobody ever noticed me until you.'

'Let's find the baby first, Susannah.'

'I think perhaps it was out in the field. Yes, I'm sure I saw it there.' She raised a lazy arm and pointed back, over her head. Her hair was spread around her head in a corn-coloured halo. She smiled sleepily and shut her eyes. The lids were sheened like dragonfly wings. 'I can see the stars today, even with my eyes closed. We should never leave this place. Never, ever leave. Look how strong we are together. Why, we can do anything. You see that, don't you? You see that…' Her voice drifted off.

He watched her fall asleep. She looked a little older now. Her cheekbones had appeared, shaping her face to a heart. She had lost some puppy fat. Light shimmered on her cheeks, wafted and turned by the tiny shields of leaves above. 'I have to go and look, Susannah,' he told her. 'There are bugs everywhere.'

'You just have to say the name,' she murmured. 'Just say the name.' But her voice was lost beneath the buzzing of crickets, the shifting of grass, the tremulous morning heat.

He rose and walked deep into the field, until he came to a small clearing in the grass. Lowering himself on to his haunches, he studied the ant nest, watching the shiny black mass undulating around a raised ellipse in the brown earth. The carapaces of the insects were darkly iridescent, tiny night-prisms that bustled on thousands of pin-legs, batting each other with antennae like blind men's canes. He shaped his hands into spades and dug them into the squirming mass of segmented bodies, feeling them tickle over his hands and wrists, running up his arms. They nipped at his skin with their pincers, but were too small to hurt. Digging deeper until his fingertips met under the earth, he felt the fat thoraxes roll warmly over his skin. Carefully he raised the mound, shaking it free of insects. A baby's face appeared, fat and gurgly, unconcerned by the bugs that ran across his wide blue eyes, in and out of the pouted lips. Raising the child high towards the fiery summer globe, he watched as the last of the ants fell away, revealing his smiling, beautiful son.

'Tyler,' he said, 'Tyler Fleet.'

And he set off back towards his sleeping wife.

'Billy. Billy, you come back.' Her lank hair hung over his face, tickling. Her plucked eyebrows were arched in a circumflex of concern. She had been crying.

'What's your problem?' he asked slowly, feeling the words in his mouth. He was lying on the cool dry dirt in front of the ghost train ride. A few passers-by had stopped to watch.

'You fell out of the carriage is what's the problem,' she said, touching his cheek with her fingers. 'You cut your forehead. Oh, Billy.'

'I'm fine. Was just a slip is all.' He raised himself on one elbow. 'No need to get so worked up.' He rubbed the goosebumps from his arms.

'I was so frightened in there, I thought I'd lost you, I panicked,' she told him. 'Look.' She held up her palm and showed him the crimson dot. 'It's my blood, not yours. I started late, that's all. I'm not pregnant, Billy. I'm so sorry.'

He realised why she had been so unconcerned at the fair. She had been happy to place her trust in him unquestioningly. It had never crossed her mind that things might not work out. He studied her face as if seeing her for the first time. 'I'm so sorry,' she said again, searching his eyes in trepidation.

'Don't worry,' he told her, pulling himself up and dusting down his jeans. 'Maybe we can make another one.' He offered his arm. 'Give me your hand.' He sealed his fingers gently over the crimson dot. She pulled him to his feet, surprisingly strong.

Molly looked up as he passed the ticket booth to the Twilight Express. There was no way of knowing what she was thinking, or if she was thinking anything at all. 'Hey Billy, Papa Jack wants you to work with him tomorrow night,' she told him. 'You gonna need to put that money by. The baby'll be back, and maybe next time you'll be ready for him.'

Then she went back to counting the change from the tickets.

The moon above the Elysium funfair shone with the colours of the sideshow, red and blue glass against butter yellow, as the calliope played on, turning wishes into starlight.

The Twilight Express was gone. It had been replaced by the Queen of the South, a Mississippi riverboat ride where passengers seated themselves on cream-coloured benches and watched as their paddle steamer slipped upriver, not past the real southland of jute factories and boatyards and low-cost housing, but an imagined antebellum fantasy of filigreed plantation houses glimpsed through Spanish moss. The candy-coloured deck looked out on pastel hardboard flats and painted linen skies that creaked past on a continuous roll as birds twittered on the tape loop.

Molly was still here at the Elysium, working the riverboat ride now. She watched him approach without pleasure or sorrow shaping her face. He supposed carnie folk saw too much to care one way or the other. To her, he was just another small-town hick.

'So you didn't leave,' she said, sweeping coins from her counter without looking up.

'Did I say I was going?' he asked defensively.

'Didn't have to.' She stacked dimes to the width of her hand, calculating the value, then swept them into a bag. 'You should bring your wife here.'

'You don't know I married her,' he said, kicking at the dry dirt in annoyance.

'Don't I, though.' Her expression never changed.

He left her counting the gate, and resolved not to bring Susannah to the Elysium. But he did, that Friday night.

He breathed in the smell of hot caramel, sawdust and sugar-floss, fired a rifle at pocked metal soldiers and hooked a yellow duck for Tyler, but wouldn't go near Molly's ride. 'I don't need to go on that,' he told his wife, watching as she held their baby to her breast. 'Not after last time.'

Susannah jiggled the baby and stood looking up at the painted riverbank. 'That was more than three years ago, Billy. The Twilight Express is gone. It's not a ghost train any more. No one's gonna fall out of the car.' She smiled at him bravely, as if it was all that could protect her from his simmering impatience.

Billy still wasn't sure what had happened that time. The accident had changed something between them. All he remembered was that she had freed him and he had elected to stay, but part of him remained regretful. He loved his boy, but the smell of the infant had lingered too long on his skin, reminding him of his responsibilities, removing any pretence of freedom. There was never time to be alone and think things through.

He worked in his uncle's feed store now, and made a decent living, but it wasn't what he had imagined for himself. Sometimes strangers passed through the local bar and talked of harsh cities they'd seen, strange lands they'd visited, and he wanted to beg them: *let me come with you.*

He loved his son, but knew there could have been a better

life. The carnival had changed all that. It took a little and gave a little back, that's what Molly had once told him.

'Come with me,' said Susannah. 'We're a team. We do things together.'

'You two are the team. Go have fun,' he said, placing a hand firmly in the small of her back, propelling her towards the steps of the Queen of the South, its minstrel music piped through speakers set on either side of the great painted boat that seemed to move forward but never travelled anywhere. 'Show Tyler the Mississippi. I'll be here when you get off.'

Susannah passed reluctantly through the turnstile, balancing the boy on her hip. From within the ticket booth, Molly caught his eye for the briefest of moments, and he read something strange in her expression. His wife looked back, the dying daylight shining in her eyes. Her glance pierced his heart. She gave a brief nervous smile and stepped inside the boat. He wanted to run forward and snatch her back before she could take her seat, to tell her he knew what he had and it was real good, but even as he thought this he wondered what else he might be missing, and then the banjo music had started, the plyboard trees were shunting past, and the steamer was gradually lost from view.

The ride was long. He grew bored with waiting and tried to knock a coconut from its shy, even though he knew it was probably nailed in place. When he returned to the ride it had already emptied out, but there was no sign of his young family. He asked Molly where they had gone, but she denied ever having seen them. None of the barkers would be drawn on the subject. He vaulted into the back of the riverboat ride, clambering through the dusty sunlit diorama, trying to see how they might have escaped through the pasteboard flats, but was pulled out by Papa Jack.

Billy yelled and stamped and made a fuss, finally called the sheriff, but everyone agreed that Susannah had gone, taking their child with her. People looked at him warily and backed away.

The heatwave broke on the day the Elysium carnival trundled out of town. As rain darkened the bald dirt-patch where the tents had stood, Billy watched the trucks drive off, and knew that he had failed the test.

The lilting sound of the calliope stole away his dreams and faded slowly with them, leaving him under clouded skies, filled with bitter remorse. Twilight died down to a starless night, and there was nothing left inside it now, just the empty, aching loss of what he might have had, who he might have been, and the terrible understanding that he had been looking too far away for the answer to his prayers.

Somewhere in another town, another state, the Twilight Express showed the way between stations for those passengers who were strong enough to stay on the ride.

exclusion zone

'She called him a *Pussy Ho* last night, screamed at the top of her voice in the middle of the street,' said Simon Rennie. 'What on earth is a Pussy Ho? Her kids were all looking on. I suppose they understood what she meant. This is North London, for God's sake, not South Detroit. They must get this patois from television shows. Why is it that only common people ever want to be American?'

8:15 am, and the Rennie household was preparing for the day ahead. The temperature was already twenty-six degrees in their apartment, too hot for cooked breakfasts, so Eva had given them fruit and cereal. Simon insisted on wearing a jacket and tie even though his office had relaxed their dress code in the debilitating heat. He stood at the great window, bowl in hand, chewing ruminatively. Even though they had been in the flat for over a year now, the view still fascinated him. King's Cross had always been an area of enormous change, and was once again reinventing itself, the land heaving up in a seismic shiver that would shake old buildings to the ground, leaving the silvered roofs of new apartments to rise above them. But even these were now hemmed with a jumble of red brick walls and chimneys where the last few Victorian terraced houses remained like surviving teeth. The worst of them, a row housing a dozen low-income families, stood between the Rennie family and the next apartment building. Simon could see their chaotic back yards, their rubbish-filled front gardens.

'I didn't specifically request to live in a gated community,' he told Eva with an air of apology. 'It just happened that the property we wanted was inside one. I've always pushed for more affordable housing in London. But really, look at them.' Simon was a partner in a firm of architects working on the area's regeneration, and found the job far more interesting than life at home.

Eva knew better than to get involved with this conversation. A retreat to the kitchen was called for, before her husband started on about the mess.

'And the litter, I mean, how can one family produce so much rubbish? The chavs do all the buying, and the middle classes do all the recycling. Come and look, they've bought themselves a giant plasma screen, and thrown the box and all the polystyrene pieces over their wall into the road. Who would consciously destroy their own environment like that?'

Celina, his daughter, sighed noisily and rose from the sofa where she had been watching a celebrity makeover show. Lately she seemed to ignore him, or do the opposite of everything he said.

'They're just messy people with a lot of kids,' said Eva. 'You make too much of it. Imagine how they feel, being able to look through the gates at us, seeing how we live.'

'They're trying to work out how to get their hands on the car park swipe-cards. Joseph told me they have to keep changing the numerical combination on the gate-pad because the kids are memorising the codes. Am I supposed to feel guilty for working harder and earning more than they do?'

'Let me know what time you're going to be home, OK?' Eva headed to the dishwasher.

Outside, Simon kicked disconsolately at the pile of crisps bags, chocolate bar wrappers, random pieces of plastic and Coke cans that lay like oversized shards of costume jewellery around the base of the freshly planted cherry tree where the chav kids played. They had stripped the bark away in a ring and discarded the pieces in the gutter, ensuring that the tree would die. Glaring up at the trellised windows on the most unruly house, he resolved to ring the council again as soon as he reached work.

He had reached the age where small acts of thoughtlessness made him disproportionately angry. Twelve affordable dwellings for large families sat in the shadow of the great wooden gate, behind which two hundred professionals, mostly single, ate and slept and worked at computer screens, and just one of the families below them caused all the trouble. There she was now, the fat woman with blonde scraped-back hair and hoop earrings, the one who usually sat on the step of number 15 with a skintight white top and leotard stretched over her lardy body. She had five or six mixed-race kids living there, and a steady parade of rowdy fathers. Simon had watched from his balcony as the black BMW Series 6 roared up to her front door, its tinted windows masking the vehicle in threatening anonymity. It was pretty obvious to Simon where a twenty-five-year-old black man got a car like that. He had seen the comings and goings late at night, watched the endless visits from the police. According to Joseph, their caretaker, Islington Council had offered them £50,000 to leave the neighbourhood, but they had refused.

Scala Partners had been the first office to move into the dusty hinterland of King's Cross, amid promises to clean up the area in time for its planned regeneration. The prostitutes and crack dealers had been shunted off the streets, only to pop up a mile away like returning weeds. Trees had been planted and traffic-calming measures installed. The backstreet laundries and stables had been reborn as uplighted offices and glassy loft apartments.

Even the porn shops and cheap accommodation outlets were moving out in the face of rent hikes. Only takeaways and backpackers' hostels still marked the area as one of transience and instability. As far as Scala was concerned, the rehabilitation programme was proving a great success. Right now, opposite the Rennie family's top-floor apartment, a concert hall was being built. Gay couples were moving in; a good sign, as they were civic-minded and raised property values. Only the shambolic council families remained with their mess, their screaming, their moral lassitude.

Another hot Friday night brought another fight on the street. Simon surreptitiously watched the scuffle from his darkened balcony as he sneaked a cigarette. The kids had been abandoned while their parents sat drinking in the back garden of number 15. They played football for a while, hammering at the gates, then sat on the kerb drinking beer and throwing food at each other. Shortly after midnight one of the mothers came out, but only to deposit a tiny child on the pavement before drunkenly weaving back to the house. At 2:00 am the black BMW pulled up, and the driver struck some kind of deal with two shifty, feral boys who had appeared at the street corner. When the fat blonde woman emerged, another argument quickly escalated until she was slapping the BMW driver around the face. His returning punch was fast and fleeting, but hard enough to knock her over. She came back at him screaming, but he held her off with ease.

Where the knife came from Simon never found out – he was too far away to see – but a moment later, the driver was lying in the gutter moaning as blood seeped from his mouth. An ambulance and four police cars arrived, and the subsequent shouting kept them awake for the rest of the night.

In the morning, even Eva had acceded his point about the nightmarish family who lived below them. Only Celina seemed resistant. 'You fucking go on about them because they disturb your plans for a perfect world,' she muttered, kicking her heels against the sofa. 'You don't really give a shit.'

'I care about how their children are growing up,' said Simon hotly, 'and you're starting to sound like them. Have you seen how aggressive the older ones are? How long will it be before they repeat the pattern of their parents' lives and start getting into trouble with the police? They have no real father, and their mother won't exercise any control over them because she doesn't even see what she's doing wrong.'

'But you want to exercise control over them, don't you?' Celina pouted.

'Perhaps you're right,' Simon conceded. 'Why should I care? Why don't we just bring back the slums, the rookeries where children prostituted themselves and the average life expectancy was twenty-eight? Their lives are already over. If we don't improve ourselves, civilisation fails.'

'So that's why you bought all this designer furniture,' said his daughter with heavy sarcasm. 'The more nice things we have, the better people we are.'

Simon felt his temper rising, and fought to control it. He had always considered himself a decent, caring liberal, but felt the ground cracking beneath him. 'I work hard so that you can do media studies at a private school, and have somewhere nice to live. If you think it's so wrong to try and protect what we have, why don't you go and live down there? You wouldn't last five minutes.'

'You have no idea how I live.' Celina jumped up from the sofa and slammed off to her bedroom.

'Why is it that the response to any serious question in this house is to storm off without providing a solution?' Simon shouted after her, but he knew that this particular skirmish was lost. In the last year or so, it had become almost impossible to engage his daughter in conversation. On the rare occasions when she wasn't out with her friends, she was locked in her room at her computer.

'You don't think she's spending her time in chatrooms?' he asked his wife. 'She keeps the door shut and won't let me in.'

'Just give her some space,' replied Eva. 'She knows what she's doing. She's very responsible.'

'She's fifteen,' said Simon gloomily. Lately, the more he tried to control the elements of his life, the further away they seemed to slide. As thunderclouds gathered over the renovated wharf apartments where the Rennie family lived, hot humid air closed about them so that the canal was glazed with a rainbow patina of oil, and even the sepia streets seemed to be sweating. Husband and wife worked listlessly at their respective computers through Saturday, while their daughter disappeared with skimpily dressed friends.

The weather finally broke that evening. Plum-coloured clouds had formed an unnerving anvil shape across the sky, and as the first fat drops of water darkened the terrace, Simon emerged from the balcony to watch. What he saw was his daughter standing on the street corner below talking with one of the older shaven-headed boys from number 15.

He had intended to control his temper, but felt his face tingling with heat as he argued with her. 'Why are you even talking to him at all?' he demanded to know. 'Are you buying drugs? Is that what you're doing?'

Celina thrust her chin out angrily. 'He just spoke to me for a second, that's all. I have to walk past him on the street every day, it's hardly surprising that he sees me, is it? And he doesn't do drugs. You just think that about all of them.'

'I'm sorry, I thought I'd seen his common-law father's chavmobile dropping coke bags off nearly every evening through the summer, it must have been my mistake.'

'What his parents do has nothing to do with him.'

'What's his name?' Simon demanded to know.

'What business is it of yours?' Celina countered.

'Just tell me.'

'It's Dred, all right? That's his nickname, anyway. He only stopped me to ask for a light.'

'And I suppose you think that's cool, hanging around with the illegitimate son of drug-dealers.'

'What do your architects do when they get together, then? They shovel coke up their noses in nightclubs and look down on the chain of people who supply it to them.'

'I'm not going to have this conversation with you now, Celina. And I don't want to see you talking to him again, you understand?'

She stood defiantly before him. 'You can't threaten me. I'm old enough to decide for myself who I want to hang out with. You've just forgotten there's anyone other than your own kind out there.'

'You have something he wants, that's all.'

'You're not going to gross me out by talking about sex, I hope.' Celina pulled a disgusted face.

'I'm not talking about that,' he said hotly. 'You like to fool yourself that this is a classless society but it's not. He sees you in nice cars, in a nice home, but you're from another planet as far as he's concerned. You've got all the things he can't have. You have nothing at all in common with him.'

He knew she held a romanticised view of herself, an Ophelia drifting through a world of scheming courtiers, but why did she not see the danger in such a situation? He knew he had handled the situation badly, but what else could he do?

He was still thinking about the problem on Sunday morning, as he stood on the terrace in his dressing gown, brushing his teeth, studying the great concrete tower of the concert hall that was slowly rising before him. He saw the thin grey line of smoke rising from its ragged top and thought nothing of it, so that the soft *whump* of the explosion caught him by surprise. A wall of heat rolled across the site, and as the roiling ash blew aside he watched the column of fierce yellow flame pulse up into the sky.

The building was too far away to be a danger, and the fire burned out in just a few minutes, but the crest of the unfinished tower was black and scattered with debris. Celina and Eva were still in their dressing gowns when the doorbell rang. He opened the door to a fire officer, who explained that although the blaze had been quickly extinguished, it had burned through a platform on the roof of the building that held half a dozen massive acetylene tanks. If it gave way, the tanks would fall through the tower's central core and explode, so they were evacuating the area immediately.

'But I'll have to get my laptop, and put a suitcase of clothes together,' he told the officer.

'There's no time,' the officer insisted. 'Just take the things at hand that you need and go.'

'Wait, what if I decided to stay?' he insisted. 'I know my rights. You couldn't stop me from being in my own home. I mean, is there really any risk?'

'The police are cordoning off the entire area. If you don't leave at once, you'll have to wait it out inside, and we won't even get a damage report from the fire department until at least Wednesday,' said the fire chief. 'The council is going to put people up in the town hall.'

'We'll stay in a hotel,' Simon decided.

'Fine, you have five minutes to vacate before we turn these streets into an exclusion zone.' The fire officer held open the door and waited while the Rennie family ran around, throwing clothes into bags.

Outside, the street was eerily empty and silent. The only sound came from fluttering strips of yellow plastic tape that had been used to cordon off the roads. Simon had tried to enter the car park, but the officers refused to grant him access because of its proximity to the site's epicentre, so he was forced to leave the compound on foot with his wife and daughter. As he passed the row of council properties, he was sure he saw a darkened figure behind bars and curtains, watching them leave. 'That family is staying put,' he told Eva. 'This is a golden opportunity for them. They'll try and break into our cars while we're gone.'

'They probably have nowhere else to go,' said his wife. 'Come on, we can afford to stay in a decent hotel for a few days. It'll be fun, like camping out, but with cable and room service.'

As they passed the junction leading to the next street, another anonymous figure darted across the road, out of sight of the police. 'Why do I feel this is the moment they've been waiting for?' muttered Simon, hefting the bag higher on his shoulder. He felt sure that feral creatures were hiding in the now-emptied buildings, waiting to make their move.

As they passed out of the police cordon, he dug out his mobile and began ringing around to find a room. Many were full because it was the week of the Wimbledon finals, but they finally managed to reserve a suite at the Charlotte Street Hotel. Celina remained silent and morose as they checked in. 'I thought at least you'd enjoy doing this,' said her father.

'Yeah, I've always wanted to stay in a fashionable hotel with no nice clothes to wear,' she snapped back.

'Patched jeans are fine, they'll think you're a rock star.' He forced a laugh.

'A true rock star wouldn't be seen dead in a place like this.'

'That's disingenuous, Celina. Rock stars might sing about starting revolutions, but live in the kind of houses bought by wealthy Tory stockbrokers.' He reached out a hand to her. 'Look, you're my daughter, you're part of me. I know we'll never see completely eye to eye, but can't we just agree to meet in the middle sometimes?'

'I do love you, Daddy, it's just—' She looked distant. 'You're too old to understand.'

They walked past the dead, bright emptiness of Simon's office, which had also been evacuated. The exclusion zone extended right around the site. 'This will be good for us,' said Eva. 'How often do we get to share each other's company any more? We can talk like we used to.'

But by 8:00 pm that night, spending the day in such close proximity to his family had begun to have a bad effect on Simon. He sat back in the restaurant chair toying with the monkfish tail that lay in sickly yellow sauce the colour of digestive juice.

He scarcely recognised his daughter this evening. She sat across from him in white make-up and black lipstick in an outfit that seemed deliberately designed to antagonise him. When had she changed from being the quiet little girl who spent all day with her books?

They argued before the dessert arrived, but by that time Simon had drunk a bottle of red wine and was feeling feisty. Something about freedom, something about property, the tide-pull of a girl testing her independence against the limits of her parents' control. Celina left the table early, although her tired apology brought them to something of a truce for the night. Simon and Eva retired to the small bar with the open fireplace and tried expensive brandies.

He couldn't sleep, though. The more he thought about leaving their apartment empty, the more it bothered him. Suppose the chavs at number 15 had really been watching him leave? He replayed the moment when he had walked past their house, the narrow eyes behind the curtain, the shadowy figures watching and waiting for him to leave. Drug-dealers, wary and ready to pounce on those they perceived to be weak and naïve. Their caretaker had left the compound along with the residents. The door codes on the main gate were regularly changed, but weren't difficult to crack. All you had to do was wait and watch while someone punched themselves inside. *They could be in there right now*, he thought. *The police wouldn't even know.* He rose and dressed, leaving Eva asleep in bed.

He took a cab to the edge of the exclusion zone, and walked its perimeters as the morning lightened through shades of blue. At the northern edge he talked to a pair of ridiculously young officers about getting back inside. 'Nobody's going in or out, mate,' warned one of them, who was leaning against their van, eating a sandwich.

'I'm not your mate, I pay your salary,' Simon said, bridling at the officer's assumption of familiarity. He headed for the lower edge and found himself in luck, for here there was a single officer, and he was busy arguing with a puzzled-looking Philippino girl, one of the cleaners who regularly came in to take care of the loft apartments. Simon slipped beneath the barrier and ran quietly behind the parked vehicles in the road. There were people at home in number 15; he glimpsed the fat woman in her lounge, watching him with impassive eyes, like a crocodile.

As soon as he had passed from the police officer's sight, he ran out into the road and looked above the gate to his apartment. Even from here he could see that there was something happening inside the lounge. As he watched, a curious red stain about a foot long appeared on the glass outer wall, slowly extending in a diagonal line. He struggled to make sense of what he was seeing. Punching in the door-code, he ran across the deserted quadrangle, past the darkened caretaker's office, into the main building.

He reached the top of the stairs and saw that the apartment's front door was ajar. He had been right to return; they had broken in to steal his family's belongings for drug money. Knowing that he was placing himself in a position of danger, yet unable to hold back, he pushed open the door to the lounge.

The red lines traversed every glass wall in the apartment. It was spray-paint. The anarchist symbols had run, dripping slaughterhouse crimson on to the carpets. Not content with stealing from him, they had to destroy what they could not own. The one who called himself Dred had a look of surprise on his face. He was standing in their kitchen, making himself a Marmite sandwich.

'What the hell are you doing in my home?' Simon asked, staring him down.

'It's not your home any more,' said Celina, stepping from behind him with the spray can in her hands. The burst of red paint caught his chin and neck, but he was able to protect his eyes. Even so, in the moment he stumbled back she was able to shut the door in his face and lock it from the inside.

He remained on the landing long after the laughter inside the apartment subsided into a far more disturbing silence.

identity crisis

I

The bony English lawyer was perplexed, but never at a loss for words. 'Señor Segura,' he began, suddenly realising he had no handkerchief with which to mop his neck, 'I hardly think there's any need to keep the boy handcuffed in this barbaric fashion. He's little more than a child.'

The police chief was more of a showman than his prisoner's legal counsel. He rolled his eyes theatrically and made a display of mock amazement. 'Mr Winthrop, you have no right to speak of barbarism here. Your English justice system has no authority in this municipality. You may only give advice to your client, nothing more. A *Procurador* will represent this man in court through a power of attorney, and until that happens he will remain under my jurisdiction. Santa Augusta is not Madrid. The people here were Franco's men. They do not care that Spain has joined the European Union. They seek only protection and justice, and it is my job to ensure that they will not be harmed by your client.'

'He has not yet been tried in a court of law, and already

you are treating him as though he has been proven guilty,' the lawyer protested.

'Your client,' the police chief almost shouted, 'is a brutal thug. We need no court of law to tell us that. I saw the evidence with my own eyes. Del Toro attacked without provocation. He exhibits no emotion, no remorse. There is no heart in him.' Here he thumped his chest to emphasise the point. 'The fact that he refuses to admit to his barbarity does not protect him.'

'Because he refuses to be bullied by a pair of policemen standing over him in a prison cell,' Edward Winthrop warned, more from force of habit than conviction. In truth, he had no idea whether the boy was guilty or not. He was only concerned with performing his duty, which usually extended to freeing drunken tourists charged with causing affray. 'To keep him chained like an animal only demeans him and encourages him to think badly of himself at a time when he needs his wits about him. You're damaging his psychological state.' He became aware that the air-conditioning had switched itself off. Within seconds, the room had grown warmer. Winthrop hated the searing summer heat of southern Spain, and was starting to perspire freely.

The police chief curled a lip. 'You lawyers should stay buried in your textbooks and not dirty your hands with these people. Why does this man have an English lawyer anyway?'

'This is a case of mistaken identity, a result of your police incompetence. I have it on good authority that the boy you're holding under arrest is not Alejandro Del Toro but a tourist named Paul McAvoy. He was born and raised in London, England and is a British citizen,' Winthrop explained, mopping sweat from his neck with a disintegrating tissue.

'I do not believe this.'

'It is true, and I'm going to prove it.'

'You cannot take him from this station.'

'He has fully co-operated with you, despite facing threats and intimidation, and he has not even been formally charged yet—'

'—a problem which we hope to rectify very shortly,' the police chief admitted.

'—so I demand that you remove his handcuffs and allow me to spend time in private consultation with him in order to help him prepare his plea.' Winthrop sensed his advantage and pressed it. He had heard about the irregular procedures that took place in these small Spanish towns, but had never before experienced it at first hand. The lawyer was based further along the coast, where a far more cosmopolitan attitude prevailed. As a representative of Her Majesty's government, it was time for him to put his foot down and show these petty officials who held the whip hand. 'Where is he being held?' he asked. 'I'm not leaving until I see him.'

Señor Segura gave a spectacular sigh and dragged himself to his feet. 'He is in the courtyard, see.' He pointed from the window. The boy was seated on a heavy oak chair with his hands tied behind his back.

'But he's in full sunlight – it must be over thirty degrees out there! This is intolerable, and in breach of his human rights as decided by the European Court. Open this door at once. Such barbarism is beyond decency.'

The police chief had just eaten lunch and was feeling sleepy. If this stupid Englishman wanted to spend his afternoon sweating it out with a piece of garbage like his prisoner, who was he to argue? He produced a ring of keys, unlocked the door and ushered the tiresome lawyer through.

Winthrop made his way across the fiery white square of gravel to where his client sat. The young man's eyes were pressed together hard, as though he was willing himself somewhere else. His blue-black hair was plastered to his forehead, and dark patches showed on his frayed linen shirt. A tin bowl of water sat at his feet, carefully placed out of reach. The lawyer went to pick it up, and found it too hot to hold. Segura reached around and unfastened his prisoner's handcuffs, pocketing them. 'You must understand I am not responsible if he tries to get away,' he warned.

'Don't worry, I really don't think there's much danger of him trying to escape. His only course of safety is to remain within the compound. I've seen the villagers waiting outside. I'm sure he wants this to be over as quickly as the rest of us.'

The police chief grimaced at the lawyer, squinted into the unbearable brightness of the sun and returned to his office, slamming the door behind him.

'Paul, we spoke on the phone, do you remember?' Winthrop leaned forward, waiting for McAvoy to open his eyes. 'We urgently need to have a conversation.'

His client remained with his head tilted back and his eyes closed. If he had heard, he gave no sign.

'Your situation isn't good. You're being held in a provincial precinct that appears to operate beyond those laws set down in Madrid. You can't stay here. The station-house has neither the staff nor the facilities to protect you. If you were to step outside these gates, you'd be lynched. I know that you are not guilty, but the entire village is against you. They're not sophisticated people, and listen to stories in the streets. You wouldn't get far on foot.'

Paul slowly raised his head and opened his eyes. Winthrop was startled by the arctic blue of his irises. He stretched his arms and flexed strength back into them. 'Can you get me out of the sun? I'm burning alive here.' He squinted up at the furnace in the sky.

'They should never have been allowed to leave you out in the sun. I'll be making an official complaint, I can assure you.'

'They've never had anything like this happen before, so

they've already decided my guilt. I guess sunburn is a form of torture that's impossible to prove. Can you get me back to my cell?' Paul pointed back to the narrow blue-painted door at the rear of the quadrangle. 'It's cooler in there.'

'Let me find you something to drink,' said Winthrop as they reached the small plastered room and seated themselves on the only piece of furniture, an old oak church pew at the back of the room. The light from the opened door formed a sharp oblong of yellow fire across the dusty floor.

'There's a jug in the corner.'

Winthrop found a pitcher of dirty warm water filled with dead flies. He strained it into a tumbler as well as he could, and let the boy drink. 'Can you tell me in your own words what happened?'

Paul's voice was little more than a dry croak. 'It's like I told you, I came here to DJ at a new beach club for the summer. They're trying to put the village on the tourist map.'

'So they built the Bar Del Mar, yes, I know. That's where you met Alejandro Del Toro.'

'I'd seen him a couple of nights before, a flashy out-of-towner with a big white Merc and a couple of girls on his arm.' He drank again, wiping water on his parched lips. 'I think he was taking money from the club. I saw him talking to the owner. Everyone seemed to know him. He took a liking to my music, and one night as I was leaving, he came over. He bought me a few drinks at the bar, then said that I now had a job at one of his clubs. I told him I didn't want it. I didn't like the look of him, this wideboy thinking he could buy me just like he did everyone else. He threatened me then – told me to give up my job at Bar Del Mar and go home. I refused, and I guess I was pretty sarcastic to him. Whatever, he came at me, but I was faster; I kneed him in the balls and he collapsed. He was pretty drunk and fell face down, that's all I know. When the police came looking for me, they held me down and took the wallet from my jacket. That was when I realised we had picked up each other's jackets at the bar. They were going crazy, shouting and pulling me around. I didn't have any photo ID in my wallet, just my name on a letter. They didn't even check to see if there were any proper witnesses. I saw the guy just before they got me into the patrol car, and his face was badly smashed up. I think the bar owner got his money back, and gave him a good kicking, knowing I'd get blamed. I wouldn't be surprised if he even switched my jacket.'

'You got out of your depth here, Paul. The police think a local low-life has beaten up a British tourist. It suits the bar owner to let them believe that, but from the villagers' point of view a bad reputation could wipe their town off the map as a holiday destination. That's why the police have been trying to intimidate you into a confession. I'm supposed to give you the pertinent regional advice set down by British Foreign Office guidelines, but you're going to need more than that to get you out. We have to prove police incompetence, and in a place like this it's not going to be easy.'

The boy was thoughtful. 'I see what you mean. I guess I took too much on face value. But listen, I have an idea.' His face was lost in shadow as he laid his head back against the cool dark wall.

'What sort of idea?' asked Winthrop.

Paul twisted his head, checking the police chief's window from the open door and beckoned to the lawyer, to let him in on the secret.

Against his better judgement, Winthrop found himself drawn towards the boy. Paul shuffled himself forward, leaning low.

'I'll use another identity,' the boy said, his voice dropping to little more than a whisper. 'I won't use the name McAvoy. I'll be someone else.'

'I don't understand,' the lawyer admitted. 'Who will you be?'

'I'll be you.' His arms flashed forward and his hands locked around Winthrop's throat, his thumbs pressing in hard, sealing breath inside his larynx. He pushed until the tendons in his wrists ached, holding the position until the lawyer began to lose consciousness, then he pushed harder still, until he heard the sound of walking on dry leaves, the breaking of small bones. He caught the body before it fell forward, ransacking pockets and removing his victim's belt with practised speed. He had been waiting for this moment since his capture, waiting for time and circumstances to collide. Winthrop wouldn't be able to speak when he came round; Paul had been taught the trick by an old army friend.

Some part of Señor Segura's brain registered an unusual sound and brought his barely remembered military training to the surface. He rose from his chair and headed for the window, only to find Alejandro still asleep in the fierce heat of the quadrangle, his head now shielded by the lawyer's hat. There was no sign of Winthrop. *So much for the big English lawyer*, he thought, checking his watch. *Here for less than fifteen minutes.* He called the duty officer over. 'Go and wake up Del Toro before he gets heat-stroke. We can't let him die, more's the pity.'

With the lawyer's briefcase raised high to protect him from the sun, McAvoy made his way through the sullen crowd of villagers towards the hired white Seat. The idiot had parked it out of the shade, and the gear-stick was too hot to touch. He dug into Winthrop's jacket – the jacket he now wore – and found a handkerchief, stained with the lawyer's sweat, to wrap around the stick.

It annoyed him that he had gone to all the trouble of selecting and stealing the Spaniard's identity, only to be picked up for attacking himself. Blaming the bar owner was a nice touch, though. He was just a penniless English traveller who should never have been noticed. He hadn't considered that the assault might be seen as detrimental to tourism.

He started to pass signs for the motorway long before the alarm was raised at the police station of Santa Augusta. He checked the wallet in the jacket, and found it full of credit cards, plus about seven hundred euros in cash. He wondered if the lawyer had been on the take. You couldn't trust anyone nowadays.

'I am Edward Winthrop,' he told himself, knowing that if he repeated the name often enough, he would come to believe it. The identity would do until he found someone better. His father used to tell him that in the course of his life every man had at least three jobs. To this, Paul could now add a new rule. If he was careful, any man could have hundreds of lives.

As he headed towards a quiet section of the French border, he thought: *next time, I'll go for an Eastern European, providing they have plenty of cash on them.* And he would head for an urban area. In cities of strangers, identity was no longer something private and lasting, like a fingerprint, it was merely a passing privilege, a carapace of interest to just a handful of people. *Thank God for the fractures caused by global mobility,* he thought, *I'm surprised no one else has realised how much freedom they create. There was a time when everyone knew what to expect from each other. Now nobody really knows anyone at all.*

Paul found the lawyer's amber driving glasses behind the sunshade, and smiled to himself as he indicated and accelerated into the fast lane. He looked across at the other drivers and thought: *you choose the life you want. Long and dull, or short and dangerous.*

Laughing, he stamped on the gas.

II

The signs had been clearly marked, but somehow he took a wrong turn. As the traffic thinned out and the road climbed, he realised that he was headed inland. The lawyer had an old-fashioned cassette deck and the worst selection of damned albums he'd ever heard.

He didn't need gas but he was thirsty, and after thirty miles of dirt-brown scenery with only the odd bull to break the horizon, the shaded avenue of trees leading into the little town was cool and welcoming. There was no one in the booth at the Fina station, so he walked back along the road and looked down through the hills, smelling orange blossom and frying steak. The town had no name, and looked closed up, but when he stood still in the middle of the road he could hear faint conversation and laughter, the clink of glasses, the warmth of conviviality. He suddenly remembered that it was Sunday lunchtime, and that sometimes you could still find whole towns who would meet for lunch together.

Following the sound and smell of cooking, he came to a pair of grey wooden doors, with a small studded door inset, an old building that doubled as town hall and community dining spot. He saw why when he pushed the door wide. The cobbled courtyard overlooked the valley, and was filled with villagers seated at trestle tables, dining on suckling pig and roasted figs. A couple of villagers looked up and noted him, but most were too busy with their neighbours and children. Coloured streamers covered the tables, and everyone was wearing carnival masks. There were papier mâché frogs and cats, cows and locusts, harlequins and pierrots. *Another saint's day,* he thought. *Catholics are always celebrating something.*

He walked to the rear of the courtyard where the food was being prepared, and stood before the serving table. A girl in a white peasant blouse worked at the spit. When she turned around, he saw she was wearing a red fox mask. She raised it on to her cropped black hair, revealing electric blue eyes. A Celtic tattoo wound across her bare brown midriff and disappeared into her low-cut jeans.

'*Si, Señor? No conseguimos a muchos turistas aqui, usted tienen gusto algo comer?*' she asked, smiling at him.

'I don't – do you speak English?'

'God, I so do.' She looked incredibly relieved, anxious even. 'Well, I certainly don't speak very good Spanish. Nobody ever comes by here. I was beginning to think—' She fanned a spatula at him, looking over his shoulder at someone on the other side of the courtyard. 'How did you find this place? There's no signs, nobody knows this place exists.'

'It was an accident,' Paul admitted. 'I kind of got lost. Sounds like you did too.'

'No, I – that is, I really didn't mean to come here. My boyfriend and I were driving through at the beginning of the summer and our rented Seat broke down on the mountain above. We just coasted into the town. Everyone seemed really friendly, so we stayed. I just didn't realise – look, I have to keep serving or I'll get in trouble. I'll bring you some food in a minute, OK?'

'Sure, but what's your name?'

'Elissa, what's yours?'

'Paul,' he answered, taking the roll of napkin from her and making his way to an empty section of table. Damn, I used my real name, he thought. I must be slipping. She was cute, though. He helped himself to the pitcher of cool red wine that stood before him, and watched a trio of children in rabbit masks chasing each other between the chairs.

It was pleasant in the courtyard, and the sun dappling through the overhead vine leaves shifted patches of warmth across his face, making him drowsy. He drained his glass and refilled it, listening to jokes and gossip shared in rapid-fire Spanish.

'I hope you're hungry.' The plate appearing before him overflowed with curls of suckling pig-meat. Elissa seated herself beside him, pulling over a blue ceramic bowl filled with tomatoes and onions. She poured herself a drink and watched as he ate. 'Hey, slow down, there's plenty more.'

He realised he hadn't eaten for nearly two days. Now, it seemed, he had everything he wanted: freedom, food, wine – and perhaps a woman. 'So where's your boyfriend now?' he asked with a full mouth.

'Over there somewhere, the one in the black bull mask – but we're not together any more.' She waved a vague hand across the courtyard, keen to change the subject. 'How's the food?'

'It's good. You're not eating?'

'I ate earlier. They've got me serving here every Sunday.'

'You sound like you don't enjoy it.'

She leaned in confidentially. 'I know, it's very picturesque, but these people – it's not like it looks.' She bit a ruby lip, studying him.

'Too many saints' days, huh?'

'Kind of. Where are you headed?'

'France. Thought I'd hit the Riviera for a while.'

She looked around, then ducked her head. He sensed desperation when she spoke. 'Take me with you.'

'I'm not looking for a travelling companion.'

'Just for a few days. Until I'm clear of this place.'

'It can't be that bad.'

'You have no idea.'

You're wrong there, he thought. *I know what it's like to keep moving.* She was the finest-looking woman ever to suggest climbing into his passenger seat. The fact that she wanted something from him could be turned to his advantage. 'Suppose I agree to take you. What do I get in return?'

'Use your imagination, Paul.' Her eyes held his, their meaning clear. Before he could reply, they were joined by two stocky Spaniards who were obviously brothers. One wore the mask of a rat, the other a monkey.

'Elissa. The fire is nearly out.'

'Javier, Lazaro – I'm taking a break.' She looked uncomfortable. They crowded in on either side of her, helping themselves to wine. 'Who is your friend?'

'Paul's just passing through. He found the place by accident.' She was obviously trying to distance herself from him. She was clearly in some kind of trouble and looking for a way out. It crossed his mind that he had finally met somebody like himself.

'Welcome, Paul. Welcome to our village,' said Lazaro. 'You like our fine woman?'

He could see that Lazaro was massaging her thigh as he spoke. Elissa had frozen. 'She's a very attractive young lady,' he deadpanned.

'Perhaps you would like to know her better,' said Javier, reaching a paternal arm around her shoulder and squeezing it. The two men stared at him, smiling broadly.

What the hell is going on here? thought Paul.

'Elissa, you should be friendly to your guest,' said Lazaro. 'Show him some hospitality.' The back of his hand brushed her right breast as he looked across at Javier. As if on a prearranged signal, they rose together.

Paul waited until they had moved to a far table at the edge of the courtyard's balcony. 'What's happening?' he asked. 'Is that why you want to get out of here? Because of those guys?'

Elissa glanced across the tables uncomfortably. 'My boyfriend, Marc,' she began. 'He was using a lot of drugs when we arrived.' She turned her wineglass, wondering whether to trust him.

'The car didn't exactly break down, we ran off the road. Javier and Lazaro helped us out. We agreed to stay here and do bar work to pay off the cost of repairing the car. I thought it would straighten Marc out, and he was doing well, even though he's been really sick. But one night he saw where Lazaro kept the till. Now they won't let us leave until we pay back the full amount he stole. They treat us like they own us, like we're their slaves. They said if I try to leave they'll really mess Marc up, but he and I are apart now. It's time he became responsible for his own screw-ups.' She traced his spine with a fingernail. 'I'd do anything to get out of here, Paul. Anything.'

Paul always backed off when he felt pressured. He threw back the remains of his red wine while measuring his response. 'I'd love to help you out, Elissa, but I can't take you with me.' Refilling his glass, he rose from the table and headed over to the balcony, where a wizened old accordionist had begun to play. Several of the villagers, masked as a cat, a cow and several chickens, had begun to dance in a graceful, stately fashion around the courtyard. In the valley below, afternoon sunlight illuminated the low mist that had risen from the olive groves.

He leaned on the railing and drank. As the polka changed to a mournful waltz, he looked back to see Elissa hiding her tears behind the fox mask. Then she was being pulled to her feet and made to dance against her will. It looked like any ordinary Spanish village, but there were issues of power and manipulation here that excited him. In that moment, he knew he wanted her very much.

He watched her moving through the throng of dancers, glancing over at him, but lost her as the villagers closed around. When Javier's meaty palm landed on his shoulder, he jumped, spilling his wine. 'So, you like our village?' he asked, leaning in too close.

'Sure, it's very – old world,' he replied, feeling a little drunk. 'Where is Elissa?'

Javier pouted playfully, tipping his head from side to side. 'I think she wants some kind of a favour from you, Paul, but who knows what women think, eh?' He nudged Paul lasciviously. 'She said to say she is waiting in the barn.' He thumbed a dirty nail in the direction of the wooden building behind the courtyard. Paul turned to follow her, but Javier placed a hand on his chest. 'I don't think you should go there if you are looking for a girlfriend, because she is *puta* – you know? Not a good girl. She like to be dirty, to be taken – you know—' He made a thrusting motion with his hips. 'Intimacy from the rear, so she don't look in your eyes.' His laugh followed Paul across the courtyard.

As he pushed open the barn door he felt a twinge of guilt, but it was quickly replaced by a flush of lust. She was waiting for him on the hay bales beyond the single shaft of sunlight that fell through the broken roof. Lazaro was holding her right wrist while she struggled feebly. The alcohol was making his heart pound, thickening his senses.

This is a sex game, thought Paul, rising to the challenge. *He's got power over her, he gets his kicks from seeing her used.* He advanced, watching as Javier pushed her down into the hay and flipped her on to her back, raising her skirt with a sly forefinger. She was wearing no pants. Something didn't look right about her.

He knew he should ask if this was what she wanted, and the thought of Lazaro watching while he had sex with her filled him with disgust, but he could no longer control himself. Dropping to his knees he unbuckled his jeans and slipped a hand between sweat-moistened buttocks. He could hear hoarse breathing through the fox mask, and told himself that that meant she was taking pleasure from this encounter. He continued even though she eventually begged him to stop, but the mask muffled her guttural cries. The violence of his actions inside her surprised him. Afterwards, as he pulled out and rolled off he saw blood, and was disgusted with himself. Clambering from the hay bales and struggling with his belt, he tried to remember where the car was parked, and mentally measured how long it would take to escape to it.

That was when the barn door opened, and in the frame of dying sunlight he saw Javier holding on to the tearful Elissa, who was shivering in her underwear.

Lazaro was no longer laughing as he pulled off the red fox mask. Paul found himself staring at a young man with duct-tape across his mouth, dressed in his girlfriend's clothes, his genitals taped up against his stomach. As Javier threw the drugged Marc onto his semi-naked girlfriend, he and Lazaro exchanged a look of satisfaction. They had heard about an English boy who had attacked a Spanish brother, and providence had delivered him into their hands.

They were still enjoying the joke as Paul stumbled from the barn towards the lawyer's car, wondering what kind of man he had finally become.

He had a short time to consider the question as he slumped beside the slashed tyres of the vandalised Seat, and then the brothers came for him with knives.

red torch

The rain had fallen all morning, and by 3:00 pm it was already nearly dark. He had kicked around the house getting under his mother's feet, and visited the local library, but the book he wanted, on the history of British horror films, was still out on loan. He checked the *South East London Mercury* cinema listings, and realised that he had seen every film on release. At the Greenwich Granada, *You Only Live Twice* and *Thunderball* were showing in a double bill, but he had seen each of them several times, and the former had already started. They always showed re-releases on Sundays at the Granada.

Still, with nothing better to do, he made his way to the cinema and, as the films had 'A' certificates, waited for someone to take him in. Taking his place in the stalls, he waited for his eyes to adjust to the darkness and looked around, his pulse quickening. He was almost fourteen, and spent all his pocket money at the pictures. He especially liked spy films, the *Man From Uncle* series, the Bonds, even James Coburn's Flint movies. He longed to travel to the casinos where 007 met his women, the grand mountain roads and mansions where he faced his adversaries, but settled for vicariously experiencing them on the great screen of the old cinema.

Still, it was not why he had come today.

He had seen her before, watching him in the penumbral auditorium, and had felt a prickling warmth beneath her gaze, a confusion, a desire. He wanted to follow the warm red glow of her torch down the aisle, back to the little room where she waited between shows.

He sat fidgeting as Bond flipped a rock on to the volcano's green lake surface, only to discover that it was made of steel. By his rough guess, that left the final battle against Blofeld, which lasted about twenty minutes; not long to wait. As the credits rolled, he looked around and saw her carefully making her way down to the front of the auditorium. She moved slowly because the floor was raked and she wore white high heels. Positioning herself between the aisles, she patiently waited for the house lights to rise. The bulb hidden in her white tray illuminated choc ices, ridged plastic cartons of fluorescent orange drink, wafers and tubs, but shrouded her face in shadow. Her proudly raised chin and disdainful air suggested that she might have been displaying ancient Egyptian artefacts, even though the effect was slightly tarnished by the fact that she was chewing gum.

Her strapped heels, the little Grecian skirt and her illuminated tray of offerings gave her the appearance of an electric goddess. Her blonde hair was fixed with a red plastic bow to keep her fringe out of her eyes, but the sides fell to her shoulders in an old-fashioned style. She wore a short pink nylon blouse buttoned down the front, and a glittery white patent leather belt. The first two buttons were undone, so that the rise of her pale breasts shone in the overhead spotlight. When he thought about undoing the remaining buttons, he could scarcely catch his breath.

Was she aware of her own strange perfection? Despite the fact that she had obviously been chosen by the management to entice men from their seats, she seemed not to notice her surroundings, as if her spirit was still far away in Okanawa, with James Bond. Would she travel with him to Florida for the second half of the double bill, and swim in warm seas during his undersea battle with Emilio Largo's henchmen?

The cinema was almost empty; the double bill had been playing every Sunday for a month now. He knew he could wait until she began her walk back up the aisle of the great auditorium, but there was a risk that he might fail to attract her attention, and his opportunity would be missed. He rose a little unsteadily from his seat, checked that he had money in his pocket and made his way to the edge of the stage.

He had bought ice creams from her many times before, but she had barely noticed him. This time, though, he felt sure it would be different. It simply took an act of courage on his part to talk to her. He waited until all of her customers had been served, then presented himself before her, staring down at the selection of fiercely coloured ice-cream boxes. Caught in the low light of the tray, her eyes were lost in darkness as she rhythmically chewed, waiting for his order. Her red lips sparkled with frosted gloss.

'I'd like—' he began. 'I see you here every week—' His words emerged with awkward bluntness. 'You're so—' He put his money away.

'You don't want an ice cream, do you?' Her lips shone fiercely in the spotlight. She breathed out, a long slow sigh, and clicked off her tray light. 'Well, come on then.' She beckoned to him and led the way along the side of the stage to the exit door below the great dark screen.

The room was coated in chipped scarlet paint, the colour of drying blood. The midnight blue carpet was shaded with geometric shapes, the same that covered the rest of the cinema. In front of him stood a G-Plan coffee table, upon which were a pair of blue and white coffee mugs and a copy of last year's *Film*

Review. On the magazine's tattered cover, Robert Vaughn and Elke Sommer clutched heartwarmingly at a Scottie dog. Vaughn was taking a break from his role as Napoleon Solo to star in *The Venetian Affair*. The posters for the film ('Vaughn! Venice! Voom!') were already up in the Roxy's foyer; despite himself, the boy wanted to see it.

He rushed at her almost before she had a chance to get the door shut. Her lips felt greasy on his neck. He wondered if her sparkly lipstick would leave a mark like a brand. Her nails were crimson plastic, and flicked open his shirt buttons with a series of tiny clicks. She seemed to know exactly what would happen. Her hand went to his fly, unzipped it and thrust inside, feeling around. Her fingers closed around his erection and dragged it out, smoothly negotiating the Y-front fold of his pants. Somehow she had unfastened her skirt, dropped it and kicked it aside with her foot without even having to look down. He was surprised to realise that there was nothing intimate or erotic about the business; it wasn't the way James Bond and his girls made love. He passed the brief minutes in a state of shock.

'That's the beauty of the "A" certificate,' said the usherette afterwards, shoving aside a stack of *Film Review*s to make a seat for herself. '*No admittance without an adult*. So young lads like you are forced to hang around on street corners picking up strangers to take you inside. God bless the British Board of Film Censors, I say.' She curled the false eyelash around her left lid and admired the result in the damp-blotched mirror. Tom Jones could be heard belting out the title track to *Thunderball* from the auditorium beyond the room.

'There's nothing like James Bond to bring out the lonely ones,' the usherette explained, smearing away an unruly edge of lipstick. 'Me, I'm more of a Doris Day fan myself. Earlier generation, see.' Reaching over to the gramophone, she flipped the single and reset the Dansette to play 'Move Over Darling'.

The boy was having trouble catching his breath now. He supposed the worst was over – nothing could be more terrible than the shock he had experienced in those moments after she had pulled away from him in the small room behind the screen, after she had turned the lights on.

'You don't have to look so disgusted. I know what you're thinking. But it's good to go with an older woman the first time. Don't bother me none. It's not like you're going to run around your school telling everyone, is it? Boys never tell.' She was rebuttoning her pink dress, straightening her skirt, adjusting her thick support hose, admiring herself in the mirror. A perfect usherette, blonde and rouged and uniformed, just so long as the lights were kept low. 'The worst part's being on your feet all day. I've got bunions you wouldn't believe. But I like this job, the lights are kind on my eyes, and it's good to see the young lads enjoying themselves. You'd be surprised how many of them have a wank during the picture. Pity to waste all that energy, I always say.'

Her tray stood on the dressing table, filled with melting tubs and Drink-On-A-Stick lollies. The confectionery looked fake in the harsh light. The tubs were too brightly coloured, like packets of plasticine.

'You're probably sorry you're missing the film. James Bond will be in the swimming pool with the shark in a few minutes. He isn't really in Florida, you know, they filmed it up at Pinewood, just outside of London. He used to be a milkman before he became an actor. Those car chases and fight scenes are done with back-projections. It's all an illusion. You notice the tricks when you get up close, like I do. You can sit through and see it again if you like.' She glanced at him, barely interested now. 'The embarrassment will soon fade. Go to the bathroom and wash yourself, you got some on your trousers. Then go back to your imaginary heroes. Concentrate on the film and forget it ever happened. I won't mind, love.'

He hated her. He wanted to kill her. A searing heat rose inside him – something had changed for ever. He couldn't stop himself from shaking as she came over and ran her hand across his chest. He should have looked at the skin of her hands, older than his mother's.

'Loss of innocence is part of growing up,' she said, reading his mind. 'You're not a boy any more, and you feel humiliated. You wanted something and you got it, and now you feel dirty.' She studied him coolly, noting the contempt in his eyes. 'I understand how it is. I had a boy your age once, but he died.'

He wanted to jump at her, attack her, but found himself barely able to move without collapsing. She tapped at her chin with crimson-painted nails, considering him with an amused half-smile that created fault-lines beneath her make-up. 'I don't just work at the Granada, you know. I do the Roxy, the Gaumont, the ABC. I move around. There are so many cinemas, and there are so many boys like you.'

Under the harsh lightbulb she was pathetic, grotesque; he saw that now as she opened the door. He wondered how he could have been so easily fooled. But the cinema was dark, and she had smiled conspiratorially in the glow of her tray-light, and he had followed the warm red torch.

She took two small oval sponges from her dressing table and pushed them down inside the top of her tunic, over her flat chest, checking the result in the mirror.

'That's better. Wouldn't be much of an usherette without nice tits, would I?' She straightened her nylon wig, lost in admiration of her own image as the boy stumbled from the room, out through the side exit and into the absolving rain.

turbo-satan

It was a Saturday afternoon in East London when Mats reordered his world.

Balancing under leaking concrete eaves, looking out on such dingy grey rain that he could have been trapped inside a fishtank in need of a good clean, he felt more than usually depressed. The student curse: no money, no dope, no fags, no booze, nothing to do, nowhere to go, no one who cared if he went missing for all eternity. He had chosen to be like this, had got what he wanted, and now he didn't want it.

Withdrawn inside his padded grey Stussy jacket, he sat beneath the stilted flats, on the railing with the torn-up paintwork that had been ground away by the block's Huckjam skateboarders who ripped up their own bones more than they flipped any cool moves, because this wasn't Dogtown, it was Tower Hamlets, toilet of the world, arse-end of the universe, and every extra minute he spent here Mats could feel his soul dying, incrementally planed away by the sheer debilitating sweep of life's second hand. London's a great place if you have plans, he thought, otherwise you sit and wait and listen to the clocks ticking. He should never have turned down his father's offer of a monthly cheque.

'You're late,' he complained to Daz, when Daz finally showed up. 'Every minute we're getting older, every hour passed is another lost for ever. Don't you wonder about that?'

'If you think about it you'll want to change things and you can't, so the gap between what you want and the way things actually are keeps growing until you drive yourself insane, so actually no, I don't,' said Daz. 'Have you got any fags?'

They were first-year graphic art students. The college was locked for the duration of the Christmas break because vandals had turned the place over and all passes had been rescinded until a new security system could be installed, so Mats was sleeping on Daz's mother's lounge sofa because he didn't want to spend Christmas with his parents, not that they cared whether he showed or not, and Daz's mother was away visiting her boyfriend in Cardiff, possibly the only place that gave Tower Hamlets a run for its money in the race to become Britain's grimmest map location.

'It'll be a new year in two days' time, and I have absolute zero to look forward to,' Mats complained. 'I hate my life. All the crappy art appreciation classes I took at school are never going to give me the things I want. Kids in Africa have a better time than I do.'

'I don't think they do, actually,' Daz suggested.

The two students had so little in common it was perhaps only proximity that connected them. Matthew's parents were not, in truth, missing him. Having given in to their son for too long, they had allowed him to attend art college in the hope that he would eventually weary of trying to be outrageous. His parents were not outraged, or even vaguely shocked, by his attempts to test the limits of their liberality. If truth be told, they found him rather boring, a bit of an angry student cliché, incapable of understanding that the world's axis was not set through his heart. Mats considered himself more sensitive than those around him, but his convictions had the depth and frailty of autumn leaves. His parents could see he was adrift but had run out of solutions. They were comforted by the knowledge that he could only fall as far as his trust fund allowed, and were happy to let him get on with the gruesome task of self-discovery. What he really wanted, he told them unconvincingly, was to become a citizen of the world. Finally they shrugged and left him alone.

'The problem is that I haven't been properly equipped to deal with the future,' Mats continued, 'and there's no nurture system for highly sensitive people.'

Daz had heard all this before, and had other things on his mind: his sister was pregnant and broke, his mother increasingly suffered mental problems and was probably going to lose her flat. Oddly, listening to Mats moaning about his life didn't annoy him; it had a curiously calming effect, because his fellow student was so fake that you could make him believe anything. Conversely, Daz attracted Mats because he was real. There was a loose-limbed lying craziness that sometimes took Daz to the brink of a mental breakdown, which was all the more frightening because his nerve endings crackled like exposed live wires. It took guts to be nuts, and Daz was braver than most.

Mats hadn't stopped complaining for almost twenty minutes. 'I mean,' he was saying now, 'what's the point in creating real art when it's denied an impact? I don't know anything that can change anything.'

'I do,' said Daz, cutting him off. 'I know a trick.'

'What kind of a trick?'

Daz jumped up and brushed out his jeans, then headed into the rain-stained block of flats behind them.

'Where are you going?' asked Mats as they passed through the dim concrete bunker that passed for the building's foyer. Daz just grinned, dancing across orange tiles to smack the lift buttons with the back of his fist.

'There's only one place it works,' said Daz, stepping into the lift, three narrow walls of goose-fleshed steel that reeked of urine and something worse. He pumped the panel, firing them to the top floor. When they got out, he pushed at the emergency exit and took the stairs to the roof three at a time. Montgomery House was required to keep the door unlocked in case of fire evacuation. Mats didn't like thirty-storey tower blocks, too much working-class bad karma forced upright into one small space, but he felt safe with Daz, who had chased storms from the stairwells since he was two foot six.

'Is it cool to be up here?' Mats asked, all the same. The hazing rain had dropped a grey dome over the top of the block. He walked to the edge of the roof and looked down, but the ground was lost in a vaporous ocean.

'There's some kids run a pirate station from one of the flats, that's that thing over there.' Daz pointed to the makeshift mast attached to the satellite TV rig propped in the centre of the gravelled flat-top. 'Touch their stuff and they'll cut you up; no one else ever comes up here.' The wind moaned in the wires strung between the struts of the satellite mount. Five blocks, all with their own pirate sounds. 'When they're not chucking vinyl, they're taking each other's signals down with bolt-cutters. Give me your mobile.'

'Fuck right off, I got about three calls left before it stiffs.'

'Come on, check this,' said Daz, snatching the mobile away from Mats. He flipped it open and punched in 7-2-8-2-6, waited for a moment, held it high, punched in the same numbers again, waited, held it high again, did it twice more, making five numbers five times, then turned the phone around so that Daz could see.

Behind them, the makeshift transmitter released a melancholy hum, like a phasing analogue radio. Mats could feel the crackle of electricity rustling under his clothes, as though he was about to be hit by lightning. Something had happened to the phone's screen; the colours had turned chromatic, and were cascading like psychedelic raindrops on a window.

'You screwed up my phone, man. What did you do?'

'7-2-8-2-6, you figure it out.'

'I don't know,' Mats admitted. 'You paying your congestion charge?' A lame joke, seeing as neither of them owned any kind of vehicle.

'Try texting the number, see what comes up.'

Mats went to Messages, and tapped in the digits. 'Oh, very mature. How do I clear the screen?'

'Can't, you have to put in a text message to that number to get rid of it.'

'What is it, a glitch in the system?'

'Must be, only works on a Nokia, and only when you're near a mast, getting a clear signal.'

'I don't get it, what's the point?'

'You didn't type in the text yet.'

'OK.' Mats' fingers hovered over the pinhead keys. 'I don't know what to write.'

'C'mere.' Daz pulled him under the hardboard shelter beneath the illegal transmission masts. 'Ever wonder why ancient curses used to work? 'Cause they're ancient. Victims sickened and died; they wasted away when they discovered they were cursed. Belief, man.' He thrust his outstretched fingers at Mats' brain, then his own. 'There's no belief any more, so curses no longer work. Who do you believe now? Do you think God will answer your prayers and sort out your life? No. Do you buy the whole Judeo-Christian guilt-trip? No. Do you believe your computer when it tells you your account's overdrawn? Yes. The new world order can't survive on images of demons and the fiery pit, 'cause we're just slabs of flickering code running to infinity. The only things you have faith in are digitised. Digital society needs digital beliefs. Most people's brains are still hardwired to analogue. Not our fault, that was the world we were born into, but it's all gone now. So change your perception.'

Mats glared at the tiny silver handset. 'What, with this?'

'What I think? A programmer somewhere spotted an anomaly in his binary world and opened up a crack, a way through. Then he leaked it. A five-digit number punched in five times, somewhere near a powerful signal, near a transmitter, all it takes to open the whole thing up. Send the message. Make it something that could alter the way you see the world.'

'Like what?'

'I don't know, use your imagination.'

Mats stared at the falling rain. Unable to think of anything interesting, he typed *My parents live in a big house in the country*, then sent the message to 7-2-8-2-6.

Message Sent

'Now what?'

'That's it, dude.' Daz was grinning again.

'You *fuck*.' Mats angrily stamped to his feet and shoved his way into the downpour. 'You almost had me believing you.'

He took the lift to the ground and walked off towards the bus stop, annoyed with himself for being so stupid. While he was waiting for the bus he rang his father, thinking that maybe he could tap his old man for a cheque after all, despite having failed to return home for the holidays. He'd told his mother he couldn't come back for Christmas because there was no God, and how could they all be so fucking hypocritical? He stared absently at the falling rain, waiting for the call to be answered. His mother picked up the receiver. When she realised who was calling, she adopted a tone that let him know she would be displeased with him until they were all dead.

'Just let me talk to Dad.'

'You'll have to hold on for a minute, Matthew,' she warned. 'Your father's in the garden fixing the pump in the pond.'

Which was interesting, because they didn't have a pump, a pond or a garden. They lived on the fourth floor of a mansion block in St John's Wood.

'What are you talking about?' he asked.

'The garden doesn't stop growing just because it's raining,' she answered impatiently. 'Hold on while I call for him.'

Mats snapped the phone shut as if it had bitten him. He fell back on the bus stop bench in awe. In the distance, a bus appeared. He felt his flat pockets, knowing there was no more than sixty pence in change, not enough for the minimum fare, and the bus driver got so weird if he tried to use a credit card. Money – he needed money.

It was a good reason to go back and try again.

He ran to Montgomery House and hopped the lift, but found that Daz had left the roof. Stepping out into the rain and flipping open the mobile, he redialled 7-2-8-2-6, adding text: *Bus driver gives me ten pounds*, punched 'send'. Then he shot back down, jumped on the next bus, and waited to see what would happen.

Red doors concertina'd back. The wide-shouldered Jamaican driver had surprisingly dainty hands, which she rested at the lower edge of her steering wheel. She did not move a muscle as he stepped up and stood before her, never raised her eyes from the windscreen before hissing the doors shut. Then she reached into her cash dispenser and handed him two five-pound notes as if they were change.

He stayed on until reaching the City, the phone burning a patch in his pocket. Alighting near the Bank of England, he tried to understand what might be happening. Altered perception, Daz had said, Daz, who had not replaced his own mobile since it was stolen, so why hadn't he altered perception to make himself really, really rich?

Why wouldn't you? There had to be some kind of problem with that, didn't there? How specific did you have to be, Tom Thumb's Three Wishes-specific, get the wording exactly right or else you end up with a sausage on your nose? What were the parameters? Was there a downside, some kind of come-uppance for being greedy, for failure to perform a good deed? Did the devil appear, hands on hips, laughing hard at man's foolishness? Already he had forgotten talk of binary existence and was replacing it with the lore of fairy tales, a language of quid pro quo cruelties, kindnesses and revenges, *because that's what is clearly fuckin' called for in this situation*, he thought, sweating at the seams.

Obviously, he needed to try again. There was a transmitter mast at Alexandra Palace, but what about mobile masts? There had been some kind of argument about placing one halfway up Tottenham Court Road, so that was where he headed next.

He couldn't get high above the ground, but he climbed to the second floor of Paperchase and stood near the rear window, close enough to see the phone mast, hoping it was close enough to register. Flipping open the mobile, he examined the screen. The pulsing chroma-rain had cleared itself after the transmission of the last message. Suddenly, his sealed existence had unfolded into a world of possibilities. Suppose he could do anything, anything at all? He could save the world. End starvation and poverty. Reverse climate change. Bring back the Siberian tiger. Build a special community in the Caribbean where artists from all over the world could live and work together in peace, free from the pressures of society.

Fuck that shit. What about the things he really wanted?

The exhilaration welled inside his gut as he realised that he could be a good six inches taller for a start, go from five eight to at least six two. His height had always bugged him. And a better physique, get rid of the beer belly. No, wait. He needed to think carefully before doing anything else. His priorities were ridiculous and wrong. What he wanted most, what he needed more than anything, was a girl – no, not a girl, a woman. *Women.* Lots of them. He wouldn't force them to like him, just provide them with the possibility, *wishes go bad when they're forced*, he thought. But what he really needed was money, lots of money, because it could buy you freedom; he'd be able to travel because that was how to make yourself truly free, go around the world and hang out with whomever you liked; it was all a matter of slipping through the cracks in perception.

Whatever he asked for had to be something he wanted very badly. As quickly as the possibilities occurred, they faded away, leaving behind a fog of appalled anxiety. If it was so easy, why hadn't Daz done it? Why was he still hanging out at his mother's council flat?

He punched out Daz's number and asked him.

Daz sounded surprised. 'That's your perception, Mats. I only feature in your world as some kind of sidekick, a support to the main act. But that's not the way I see it from my side, compadre. I'm the big event – you barely exist. You see, once you're *really* through to the other side, the digital world, that's when you discover who you should really be, and you're free. You get the life you always deserved, probably the life you have right now but simply can't see. Figure it out, Mats, the answer's right in front of you. Just help yourself.' The line went dead. Was he stifling a laugh as he rang off? It sure as hell didn't sound like Daz talking. He couldn't usually string two clear thoughts together without aid.

Mats had walked the upper floor of the store half a dozen times before he understood what he was supposed to do. Gardens, buses, looks, girls, money, all small-time stuff, changing single elements, not rewriting the hard drive. He pulled the phone from his pocket, flipped it open and punched in the number again.

7-2-8-2-6

He watched as the letters came up once more.

S-A-T-A-N

A broadband hotline to the devil, a kind of turbo-Satan, a programmer's joke, not even that – a child's idea of a secret, something so obvious nobody even thought to try it. *You're supposed to send it to yourself,* he thought, *that's all you have to do, like making a wish.* This time, instead of texting a request, he simply typed in his own phone number, then pressed 'send'.

Message Sent

What now? The screen was teeming with colours once more, but now they were fading to mildewed, sickly hues; something new was at work. For a moment he thought he saw Daz outside the window, laughing wildly at something preposterous and absurd. He felt bilious, as if he had stepped from a storm-shaken boat. The pale beechwood floor of the store tilted, then started to slide away until he was no longer able to maintain his balance.

He landed hard, jarring his arm and hip, but within a second the wood was gone and he had fallen through – he could feel the splinters brushing his skin – until the ground was replaced with something soft and warm. Sand on clay, earth, small stones, heat on his face, his legs. His eyes felt as if they had been sewn shut. He lay without moving for a moment, feeling the strange lightness in his limbs. Then he reached out a hand to touch his bruised thigh.

Stranger still: it was not his leg, but one belonging to a child, thin and almost fleshless – and yet he could feel the touch of his fingers from within the skin.

So bright. He could see the veins inside his orange eyelids. Yet there was something else moving outside. He sensed rather than saw them, dozens of black dots bustling back and forth.

He ungummed his eyelids and opened them. Flies, fat black blowflies lifted from his vision in a cloud and tried to resettle at once. He brushed them away with his hand, and was horrified to discover the brown, bony claw of a malnourished child. The effort required to pull himself upright was monstrous. Looking down at his legs, he found that instead of the pre-stressed lowriders he always wore, his twisted limbs were encased in ragged, ancient suit-trousers.

He found himself sitting exhausted beneath a vast fiery sun on a ground of baked mud, waiting for the charity worker in front of him to dole out a ladle of water from a rust-reddened oil drum. Staring down into the opalescent petrol stains on the rancid liquid, he saw his opposite self: an encephalitic head, fly-crusted eyes, cracked thin lips, sore-covered ribs thrust so far forward that they appeared to be bursting from his skin, the knife of perpetual hunger twisting in his swollen stomach. Looking around, he saw hundreds of others like himself stretching off into the dusty yellow distance, the marks of hunger and disease robbing them of any identity. He would have screamed then, if his throat had not been withered long ago to a strip of sun-dried flesh.

Daz made his way along the balcony of Montgomery House, avoiding pools from the dripping ceiling, swinging the cans of beer he had withdrawn from his secret stash behind the bins. He had half expected Mats to trail him back to the flat, but perhaps he was off sulking somewhere about the phone joke. That was the great thing about people like Mats: you could tell them any old shit, and at some primitive level, even when they said they didn't, they actually believed you, heart and soul.

the uninvited

The elaborate silvered gates stood wide apart, ready to accept guests. You couldn't arrive on foot, of course; there was nowhere to walk, except in the drive or through the sprinkler-wet grass, and you would have looked foolish climbing towards the house in the headlights of arriving cars.

Inside, the first thing I saw was an avenue of rustling palms, their slender trunks wound with twinkling blue and white lights, like giant candy sticks. Two robotically handsome valets in gold and crimson jackets were parking the cars, mostly sparkling black Mercedes, Daimlers, Volvos. The staircase was flanked by six teenaged waitresses in tiny red Santa outfits tentatively dispensing delicate flutes of champagne. A floodlit house, oblong, low and very white, was arranged on two levels between banked bottle-green lawns. I could hear muted laughter, murmuring, a delicate presence of guests. I saw silhouettes passing before the rippled phosphorescence of a pool with translucent globes pacing its perimeter. There was no sign of our host, but on the patio a butler, chef, bartenders and waiters were arranged behind banks of lurid, fleshy lobster tails and carrot batons.

There was a muffled beat in the air, the music designed to create ambience without being recognisable, Beatles songs rescored for a jazz trio. It was the end of the sixties, the age of Aquarius. Smokey Robinson and Dionne Warwick were in the charts, but there were no black people there that night except me.

In Los Angeles, parties aren't about letting your hair down and having fun. They're for networking, appraising, bargaining, being seen and ticked from a list. There were two kinds of guest roaming the house that night: ones who would have been noticed by their absence, and others who had been invited merely to fill up dead space. It goes without saying that I was in the latter group. Only Sidney Poitier would have made it into the former.

It was the home of Cary Dell, a slow-witted middleweight studio executive at MGM, and I remember seeing plenty of almost-familiar faces: Jacqueline Bisset, Victoria Vetri, Ralph Meeker, a couple of casting directors, some black-suited agents lurking together in a corner, fish-eyeing everyone else. The important people were seated in a semi-circular sunken lounge, lost among oversized purple cushions. The area was so exclusive that it might as well have had velvet ropes around it. Everyone else worked hard at keeping the conversation balloon-light and airborne, but couldn't resist glancing over to the pit to see what was going on at the real centre of the party.

There was another kind of guest there that night. Dell had invited some beautiful young girls. No one unsavoury, they weren't call-girls, just absurdly perfect, with slender waists and basalt eyes. They stood together tapping frosted pink nails on the sides of their martini glasses, flicking their hair, looking about, waiting for someone to talk to them.

Parties like this took place all over the Hollywood hills; the old school still arrived in tuxedos and floor-length gowns, but studios had lately rediscovered the youth movie, and were shamelessly courting the same anti-establishment students they had ridiculed five years earlier. I had made a couple of very bad exploitation flicks, usually cast as the kind of comic sidekick whose only purpose was his amusing blackness. Back in those days I believed in visibility at any cost, and always took the work.

I had a feeling I'd been added to the guest list by Dell's secretary in order to make up numbers and provide him with a sheen of coolness, because I wore fringed brown leather trousers and had my hair in an Afro, and hadn't entirely lost my Harlem jive. He sure hadn't invited me for my conversation; we'd barely spoken more than two words to each other. If we had, Dell would have realised I came from a middle-class family in New Jersey, and I might not have got the work.

I remember it was a cool night towards the end of November. The wind had dropped, and there were scents of patchouli and hashish in the air. The party was loosening up a little, the music rising in volume and tempo. Some of the beautiful girls were dancing together on a circular white rug in the lounge. I had been to a few of these parties and they always followed the same form, peaking at ten-thirty, with the guests calling for their cars soon after. People drank and drove more in those days, of course, but nobody of any importance stayed late because the studios began work at 4:00 am.

I was starting to think about leaving before undergoing the embarrassment of waiting for my battered Mustang to be brought around the front, when there was a commotion of raised voices out on the patio, and I saw someone go into the pool fully dressed: a gaunt middle-aged man in a black suit. It was difficult to find out what had happened, because everyone was crowding around the water's edge. All I know is, when they pulled him out of the chlorine a minute later, he was dead. I read in the *Los Angeles Times* next day that he'd twisted his neck hitting the concrete lip as he went in, and had died within seconds. He was granted a brief obituary in *Variety* because he'd featured in a lame

Disney film called *Monkeys, Go Home*. I remember thinking that the press reports were being uncharacteristically cautious about the death. I guess nobody wanted to risk implying that Dell had been keeping a disorderly house, and there was no suggestion of it being anything other than an unfortunate accident. Dell was a big player in a union town.

As I drove back to the valley that night, passing above the crystalline grid of the city, I passed one of the beautiful girls walking alone along the side of the road with her shoes in her hand, thumbing a ride, and knew she'd come here from the Midwest, leaving all her friends and family behind just so she could be hired as eye-candy to stand around at parties. I remember thinking how nobody would miss her if she disappeared. I felt sad about it, but I didn't stop for her. Black men didn't stop to pick up white girls back then; you didn't want a situation to develop.

The work dried up for a couple of months, but on a storm-heavy night in February I was invited to another studio party, this time a more low-key affair in Silverlake, where single palms crested the orange sky on the brows of hills, and Hispanic families sat in their doorways watching their kids play ball. You can tell poorer neighbourhoods by the amount of cabling they carry above their houses, and this area had plenty. I pulled over by an empty lot and was still map-reading under the street lamp when I heard the dull thump of music start up behind me, and realised the party was being held in a converted brownstone loft – they were pretty much a novelty back then – so I parked and made my way to the top floor.

The building's exterior may have been shabby, but the inside was Cartier class. The whole top floor had been stripped back to brickwork and turned into one big space, because the owner was a photographer who used it as his studio. He handled on-set shoots for Paramount, and had coincidentally taken my headshots a couple of years earlier. It was good to think he hadn't forgotten me, and this event was a lot friendlier than the last. I recognised a couple of girls I'd auditioned with the month before, and we got to talking, then sharing a joint. The music was Hendrix – *Electric Ladyland*, I think. Pulmonary gel-colours spun out across the walls, and the conversation was louder, edgier, but it was still a pretty high-end layout.

It was the photographer's thirtieth birthday and he'd invited some pretty big names, but it was getting harder to tell the old money from the new, because everyone was dressed down in beads and kaftans. The new producers and actors were sprawled across canary-yellow beanbags in a narcoleptic fug, while the industry seniors stuck to martinis at the bar. I was having a pretty good time with my lady-friends when I saw them again.

Perhaps because nobody had noticed me at Dell's house, I noticed everything, and now I recognised the new arrivals as they came in. There were four of them, two girls and two men, all in late teens to mid-twenties, and I distinctly recalled them from Dell's Christmas party because they'd stood together in a tight group, as though they didn't know anyone else. They were laughing together and watching everyone, as though they were in on a private joke no one else could share.

I admit I was a little stoned and feeling kind of tripped out, but there was something about them I found unsettling. I got the feeling they hadn't been invited, and were there for some other purpose. They stayed in the corner, watching and whispering, and I wanted to go up to them, to ask what they were doing, but the girls were distracting me and – you know how that goes.

I left a few minutes after midnight, just as things were starting to heat up. I went with the girls back to their hotel. They needed a ride, and I needed the company. When I woke up the next morning, they had already vacated the room. There was only a lipstick-scrawled message from them on the bathroom mirror, plenty of kisses but no contact numbers. I picked up the industry dailies in the IHOP on Santa Monica, and there on page 5 found a report of the party I'd attended the night before. Some high-society singer I'd vaguely recalled seeing drunkenly arguing with his girlfriend had fallen down the stairs as he left the party, gone all the way from the apartment door to the landing below. He was expected to recover but might have sustained brain damage. Fans were waiting outside his hospital room with flowers.

Two parties, two accidents – it happens. There were studio parties all over town every night of the week, but it felt weird that I'd been at both of them. You had to be invited, of course, but there wasn't the strict door policy that there is now, no security guards with headsets, sometimes not even a check-list. People came and went, and it was hard to tell if anyone was gatecrashing; the hosts generally assumed you wouldn't dare. They were insulated from the world. I remember attending a shindig in Brentwood where the toilet overflowed through the dining room, and everyone acted like there was nothing wrong because they assumed the maids would clear it up. Hollywood's like that.

Maybe you can see a pattern emerging in this story, but at the time I failed to spot it. I was too preoccupied: with auditions, with my career, with having a good time. The town felt different then, footloose and slightly lost, caught between classic old-time movie-making and the rising counter-culture. They needed to cater to the new generation of rootless teens who were growing impatient with the world they'd been handed. The producers wanted to make renegade art statements but didn't know how, and they couldn't entirely surrender the movies of the past. People forget that *Hello Dolly!* came out the same year as *Easy Rider*.

Strange times. In Vietnam, Lt William Calley's platoon

of US soldiers slaughtered five hundred unarmed Vietnamese, mainly women and children, at My Lai. Many of us had buddies over there, and heard stories of old women thrown down wells with grenades tossed in after them. Those who were left behind felt powerless, but there was an anger growing that seeped between the cracks in our daily lives, upsetting the rhythm of the city, the state and eventually the whole nation. I'd never seen demonstrations on the streets of LA before now, and I'd heard the same thing was happening in Washington, in Chicago, even in Denver.

But nothing affected the Hollywood elite; they hung on, flirting with subversion when really, what they wanted to make was musicals. They still threw parties, though, and the next one was a killer.

This was the real deal, a ritzy Beverly Hills bash with a sizeable chunk of the A-list present, thrown in order to promote yet another *Planet Of The Apes* movie. The sequels were losing audiences, so one of the executive producers pulled out the stops and opened up his mansion – I say his, but I think it had been built for Louise Brooks – to Hollywood royalty. This time there were security guards manning the door, checking names against clipboards, questioning everyone except the people who expected to be recognised. Certainly I remember seeing Chuck Heston there, although he didn't look very happy about it, didn't drink and didn't stay long. The beautiful girls had turned out in force, clad in brilliantly jewelled mini-dresses and skimpy tops, slyly scoping the room for producers, directors, anyone who could move them up a career notch. A bunch of heavyweight studio boys were playing pool in the smoke-blue den while their women sat sipping daiquiris and dishing dirt. The talent agents never brought their wives along for fear of becoming exposed. I'd been invited by a hot little lady called Cheyenne who had landed a part in the movie purely because she could ride a horse, although I figured she'd probably ridden the producer.

So there we were, stranded in this icing-pink stucco villa with matching crescent staircases, dingy brown wall tapestries and wrought-iron chandeliers. I took Cheyenne's arm and we headed for the garden, where we chugged sea breezes on a lawn like a carpet of emerald needles. Nearby, a fake-British band played soft rock in a striped marquee filled with bronze statues and Santa Fe rugs. I was looking for a place to put down my drink when I saw the same uninvited group coming down from the house, and immediately a warning bell started to ring in my head.

It was a warm night in March, and most people were in the torch-lit garden. The Uninvited – that's how I had come to think of them – helped themselves to cocktails and headed to the crowded lawn, and we followed.

'See those people over there?' I said to Cheyenne. 'You ever see them before?'

She had to find her glasses and sneak them on, then shook her glossy black hair at me. 'The square-jawed guy on the left looks like an actor. I think I've seen him in something. The girls don't seem like they belong here.'

'What it is, I'm beginning to think there's some really harmful karma around them.' I told her about the two earlier parties.

'That's nuts.' She laughed. 'You think they could just go around picking fights and nobody would notice?'

'People here don't notice much, they're too busy promoting themselves. Besides, I don't think it's about picking fights, more like bringing down a bad atmosphere. I don't know. Let's get a little closer.'

We sidled alongside one of the men, who was whispering something to the shorter, younger of the two girls. He was handsome in a dissipated way, she had small feral features, and

I tried figuring them first as a couple, then part of a group, but couldn't get a handle on it. The actor guy was dressed in an expensive blue Rodeo Drive suit, the other was an urban cowboy. The short girl was wearing the kind of cheap cotton sunflower shift they marked down at FedCo, but her taller girlfriend had gold medallions around her throat that must have cost plenty.

Now that I noticed, they were all wearing chains or medallions. The cowboy guy had a ponytail folded neatly beneath his shirt collar, like he was hiding it. Something about them had really begun to bother me, and I couldn't place the problem until I noticed their eyes. It was the one thing they all had in common, a shared stillness. Their unreflecting pupils watched without moving, and stayed cold as space even when they laughed. Everyone else was milling slowly around, working the party, except these four, who were watching and waiting for something to happen.

'You're telling me you really don't see anything strange about them?' I asked.

'Why, what do you think you see?'

'I don't know. I think maybe they come to these parties late, uninvited. I think they hate the people here.'

'Well, I'm not that crazy about our hosts, either,' she said. 'We're here because we have to be.'

'But they're not. They just stand around, and cause bad things to happen before moving on,' I told Cheyenne. 'I don't know how or why, they just do.'

'Do you know how stoned that sounds?' she hissed back at me. 'If they weren't invited, how did they get through security?' She reached on tiptoe and looked into my eyes. 'Just as I thought, black baseballs. Smoking dope is making you paranoid. Couldn't you just try to enjoy yourself?'

So that's what I did, but I couldn't stop thinking about the guest dying in the pool, and the guy who had fallen down the stairs. We stayed around for a couple more hours, and were thinking about going when we found ourselves back with the Uninvited. A crowd had gathered on the deck and were dancing wildly, but there they were, the four of them, dressed so differently I couldn't imagine they were friends, still sizing things up, still whispering to each other.

'Just indulge me this one time, OK?' I told Cheyenne. 'Check them out, see if you can see anything weird about them.'

She sighed and turned me around so that she could peer over my shoulder. 'Well, the square-jawed guy is wearing something around his neck. Actually, they all are. I've seen his medallion before, kind of a double-headed axe? It means *God Have Mercy*. There are silver beads on either side of it, take a look. Can you see how many there are?'

I checked him out. The dude was so deep in conversation with the short girl that he didn't notice me. 'There are six on each side. No, wait – seven and six. Does that mean something?'

'Sure, coupled with the double axe, it represents rebellion via the thirteen steps of depravity, ultimately leading to the new world order, the *Novus Ordor Seclorum*. It's a satanic symbol. My brother told me all about this stuff. He read a lot about witchcraft for a while, thought he could influence the outcome of events, but then my mother made him get a job.' She pointed discreetly. 'The girl he's talking to is wearing an *ankh*, the silver cross with the loop on top? It's the Egyptian symbol for sexual union. They're pretty common, you get them in most head shops. Oh, wait a minute.' She craned over my shoulder, trying to see. 'The other couple? She's wearing a gold squiggle, like a sideways eight with three lines above it. That's something to do with alchemy, the sign for black mercury maybe. But the cowboy, he's wearing the most potent icon. Check it out.'

I looked, and saw a small golden five lying on his bare tanned chest. Except it wasn't a five; there was a crossed line above it. 'What is that?'

'The *Cross of Confusion*, the symbol of Saturn. Also known as the *Greater Malefic, the Bringer of Sorrows*. Saturn takes 29 years to orbit the sun, and as a human life can be measured as just two or three orbits, it's mostly associated with the grim reaper's collection of the human soul, the acknowledgement that we have a fixed time before we die, the orbit of life. However, we can alter that orbit, cut a life short, in other words. It's a satanic death symbol, very powerful.'

I got a weird feeling then, a prickle that started on the back of my neck and crept down my arms. I was still staring at the cowboy when he looked up and locked eyes with me, and I saw the roaring, infinite emptiness inside him. I never thought I was susceptible to this kind of stuff, but suddenly, in that one look, I was converted.

We were still locked into each other when Cheyenne nudged me hard. 'Quit staring at him, do you want to cause trouble?'

'No,' I told her, 'but there's something going down here, can't you feel it? Something really scary.'

'Maybe they just don't like black dudes, Julius. Or maybe they're aliens. I really think we should go.'

Just then, the Uninvited turned as one and walked slowly to the other side of the dancing crowd until I could no longer see them properly. A few moments later I heard the fight start, two raised male voices. I'd been half expecting it to happen, but when it did the shock still caught me.

He was in his late fifties, balding but shaggy-haired, dressed in a yellow *Keep On Truckin'* T-shirt designed for someone a third his age. I saw him throw a drink and swing a fat arm, fist clenched, missing by a mile. Maybe he was pushed, maybe not, but I saw him lose his balance and go over on to the table as if the whole thing was being filmed in slow motion. The kidney-shaped sheet of glass that exploded and split into three sections beneath him sliced through his T-shirt as neatly as a scalpel, and everyone jumped back. God forbid the guests might ruin their shoes on shards of glass.

He was lying as helpless as a baby, unable to rise. A couple of girls squealed in revulsion. When he tried to lift himself on to his elbows, a wide, dark line blossomed through the cut T-shirt. He flopped and squirmed, calling for help as petals of blood spread across his shirt. The music died and I heard his boot heels hammering on the floor, then the retreating crowd obscured my view. Nobody had rushed to his aid; they looked like they were waiting for the Mexican maids to appear and draw a discreet cloth over the scene so that they could return to partying.

Why didn't I help? I have no answer to that question. Maybe I was more like the others back then, afraid of being the first to break out of the line. I feel differently now.

Cheyenne was pulling at my sleeve, trying to get me to leave, but I was looking for the Uninvited. If they were still there, I couldn't see them. They'd brought misfortune to the gathering once more and disappeared into the despairing confusion of the Los Angeles night.

As I had twice before, I found myself searching the papers next morning for mention of the drama, but any potential scandal had been hastily hushed up. I lost touch with Cheyenne for a while, even began to think I'd imagined the whole thing, because the next month my career took off and I stopped smoking dope. I'd landed the lead role in a new movie about a street-smart black P.I. called Dynamite Jones, and I needed to keep my head straight, because the night schedule was punishing and I couldn't afford to screw up.

We wrapped the picture in record time, without any serious hitches, although my white love interest was replaced with a black girl two days in, and our big love scene was cut to make sure we didn't upset the heartland audiences. Perry Sapirstein held the wrap party at his house on Mulholland because they were striking the set and we could keep the studio space. I figured it was a good time to hook up with Cheyenne again – she'd been in Chicago appearing in an anti-war show that had tanked, and wanted to get a little more serious with me while she was waiting for another break out West.

I thought I'd know everyone there, but there were still some unfamiliar faces, and of course, the Beautiful Girls were out in full force, hoping to get picked for something, anything before their innocence faded and their faces hardened. The Hollywood parties were losing their appeal as I got used to them. I could see the establishment would never be unseated from their grand haciendas. They flirted with rebellion but would revert to type at the first opportunity, and everyone knew it.

I'd forgotten all about the Uninvited. People were caught up in the events unfolding in Vietnam, and fresh stories of atrocities on both sides were being substantiated by shocking press footage that brought the war to everyone's doorstep. I didn't meet anyone, ever, who thought we should be there, but I was in liberal California, and it would take some time yet for the mood to sink in across the nation. The sense of confusion was palpable; hippies were hated and feared wherever they went, and the young were viewed with such suspicion beyond the Democrat enclaves that it felt dangerous to step over state lines. Folks are frightened of difference and change, always were, always will be, but back then there were no guidelines, no safety barriers. There was no one to tell us what was right, beyond what we felt in our hearts.

We couldn't see how far we were blundering into darkness.

Even in the strangest times, somebody will always continue to throw a party and act like there's nothing wrong. So it was on Mulholland, where the gold tequila fountains filled pyramids of sparkling salt-rimmed glasses, and invisible waiters slipped between the guests with shrimps arranged on pearlised clam-shells.

Everything was strange that last night I saw them. I remember being freaked by shrieks of hysteria that turned into bubbles of laughter, coming from the darkened upstairs floor of the house. I remember the hate-filled glare of a saturnine man leaning in the corridor by the bathroom. I remember going to the kitchen to rummage for some ice and seeing something written in maple syrup on the bone-white door of the fridge, the letters running like thick dark blood. I peered closer, trying to read what it said, expecting something shocking and sinister, only to feel a sense of anticlimax when I deciphered the dripping, sticky word:

HEALTH

So much for Lucifer appearing uninvited at Hollywood parties.

But the second I dismissed the idea as dumb, a scampering, shadowy imp of fear started scratching about inside my mind again. The more I thought about it, the more the room, the house and everyone in it felt unsafe, and the sense kept expanding, engulfing me. Suddenly I caught sight of myself reflected in the floor-to-ceiling glass that separated the kitchen from the unlit rear garden, and saw how alone I was in that bright bare room. There was no one to care if I lived or died in this damned city. Without me even realising it, everything in my world had begun to slip and slide into a howling, empty abyss. There were no friends, no loyalties, no good intentions, only the prey and the preyed upon.

No haven, no shelter, just endless night, unforgiving and infinite.

If this was the effect of giving up marijuana, I thought, I really needed to start smoking again.

But the line of safety was thinner then. We felt much closer to destruction. These days we live with the danger while cheerfully ignoring the data.

I once attended a class on the structure of myths at UCLA where we discussed the theme of the uninvited guest, the phantom at the feast, the unclean in the temple, the witch at the christening, the vampire at the threshold, the doomsayer at the wedding, and all these myths shared one element in common: someone had to invite them in to begin with. I wondered who had provided an unwitting invitation here in California.

I remember that night there was a very pretty blonde woman in the lounge – although I only saw her from the back – whom everyone wanted to talk to. One of her friends was drunkenly doing a trick with a lethal-looking table knife, and I thought *what if he slips?* And just as I was thinking that, I became aware of them, standing right alongside me. I turned and found myself beside the square-jawed one who looked like an actor. His grey deep-set eyes stared out at me very steadily, holding the moment. The light was low in the main hall, which was lit only by amber flames from an enormous carved fireplace. I saw the Satan sign glittering at his buddy's neck, and he smiled knowingly as I flinched.

'Who the hell are you?' I half-whispered, finally regaining my composure.

'Bobby.' He held out his hand. 'You're Julius.'

'How do you know who I am?'

'I have friends in the business. We know a lot of people.'

I didn't like the way he said that. 'I've seen you before,' I told him. 'Seen your friends, too.'

'Yeah, they're all here. We hang out together.' He pointed. 'That's Abby, Susan, Steve.'

They all looked over at me as if they'd picked up on their

names being spoken. The effect of them moving with one shared mind was unnerving. I meant to say 'Who do you know here?' but instead I asked 'What are you here for?'

Bobby was silent for a moment, then smiled more broadly. 'I think you know the answer to that. We're here to taste death.'

'What do you mean?'

He looked away at the fire. 'You have to know what dying is before you can know life, Julius.'

'I don't understand you.'

'I mean,' Bobby leaned in close and still, his eyes filling with morbid compassion as they stared deep into mine, 'we're leading the rise to power. We've already started the killing, and this city will become an inferno of revenge. The streets will run with blood. There will be a new holocaust, revolution in the streets, and the world will belong to the Fifth Angel.'

'Man, you're crazy.' I shook my head, suddenly tired of this white supremacy crap. I'd just spent two months mofo-ing around in some Stepin Fetchit role given to me by rich white boys, and I guess I'd just had enough. 'Bullshit,' I told him. 'If the best thing you can do to start a revolution is shove a few drunks around at parties, you're in trouble. I saw you at Dell's place. I know you pushed that guy into the pool and broke his neck. I saw you in Silverlake, and at the house on Canon Drive where that guy was cut on the table. I know you don't belong here, except to bring down chaos.'

'You're right, we don't belong here any more than you do,' he said, distracted now by something or someone moving past my left shoulder. 'There's no difference between us, brother. The rest of them are just little pigs.' He exchanged glances with the others, and the two girls turned to go, slipping out through the crowd. He pushed back to take his leave with them.

'Wait,' I called after him, anxious to keep him there. 'How did you get in through security?'

Bobby looked over his shoulder, quiet and serious. 'We have friends in all the places we're not invited.'

'Nothing's going to happen tonight, right? You've got to promise me that.'

'Nothing will happen tonight, Julius. We're leaving.'

'I don't get it.' I was calling so loud that people were turning to stare at me. 'Why not tonight? You made this stuff happen before, why not now, right in front of me? Let me see, Bobby, I want to understand. You think you can summon up the devil?'

His eyes were still focused over my left shoulder. 'The devil is already here, my friend.'

I twisted around to see who he was looking at, but when I looked back he had gone. They had all gone. And the tumble of the party rushed into my ears once more. I heard the blonde girl laughing as the man fumbled his knife trick, and the point of the blade fell harmlessly to the floor, where it stuck in the wood.

When the girl turned around, I saw that she was heavily pregnant, and heard someone say, 'Come on, Sharon, I'm going to drive you home, it's late. What if Roman calls tonight?'

She lived on 10050 Cielo Drive, I heard her say. And she had to get back, because the next night she was expecting her friends Abby and Jay, and they'd probably want to stay late drinking wine. She wasn't drinking because of the baby. She didn't want anything to happen to the baby.

The next day was August 9th, 1969.

It was the day our bright world began its long eclipse.

They caught up with Charlie and his gang at the Spahn ranch, out near Chatsworth, but by then it was too late to stop the closing light. There were others, rootless and elusive, who would never be caught.

I remembered those parties in the Hollywood hills, and realised I had always known about the rise of the Uninvited. Much later, I read about Manson's children writing *Helter Skelter* on their victim's refrigerator door, only they had misspelled the first word, writing it as *Healther*.

I saw how close I had come to touching evil.

The world is different now. It's sectioned off by high walls, no-go zones, clearance status, security fences, X-ray machines. The gates remain shut to outsiders unless you have a pass to enter. The important parties and the good living can only continue behind sealed doors. At least, that's what those who throw the parties desperately need to believe. That's what *I* need to believe.

I married Cheyenne. We have two daughters and a son. Against all reason, we stayed on in California.

And we no longer know how to protect ourselves from those who are already inside the gates. I guess we lost that right when we first built walls around our enclaves, and printed out our invitations.

the spider kiss

Two dead, a house trashed, a trail of food, garbage and excrement. Jackson pushed back his baseball cap and scratched his sweating forehead. 'It's going to be a long night, man. I don't know what we're dealing with here.' He looked at the woman in the pink quilted housecoat and yellow plastic curlers. 'Ask her again, Dooley.' He didn't see why he should have to deal with witnesses when he had a new partner to break in for the job.

Dooley approached the frightened woman and eyed her with something approaching sympathy. 'I don't know, Matt, maybe we should get her some counselling first. She looks pretty shaken up.'

'Just fuckin' ask her, OK?'

Dooley tried to look official but he was wearing an XXL sunset-orange Hawaiian shirt. They had both been off duty when the call had come through. 'Tell us what you saw once more, ma'am. Take your time.'

'I told you, I was watching a rerun of *American Idol* when I heard a noise out in the yard. I thought it was an animal. We had a 'gator come through here last fall. I turned down the TV, put on the light and this guy came out—'

'Describe him?'

'Big, heavy, balding, fat belly, around forty. He'd been going through my garbage, had grass cuttings and doggy doo all around his mouth, it was just gross. Stared right at me, but kind of didn't see me, like he was on drugs, you know?'

'And you say he was wearing—'

'That was the weirdest thing – he had no pants on, just a Miami Dolphins shirt. And then he squatted and took a dump. Right in front of me on the lawn. He took a dump and wandered off next door. That was when I called 911. And now I've missed the rest of the show.'

'Nice,' said Jackson. 'Glad I already had supper. Tell her to fuck off.'

'Thank you, ma'am. We may need to talk to you again.'

'No we won't, she's a fucking moron, come with me.' Jackson beckoned to his new partner, lowering an avuncular arm around him. 'Then this guy walks – get this – *walks* – through the glass patio doors, bam, smash, into the next house where the victims are sleeping, and pulls 'em out of bed. And he kind of – *scratches* – at their faces in a frenzy. They got no features any more, Dan. Cocksucker didn't give a fuck about leaving traces or cutting himself, he just walked away. The woman's teeth are spread out there all over the fucking drive. He must be spouting blood, but no one saw where he went.'

'I don't think anyone wanted to look too closely. You want to do a search before the rest of the department gets down here?'

'Fucking right I do. Was a time when the Miami PD would let Homicide take care of things themselves, without dragging every so-called fucking expert off the bench to take a look. Everybody's a fucking big shot. See that?' Matt Jackson pointed to the bedroom lights flicking on in the identical white clapboard houses on the other side of the road. 'Gawkers'll be uploading the whole thing into blogs any second now. It'll be on fucking Yourspace or Mytube or whatever the fuck it is before we get back. Let's get it.'

Heavy blood spatters made the trail on the blacktop easy to follow. 'He must have cut himself real bad,' said Dooley.

'You mean like, when he tore the woman's teeth out of her head? No shit, Dooley.' Jackson scratched his hairy belly and pulled at his shorts, hitching them higher. Everything he said was coated in layers of world-weariness that you had to be careful about unwrapping. 'Hey, check this out.' He waved his torch in the direction of the scarlet splashes. They turned into an unlit vacant lot, following the trail. 'No way am I climbing over a fucking chicken-wire fence. My wife bought me this shirt. You go.'

'Jesus, Matt, I know I'm new around here but why do I have to—'

'You're an African-American with ginger hair and an Irish name, you got some way to go before I start trusting you. Just get over there.' Jackson cradled his hands, giving his partner a leg-up.

Dooley dropped to the other side and continued to follow the trail. He disappeared into an oleander bush, then called out. 'Oh man, you're going to love this. He's buried himself.'

'What do you mean?'

'I mean he's in the fucking ground.'

'Then cuff him up and bring him out.'

'I don't think I can do that. You'd better come and see.'

Jackson snagged his shirt on the top of the fence and tore off a button. He was still cursing under his breath when he came upon Dooley and their quarry. His torch revealed a fat naked butt. The top half of the guy's body had been wedged into grass and earth.

'Christ, it looks like he dug himself a burrow using his head. Take a leg, let's get him out.' They each grabbed an ankle and pulled. As the body emerged, they realised they were looking at a very dead man. He had bulldozed himself into the ground, grinding the flesh from his face and filling his mouth with hard dry soil.

'Another fucking crazy on crystal meth,' said Jackson, turning away. 'For this I missed the last quarter of the game?'

Next morning, he and Dooley were sweating beneath a wheezy air-conditioner in their Calle Ocho office, trying to concentrate on a bunch of forms the Miami Police Department required them to fill out. 'It doesn't make sense,' Dooley complained. 'Everyone in the neighbourhood knew this guy. He never took a drug in his life, a regular churchgoer, a restaurant critic at the local paper, for Christ's sake, and suddenly he starts eating dogshit and leaves? What would make him go nuts like that?'

'You mean apart from the temperature and the fact that people spazz out all the time around here? You've already been working in this unit for long enough to know that nothing we deal with makes sense. That Baptist minister last week who thought he could fly, the one who threw himself off the AT&T building? He was supposed to be a regular kind of guy, but the medics had to lift him off the sidewalk with barbecue tongs. Who knows?'

'Well, something weird's going on, and it's not just because of the heat,' said Dooley, wiping air-con dust from his computer screen. 'We got another call coming in right now.'

They arrived at the San Paulo deli on 3rd to find the owner, a tiny Cuban guy called Jacinto, standing in the wreckage of his store, fending off a customer with an aluminium stool. Jackson knew Jacinto. He ate there sometimes, even though the food was awful. 'What the hell's going on here, Jacko?' he asked. 'What'd you do to this guy, poison him?'

'He was eating his lunch and just went crazy,' Jacinto

explained, setting aside the stool in relief. 'Stuck his hands in the fish tank and started biting the heads off my crawfish.'

'OK, we'll take over now,' said Dooley, drawing his gun from its holster.

'Hey, Dan, don't overreact, OK?' said Jackson. 'Trust me, you don't want the fucking paperwork. Try giving him a verbal warning before you decide to blow his fucking head off.'

They looked back at the angry diner, a skinny young Asian who was frothing bubbles from his nostrils and rocking back and forth. His white shirt was torn in half, he was wearing one black trainer, and his cheeks were smeared with blood from the sharp shells of the crustaceans he had bitten. Every few seconds he screamed like a seagull. 'This one has definitely been smoking crack,' said Jackson.

'No,' Jacinto shook his head, 'I know him, a good man, Mr Yuan is a teacher at my son's school for five years now.'

Jackson scrunched up his eyes and tilted his head to one side, trying to square the foaming, squawking madman before them with Jacinto's ID. He was still considering the problem when Mr Yuan charged at them. He and Dooley braced themselves, preparing to fire warning shots, but the teacher leaped on to the counter and soared over their heads, sending himself face first through the deli's deafening plate-glass window.

'Fuck me,' said Jackson, running out through the falling shards to the spot where the bloody body had touched down. 'What the fuck is happening around here?'

'Like you said, when the heat rises this town goes postal,' Dooley replied.

'Get the medics, no way am I touching this guy.' Jackson tried to stuff his shirt back into his pants as he knelt, but he'd put on weight lately. 'I'm getting too old for this shit. I spend my days sitting in a car that smells like a hot gym shoe, eating cow-parts from street vendors with names I can't even pronounce. South

Beach PD is looking to set up new specialist units. The money's good. I could apply for a position there. Be a fucking sight easier stopping fags from bitch-slapping each other outside bars than staying here to act as pest control for the locals.'

'Maybe this is just a blip,' said Dooley. 'It'll pass.'

But it didn't pass; in the next few days, things got much worse.

'You want to know how many crazies we've had in the last two weeks?' asked Jackson, throwing the remains of his hot dog in the nearest bin as they walked towards the Hong Kong Center. The temperature was soaring to record highs. Over a week had passed since Mr Yuan killed himself in the 3rd Street deli. 'One hundred and seven reports of life-threatening behaviour, ten fatalities, and that's just between Bayshore Drive and the I-95. One woman out on Dodge Island chewed a hole through her husband's throat and sat on top of his body until they came to take her away. They found a naked old guy down on Beethoven who had broken his neck trying to lick his own balls.'

'It's not just the heat. I think I'm starting to see a pattern here,' said Dooley, eyeing his partner with distaste as Jackson noisily sucked mustard from his nicotine-stained fingers. 'Check out this one.' He pulled a page from his back pocket and unfolded it. 'See, before I joined the force I trained to be a naturalist.'

'You mean you ran around with no fucking clothes on?'

'That's a naturist, Matt. I studied endangered species of insect. This was in the local press yesterday. Some guy locked himself in his apartment, painted his entire body with black and orange stripes, wrapped himself in duct tape and then suffocated trying to get back out of it. The attending medic said he kept making a weird ratcheting noise as he was dying.'

'What are you telling me here?'

'OK, I know how this is going to sound.' Dooley held up his hands and took a deep breath. 'There's a rare bug that's nearly extinct, called the New Forest cicada, something like that. It's black and orange. It spends eight years in a larval stage, and as it emerges from its cocoon it releases a shrill series of clicks.'

'You telling me this guy thought he was a fucking *cicada*?'

Dooley looked sheepish. 'The story just reminded me, is all.'

'Take my advice and leave it to the detective division,' said Jackson. 'We're just here to clean up the shit, and I mean that – nearly everyone we've been called to take in has dropped a log in the street after killing someone. If that's a linking MO, it's pretty fucked up. Kill someone if you have to but use a fucking toilet, for Christ's sake.'

'Maybe not so odd,' said Dooley. 'I need to talk to a guy I know.'

'OK, but remember what I said, it's not our problem. Let the other divisions sort their own shit out.'

'Don't worry, this guy's not a detective, he's a Buddhist.'

I knew Dooley was going to be trouble, Jackson thought as he took an incoming call and watched his young partner walking away.

Dooley went to see Jim Pentecost. Once they had been students together, but their careers had taken them in separate directions. Pentecost now ran a Buddhist centre from an art deco schoolhouse in South Beach. His long hair, beads and kaftan gave him the appearance of a neo-hippie, but he taught New Age philosophies even hippies would have found extreme. He clasped Dooley warmly to his chest. 'Man, it's been a long time,' he said, grabbing the cop's arm and pulling him into the building's cool interior. 'I'd like to think this is a friendly call, but I guess you're here on business.'

'Kind of,' Dooley admitted. 'Remember you used to tell me your theories about man's relationship with the animal kingdom, life balance, all that kind of stuff? You still believe it?'

'More than ever, Dan, even though it's too late now.'

'What do you mean?'

'Hell, the balance has been destroyed. Man's greed has won the day, my friend. They're ripping up the world's last unspoiled sites to make money for the stockholders.'

The pair seated themselves in a shadowed courtyard musky with the smell of incense. 'The wars of the future will be about energy, water, religious control,' Pentecost continued. 'Capitalists are the new warmongers. They have destroyed the earth's natural inhabitants, and now they will in turn be made extinct. The karmic equilibrium has been tipped against humans. It's like the ozone layer – once you pass a certain point, balance can never, ever be restored.'

'Yeah, but what does all that mean?' asked Dooley. 'I can only report from personal experience. We're seeing so much fucked-up behaviour on the streets, we can't even begin to deal with it.'

'What kind of behaviour, exactly?' asked Pentecost, intrigued.

Dooley thought for a minute, then set about describing what he had seen.

Matt Jackson pushed back the door to the old Sport World warehouse and stepped inside. The heat was grotesque; the building had trapped the day's warmth. His partner had missed the call, and the only other squad cars in the area had been called to the airport, where a man was standing on the roof of his Toyota waving a rifle around and screaming his head off, blocking the intersection at Biscayne Boulevard.

Jackson walked through corridors of fierce light and back into patches so dark that his eyes were flooded with drifting orange spots. The call had warned that a naked woman had run amok in the pet shop of a local mall before fleeing into the warehouse. Jackson figured that at least she was unlikely to be armed, and moved through the empty hall with confidence. Ahead he thought he saw a human shape, swaying back and forth at the edge of the light. She looked young and pretty fit, even though she was probably insane. *That would make her a better bet than my old lady*, Jackson thought.

'Hey there, miss,' he called. 'I'm a police officer, I'm here to help you.' He placed his palm over the reassuring warmth of his gun. The figure remained fixed to the spot. Jackson could see now that she was, indeed, naked; tanned long legs, brown hair that fell to her shoulders in a glossy curtain, slender hips, flat belly, enhanced breasts. *Holy mama*, he thought, *maybe I'll get lucky even if she is crazy*. He advanced with confidence. 'Tell you what, lady, I'm having a bad day. It's too fucking hot, I've got a case of jock itch you wouldn't believe and I could do with a cold beer.' She circled him slowly, warily, tilting her head to one side. 'What say we go outside and get one together?' he suggested with a smile.

It should have been easy after that, but he'd made a mistake, believing the woman was harmless because she was naked. Jackson got cocky and dropped his attention for a moment, just long enough for her to manoeuvre behind him with incredible speed, dropping slender, muscular arms around his chest that tightened like pincers, crushing the breath from his lungs. Even as he fought to draw air, he marvelled at her athleticism. How could she be so fast, so powerful?

As they toppled backwards, Jackson blacked out. *Shit*, he thought, *it feels like I'm having a fucking heart attack*.

When he came round, the woman had pinned his wrists together with her left hand, and was pinching his nostrils shut, smacking at his chin. Clearly, she was trying to open Jackson's mouth. She worked in silence, patiently and calmly, with great determination. Her perfumed hair brushed his sweating forehead as she drew her face close, studying Jackson carefully. She seemed to be searching for some sign of recognition. As she slowly opened her mouth, Jackson could see that there was something dark inside it, some kind of animal trying to get out.

A thin black leg appeared, seeking purchase on the woman's shiny red lip, then another, and another. Her mouth widened further, and Jackson watched in mute horror as the first of the black funnel-web tarantulas tentatively emerged.

'Karmic imbalance,' Pentecost repeated. 'I was always taught that if all the animals on earth were wiped out tomorrow, the insects would survive, but now the chain has started to falter at the very basis of life, and even many of the hardiest species of insect are dying. Insects, birds, fish and animals all have souls, although they're not the same as human beings. When the souls of men become tainted, malnourished and weak, they can be replaced with purer, more driven-to-survive life forces. What you're seeing is the start of reincarnation's replacement programme.'

'You're telling me I have to go to my boss and warn him that insects' souls are coming back inside soulless people?' asked Dooley uncomfortably, remembering the woman who had killed her husband in the manner of a praying mantis devouring her mate.

'Yes, and there's nothing you can do about it.' Pentecost sat back in shadow, resting his head against the wall. 'Not this time around, anyway.'

The woman drew close and placed her mouth directly over Jackson's, allowing the spider to extend its bristling black legs and climb across, feeling its way inside a new warm haven. Jackson felt something tickle his cheeks, but there was sweat in his eyes and he could not see clearly. The insect was wriggling desperately, its hairy legs splaying outward as it supported a bulbous venom-filled body. It tried to free itself, but the woman's full lips closed tightly over his, so that the creature was fully propelled from one mouth to the other.

The spider's torso-sac shifted back and forth across his

tongue. It was large and heavy and pregnant, a species from eastern Australia, and was followed by another, pushed in so hard by the woman's tongue that the first spider stung the inside of his cheek in distress. With horror, Jackson realised that she was feeding him. He gagged, the contents of his stomach rising to spray acidic vomit over the wriggling mass, but she kept her mouth clamped tightly over his. Jackson could feel the creatures writhing, the hairs on their legs pricking and scratching the back of his throat.

Then their poisonous chelicerae lowered into his soft red flesh, and they started to inject their lethal venom.

Who the hell is ever going to believe that the souls of dying life-forms are transmigrating to living humans? thought Dooley as he headed back into the fierce South Beach sunlight and hailed a cab. *Hey, Jackson wants to change his job. Maybe we can persuade PDHQ to let us set up a special unit; take a tip from the old Radiohead song and call it the Karma Police. Nah, that's way too whack. How do you prevent something happening if you don't know who it will get next?*

As he settled back in the taxi he watched a fat, juicy fly crawling up the window. Its iridescent wings caught the late Miami sunshine and reflected prismatic shards of rainbow light. The hairs on its legs were as glossy as needles. He had never noticed how beautiful they were before now.

Without thinking, he licked it off the window and swallowed.

heredity

I

'I see you left your last place of employment after just four months, and I do find myself wondering why that should be the case,' said Constance Connaught.

She tapped the fingers of her right hand on the teak desktop with light impatience. Her nails were clear, her hair naturally pale and immaculately, but practically, coiffured. Mrs Connaught prided herself on clarity and durability in all things, including personal appearance. She settled in her high-backed chair, which creaked faintly, the only sound in the reception room apart from the tick of the mantelpiece clock and the sussurance of softly falling rain against the latticed windows. In the still air, the scents of old wood and lavender lingered in a drowsy vapour.

Biddy Kinross coughed lightly to allow herself thinking time. 'The thing of it is, ma'am, I had some trouble with – a household gentleman.' She chose not to elucidate.

'We are speaking of Mr Edward Chatham, are we not? A fine, upstanding young man, wise, prudent, and already much respected in London society. Would it be indelicate to consider the nature of this trouble?'

An uncomfortable silence settled in the room. 'In my eyes, ma'am, my unborn child's father was not the honourable person I took him to be.'

'Am I to understand, then, that your condition was forced upon you?'

Biddy cast her eyes to her shoes, which were worn and splashed with mud. The left one had a broken strap, which she hid behind her right ankle. She had scrubbed her hands as hard as she could, but there was no disguising the redness of her skin, so she folded her fingers in her lap. 'I'm afraid it is true, ma'am,' she said softly.

If Mrs Connaught was surprised, she decided not to show it. 'I assume you attempted to repel his advances?'

'Yes, ma'am.'

'Clearly to no avail. You did not lead him on?'

'No, ma'am. I was the subject of his unwanted attention for some time, and did my best to remove myself from his presence whenever he contrived to be alone with me.'

'What happened when you discovered your condition?'

'Why, I went to see the Mistress, but she accused me – accused me—'

'You must not upset yourself, Biddy. Wipe your nose now and draw a deep breath. I have little doubt of your veracity.'

'Ma'am?'

'I believe you, Biddy. One hears of such situations arising throughout the county these days. Fine gentlemen may behave very differently when they are away from their sphere of influence. It is a most un-Christian state of affairs, and I imagine has caused you much distress. Tell me, have you asked Our Saviour to forgive you in His infinite mercy?'

'Oh yes, ma'am.'

Mrs Connaught pressed her hands flat upon the desktop and studied the young maid with care. 'Unfortunately, despite your excellent references I could not engage you in this household without the servants speaking of your condition. If I should perish in the knowledge of only two sure truths, it would be that the Lord sees all and that servants will talk.'

Biddy's face started to crumple. Her childhood friend Betsy Green had urged her upon the family of this great Staffordshire house before she was stricken with consumption. If Mrs Connaught could not take her, there was nowhere left but the workhouse in Walsall, a squalid, corrupt establishment where pretty young women quickly succumbed to the predations of their seniors.

'However, I can see a way forward which may solve your problem. My husband's mother, Lady Beatrice Connaught, has lately grown too frail to be left to her own devices. Should your face find favour with her, it might be possible to place you in her employ. She occupies the upper floor here at Clare House, and you would remain at all times in her maid's quarters unless specifically requested to descend into the main part of the house.'

'Oh, ma'am, I thank you for your kind offer, but I must ask what would happen upon—'

'Lady Beatrice does not hold with the lax morality of young women, and you would have to ensure that no sign of your condition might be discerned in her presence. That should not be too difficult to arrange, as the last maid's clothes are still here, and she was of a full demeanour.'

Biddy recalled a fond memory of her plump friend, when the two of them attended the annual Summer Fayre in Sileston, across the valley. How she must have wasted away in her final days.

'When you reach full term I will not be able to fetch the village doctor, for although he is a kindly old gentleman, Dr McNairy may not be trusted with the secrets of a house such as this. The groom, however, is a silent type, and has delivered many healthy foals for us. If, by the divine will of God's grace, he should be able to place a living child in your arms, the infant may reside in a foundling home, where you can reclaim him before two years have passed.'

'I do not deserve such kindness, Mrs Connaught. I cannot find the words—'

'Do not thank me too soon, my girl. I run the accounts of my husband's estate here at Clare, and your price is appealingly low. And you have yet to meet with the approval of Lady Connaught.' From the look on her face, Biddy imagined that this would be a formidable task. 'Tell me, child, do you have family?'

'A brother only, ma'am, two years younger. His name is George, but we rarely speak to one another. He is a groundsman at Bly.'

'A fine house. What of your parents?'

'Due to their reduced circumstances, they could not keep us. At the age of ten we were placed in service.'

'So you have had time to learn your trade. Can you read and write?'

'Most certainly, ma'am. I also have some French.'

'Well, you are quite full of surprises. Perhaps it is time for you to meet my husband's mother.'

The old lady sat so still and upright in her great oaken bed that Biddy thought she might have died. The brocaded room was filled with stale, overheated air, and Lady Beatrice Connaught wore a thick linen night-smock with a high lace collar and bonnet. Slowly, one tortoise-eye opened, followed by the other. A pair of warts sat on either side of her nose like barnacles attached to the hull of a boat. A thin grey hand appeared above the counterpane, which slid back with a crepitation of old silk.

'Approach me.' Her voice was as dry as baking paper. Biddy took a step nearer.

'Well, don't just gawp like a codfish, girl, help me up. Let me have a good look at you.'

Biddy leaned forward. Betsy's old skirt was arranged about her in broad folds. Self-conscious of her condition, she placed her hands across her lap. The old lady smelled of camphor and clove, masking something sour.

'Show me your teeth.'

Biddy opened her mouth as the old lady's hand crept to her chin and pulled the flesh about. 'It is the best way to judge the health of a maid,' she told her. 'Servants are no different from horses in that respect.'

A log dropped in the grate, making Biddy start.

'You have nothing to fear from me, Biddy,' Lady Beatrice told her. 'My reputation means little now that I am an old woman. Time brings the weight of experience to men, but it is the destroyer of a woman's only power. How the heads turned at the Duchess of Gloucester's summer ball when I arrived on the arm of her only son! Alas, our betrothal could not survive the conspiring tongues of London society. For such a marriage to be successful there must be male heirs in abundance, and their family was not blessed with fecundity. But all that was long ago. My power has been extinguished, and you, my girl, will do, just so long as you remember your place, which is here by my side whenever I call for you.'

'Ma'am, Mrs Connaught says I am to live here in your quarters.'

'She does, does she? This house has over fifty rooms, yet Constance and my useless son find themselves constricted within it. Very well, I suppose there is room enough here. You will have the attic, and make sure you keep it neat as a pin, for I can no longer climb the stairs to check upon you, and will not be taken advantage of.'

And so her new life began. Biddy was to be paid £22 a year, a wage £6 less than the salary assigned to most first housemaids. She was introduced to the rest of the serving staff as a parlourmaid, and that was the last she saw of the great house at Clare. Her world shrank to two floors: Lady Connaught's velvety, claustrophobic quarters, where the air was heavy with dust and the light of day was never admitted, and her own room in the eaves, which had bare boards and was unheated.

In this manner, Biddy's confinement slowly passed. The mansion below seemed gloomy and unhomely, more a silent mausoleum than a family house. She had occasion to visit it only thrice, and briefly on those occasions. She ventured down the great staircase once to speak to the cook about Lady Beatrice's broth, once to ask one of the footmen if he would post a letter to her brother, and once at the summoning of Mrs Connaught, who introduced her to her husband Harold, Lady Beatrice's son. Harold was dry as toast and elderly before his time. Although he was not yet forty years of age, his straining embroidered waistcoat, receding chin and unkempt mutton-chop whiskers gave him the appearance of decay and disregard. He possessed a harrumphing grandiosity that required him to stand with two fingers wedged in his waistcoat pocket, back erect, eyes hooded as he surveyed his mother's maid, inspecting her as he would one of his prized chestnut geldings. Biddy hated him from the moment their eyes briefly met.

'I am anxious to tell you the good news, Biddy,' said Mrs Connaught with uncharacteristic charity. 'We are to be sisters.' Her husband harrumphed in disapproval. 'After a fashion,' she added hastily. 'Come, this is not a matter for the ears of men.' She led Biddy to the front parlour and seated herself beside her.

'I, too, am with child. I had almost given up hope, but Dr McNairy confirmed the matter some while ago.

'Ma'am, I had no idea—'

'I was far slenderer of waist before we met. You were a stranger then, and not to be trusted with secrets. My husband has so longed for an heir to his property. Indeed, it has been a source of some difficulty between us.' She clasped the maid's hand warmly. 'So you see, my dear, you are not alone in your delicate condition. Obviously, you appreciate that the bond between us must remain a secret. But at least now, you have someone to whom you can turn. And I, in my turn, may ask your advice, for it is well known that in some ways the lower orders have more knowledge of birthing than their betters.'

Constance's amity and frankness took Biddy aback, but despite her employer's enthusiasm, she knew no bond could ever exist between them. One might as well ask the sky to join with the earth; it was not in the natural order of things. Still, the high born enjoyed the illusion of camaraderie with those they employed.

Biddy was obliged to keep the child a secret from all. Mrs Connaught, on the other hand, began to receive a steady stream of visitors and well-wishers, and talked of nothing else.

When her belly began to reveal itself, Biddy remained aloft, swathing herself in Betsy's baggy old clothes, hitching the long brown skirt high above her waist. Her days and nights were passed tending to the old lady, whose eyesight was mercifully poor. Biddy put up with her querulous complaints, her veiled insults, her unreasonable demands and her childish tantrums. She dressed and undressed her, attending to her *toilette*, listened to her diatribes against the fading light and the world's growing ills. She cut up her food and read aloud every evening until Lady Beatrice sank into her pillow and began to snore like a horse. Yet despite the demands made upon her, Biddy grew to like the old lady.

Lady Beatrice had once found favour at court, but her beauty had withered and she with it, so that she now lived with bitter memories of what might have been. The English have never cared much for their elders, and Mrs Connaught showed scant regard for her mother-in-law, rarely venturing up to see her.

Harold visited even more infrequently, preferring to spend his days among his horses and hunting dogs.

And so late summer passed into autumn. One night, soon before midnight, when the wind was howling in the eaves and the house was asleep, Biddy made her way downstairs, past the great gilt clock on the landing that had once belonged to Caroline of Ansbach, and the faded tapestries that covered the draughty servant corridors, all the way to the front door that she had never, and would never, be allowed to use. Her purpose was merely to step outside and stand in glistening dark emeralds where the garden grew wild, and feel the meadow air against her cheek.

Removing her slippers, she stood in the wet grass and pressed her hands against her growing flesh, and prayed for her unborn child. *Let this most innocent of God's creatures survive*, she asked. *Let it be my child and not take after its father.* She wished for a sign that all might be well, but was not rewarded.

Worried that Lady Beatrice might awaken and demand to see her, she returned to the great hall and made her way back to the attic. When she arrived, her worst fears were confirmed. Light showed beneath the old lady's door. Her lamp had been turned up.

'Where were you, girl?' she demanded to know. 'I have been calling for you this last quarter hour.'

'I am sorry, my lady.' Biddy cast her eyes downward, noting that the hem of her skirt was dark with dew.

'I should not be left alone. Really, it is too cruel. I had a dream.'

'It shall not happen again, my lady.'

'I dreamed – shall I tell you what I dreamed? A tiny child, running along an endless lawn towards a forest filled with great Staffordshire oaks…the tiniest child…' And then she was asleep, and the old lady's dream was dissipated. Biddy lowered the lamp once more and tucked her charge's hands beneath the counterpane.

Days turned to weeks, then months, until the arrangement of her clothing could barely conceal the form of her child. One morning, Mrs Connaught came up to visit, and mistress and servant passed a few moments together in Biddy's attic room. Constance was heavy with child, but carried her distended belly before her as a proud sign of impending motherhood. She was pleasant enough, in a distant fashion, but after she left, Biddy felt disheartened and ashamed of her own unacknowledgeable condition.

Later, as she washed the old lady's sheets and prepared to hang them on the flat roof formed by the redbrick turrets beyond her window, Biddy felt a sharp shift of weight in her stomach, and knew that her time had come. Making her way slowly down the rear staircase to the servant's quarters, she was surprised by Mrs Connaught, who understood at once and headed her off towards the back doors, into the flagstone courtyard. Although heavy with child herself, Constance moved with such lightness and grace that Biddy felt ungainly and stupid beside her. They walked beyond the stables where Harold kept his beloved horses, and arrived at the old barn, which had fallen from use after the new stables were built.

'The groom's name is William. He is a decent soul, Biddy, and will do his best to deliver your child in good health. You will be comfortable in here, where it is clean and dry enough. Remember, Our Lord commenced his life in such a place.'

Biddy was left alone while her mistress found the groom. She looked up at the doves shedding feathers in the rafters, at the bright morning prying its way through the cracked rafters, and felt new hope for her baby.

Constance returned with William, a gaunt, lipless man whose skull could be clearly discerned beneath his wind-crimsoned skin. He stared at Biddy with the look of a man more used to seeing horses than women. 'There are hale bales over in the corner, miss. We've taken the mares out to the paddock, so you'll not be troubled here.'

The contractions tightened. Her waters broke and seeped into the damp, dungy hardpack. She tried to see beyond her soaked skirts, but William pushed her back into the prickly hay. She felt the child hot in her groin as his hands descended to ease it forth. She felt movement, but heard no cry, no scream of life. The groom summoned Constance; there was an urgent fluster of activity. Something, she felt instinctively, had gone terribly wrong.

'What is it? What has happened?' she asked, but there came no answers. The doves flapped free of the rafters and sought exits to the sky. She watched the dust motes settling in the shafts of sunlight that crossed the barn, but she did not hear the squalling of a newborn child. There was a hot pain deep within her pelvis, and yet she fell asleep.

'I am so sorry,' said Constance, easing the weight of her burden as she sat beside Biddy's bed. On the table beside them, bloody cloths lay in cooling water. 'The cord was caught around your baby's neck, so that he could not catch his breath.'

'So it was a boy.'

'Indeed, and a bonny child at that. William tells me he suffered no pain. I am so sorry for you, my dear.' She patted Biddy's hand. 'By what name would you have had him baptised?'

'Thomas. Little Thomas.' Biddy looked about her. 'Where am I?' she asked.

'You are in the cook's quarters, and must stay here until you regain your strength. There is the question of a burial. Your child could not be recognised in the eyes of God. If you wish, I will arrange for him to be interred elsewhere.' Constance rose with difficulty and walked to the window. 'In the greenwood beyond, perhaps, in a pleasant glade where you may visit him.'

Three days later, Biddy visited the small clearing wherein her child had been interred. Mrs Connaught walked her to the little patch of cleared earth and allowed her a few moments of solitude before leading her back. 'You must not worry about the future,' she instructed Biddy as they approached Clare House. 'You are young and sturdy. There may yet be a happy marriage and further children for you. I have arranged a position as a lady's maid for you in a great house just beyond the next village. The Marlboroughs are old family friends, and will make sure no ill befalls you. In three weeks' time, when you are feeling entirely recovered, we will release you into their care. Cook will be along to remove your milk shortly. She has been with us since she was a child, and I trust her to ask no questions of you. I shall tell the rest of the servants that you are unwell, and are to remain with us until you are fully recovered.'

'But who will look after Lady Beatrice?' asked Biddy, concerned.

'She will have to share my own maid. Heaven knows the girl has little enough to do.' Constance pressed her hands together. 'Very well,' she decided. 'I wish a happy life for you, Biddy. We shall see each other soon, I hope.'

But they did not. Three days later, Biddy glimpsed Harold Connaught and Dr McNair striding along the hall together, and the servants spoke of Mrs Connaught giving birth to a healthy son, but it seemed impossible to see the child or its mother. Her requests were made via the second footman to the butler and the housekeeper, but no access was ever granted to Constance or her mother-in-law.

Finally, and with great reluctance, Biddy left the house. On the drive outside, she looked up at the windows where the two ladies lay in their beds, and wondered about the fickle nature of friendship. She had never expected to be treated as a true companion by either of them, and yet Mrs Connaught's kindness had given her a faint hope. The chill spring morning nipped at her bare arms, but she had refused the butler's offer of a carriage. As she left the estate, she took one last look at the patch of earth in the clearing where her baby was buried. There was no time now for sadness or looking back. She strode forward from the wood, to a new life as a lady's maid in Marlborough House.

II

Outside, summer was dying, fractured by heat-storms that rolled across the brown meadows, darkening the parched earth.

The envelope was damp-fattened vellum, the blue handwriting spidery and fine. Only George, her brother, ever wrote to her, but this was not his style. Unfolding the letter within, she found herself in receipt of a request from Lady Beatrice Connaught. There were but a few faint lines. *Perhaps you will be surprised to find me still alive after seven long years, but no more surprised than I find myself to be, I assure you. However, the doctor informs me that although I feel in the best of spirits, my body is now filled with ill humours, and I have but a few days of life left before I finally pass beyond this mortal veil. I shall not be sorry to leave, but find I cannot dismiss the kindnesses you showed me. It is with that thought in mind that I summon you to my bedside, where you shall hear something that may come as a shock to you. I entreat you to travel with the coachman who delivers this missive, and who will deliver you to the servants' entrance at Clare. It is of **paramount importance** that you do not allow my son or his wife to see you at Clare House.*

As the horse slowed to a trot, and the house appeared from behind the beeches, Biddy's sense of foreboding increased. She could not imagine what news the old lady wished to impart to her. Could illness have turned her mind, encouraging her to recall the maid who had performed acts of small benevolence in the most confining part of her life? It saddened her that a once-proud old lady now sounded so fearful and feeble.

The coachman silently held open the door to the servants' staircase, and ushered her into darkness. The stairs creaked beneath her boots, but no other sound came from the house. She followed the splinters of daylight formed by gaps in the landing shutters and made her way to the old lady's apartment.

In the seven years that had passed since she last laid eyes on her maidservant, Lady Beatrice had withdrawn and shrunk like an untended plant, so that only her blue eyes remained young. Her voice was no louder than the lightest breeze in the branches of the sycamores that lined the drive to Clare House. Beside her right shoulder lay a white silk handkerchief, spotted with crimson droplets. The unmistakable odour of death was in the room.

'Sit by me, Biddy,' she implored. Her imperious nature had faded to nothing, to be replaced by the sad, wheedling tone of someone begging to be noticed. 'You have grown into a fine woman. You were seen by no one in the house?'

'Only the coachman who delivered me, Your Ladyship.'

'Tell me of yourself. What has happened since you left this place? Do your new masters treat you well? Have you found happiness?'

'I am treated fairly,' Biddy admitted. 'Alas, I have not married. My duties leave no time for the devotions of a spouse.'

'And your lost child, do you think of him?' she asked.

'Ne'er a day passes when I do not think of my little boy, Lady Beatrice.'

The old woman reached out and seized her arm with a grey claw. 'What if I told you that your child lives?' she hissed.

Biddy was taken aback. 'What do you mean?'

'You have been the victim of a most abominable deception, and I am ashamed to admit my part in it. Your son lives on, and I, who have nothing now to lose, must unburden myself to you. My son has not the power within himself to create an heir, and as no woman may own her husband's property, Clare House must have a male, sound in mind and limb, in order to inherit the family estate. Come closer.'

Biddy placed her ear near to the old lady's mouth and listened.

'A cruel plan was conceived. Harold encouraged my daughter-in-law to seek out a maid who would bear a child, and her former maid Betsy, in all innocence, made mention of your name. You were betrayed, my child, tricked into believing that your baby died at birth, when he yet lives in the bosom of this house.'

'But how is that possible?' asked Biddy. 'What happened to Lady Constance's child?'

'There was no child, you silly girl. You remember how her supposed pregnancy began to show after yours? It was a sham. Your baby was taken from you and handed directly to her, where it was fed with the milk you surrendered.'

'Then why torture me so by revealing this terrible thing to me now?' asked Biddy, tears blurring her sight.

'Because my conscience has turned my eyes in upon myself and made me ashamed, and I must make my peace with God before I die,' she whispered. 'You must take the child from this house. Reveal the truth to him, and flee. You may yet know some happiness in your life.'

'But I have not the means—' Biddy searched for a workable solution to her predicament. 'My present employer—'

The old lady shook her hand at Biddy. 'Lift me up and search beneath my pillow. You will find all you need there.'

Lady Beatrice weighed less than a cat. Biddy raised her forward and felt beneath the pillow, removing a chamois pouch, inside which were folded several five-pound notes. 'I cannot take these, Your Ladyship.'

'It is but small recompense for the suffering you have endured. To be ravished at so young an age, then lied to about the fate of your only child. You will find the boy playing alone in the nursery, unguarded. Lady Constance and my son have been called to the next village to deal with a dispute. I can no longer walk to the window, but I heard their carriage leave. Opportunity is no lengthy visitor, my girl. You must seize your chance while you may!'

She ran down the stairs, moving as lightly and quickly as she could. The nursery was at the back of the second floor. If anyone approached from the front of the house, she would not be able to see them. Through the open door, she saw the child playing with his back to her. He had been dressed in a blue velveteen suit with a collar of cream lace, brown breeches and white knee-socks, the proper little gentleman. He turned as he heard her approach, and gazed back with the strange grey eyes she knew he would have.

'Thomas.' She knelt before him, watching as he assembled the army of lead dragoons before him. 'You don't remember me, but I am your mother.'

'You are most certainly not, and my name is not Thomas but Cedric,' the boy replied. 'You look like one of the parlourmaids, but not one I have seen at Clare.' He set the captain upright beside his hussars and some Napoleonic marshals from a different set. 'Papa promised to obtain some British infantrymen for me.' His speech was clear and confident. He had the tone of a child used to ordering servants.

Casting a fearful glance back at the open nursery door, Biddy knelt closer. 'You must listen to me, Thomas. As God is my witness, I swear I am your real mother.'

'I don't believe you. Mama has gone to Baronsfield with Papa to see about the pigs. Why do you keep using that name?'

'You may ask Lady Beatrice who I am, Thomas. She will tell you the truth.' She reached over and removed his hand from the lead soldier, placing his fingers in her palm. 'All this time I believed you had died at birth. Now we can be together again.'

'So I am to come with you?'

'Yes, my darling, yes.' She crushed him to her breast with a full heart.

Thomas pulled himself free and examined her with a critical eye. 'I do not think so. I don't know who you are, except that your shoes are worn and muddy and the hem of your skirt is torn. Even if what you say is true, why would I come with you? I am the heir of Clare House and its estate. Papa says that when I am a little older I will own all the land I can see from the gate.'

'But that is not important, my lamb. What matters is that we can be reunited as family.'

'I think you are perhaps mistaken. You should look for your child in the scullery, or in the passage where they clean the boots, where the footman allows his little boy to play.' He turned back to his army, no longer interested in this desperate woman, so ragged and old before her time.

'There, you see. You have heard it from the child himself.'

She turned to find Harold standing in the doorway, still dressed in his breeches and boots. 'I thought my mother might make an attempt to contact you. Constance wanted to keep you away, but I knew I could rely upon my boy to make the right decision.' His wife joined him, removing her grey gloves and placing them in her reticule. 'So we have come to a pretty pass when a maidservant might enter a gentleman's house for the purpose of kidnapping his son.'

'I only ask for what is rightfully mine, sir,' said Biddy, standing protectively before the boy.

Harold appeared puzzled. He searched the ceiling, looking for an answer. 'Rightfully yours? Where is the paper that assigns my son to you? There are no documents or proofs of any kind to suggest that this boy is in any way connected to you or your family, if you should have such a thing.'

'He has his father's grey eyes, sir.' She shielded him still.

'And you believe that this is enough evidence to mark him as your flesh and blood? Perhaps in your world it is all that is required, but this, madam, is Clare House, which has stood since the reign of James II, and my son, *my son,* madam, will take forth the family name to breed a great dynasty once more, because it is his rightful inheritance to do so.'

'Except that he cannot,' said Biddy, seizing the boy and raising him to her waist.

'Then I wish you would enlighten me as to the reason,' said Harold, the flush of rising anger colouring his cheeks.

'Because, sir, even you must have noticed the signs in his nature by now,' Biddy replied. 'He has his father's eyes. The eyes of my poor brother.'

Harold's mouth dropped. Constance Connaught looked as if she might fall at any second. 'You told me the father was Edward Chatham, who is a fine gentleman,' she whispered.

'I said no such thing, Madam. You made the assumption yourself. My brother George suffers from an incurable madness, and is but fit to work in the gardens at Bly. The only thing Thomas can inherit is his insanity.'

Biddy left the house with her child. Thomas was shocked by the ease with which his adoptive parents relinquished their claim on him. As Biddy reached the open doors to the drive, she felt the boy pull to her chest.

'Are you really my mother?' asked Thomas.

'Yes, I am,' Biddy replied, feeling his growing warmth through her coat.

'Then I suppose I must go with you, even though I am to be mad.' His eyes were cast down.

'I think perhaps you will not be so,' she answered him. 'George is my step-brother. He had a moment of terrible weakness, which is the source of all trouble between us, but he is otherwise healthy in mind and body. It is true that your parentage is unnatural, but madness requires something more to draw it out. The solitary life at Clare House would most likely be your greatest cause of harm. I shall not leave you so unloved and unprotected.' She looked ahead to the greenwood, and the clearing where a bundle of rags lay buried, then turned to her son. 'I hope you will come to understand, Thomas, that the lives we lead are not always at the mercy of heredity.'

Her smile held just enough hope for both of them.

let's have some fun

'This could be the answer to your problems, Steve.'

Gabriel leaned across his keyboard, tilting the screen in his direction and moving Steve to one side in a manner that suggested he would prefer his colleague to move altogether. 'It's a new one on me, but it sounds like what you're looking for.'

The dayglo banner bounced back and forth across his screen. *Let's Have Some Fun!* On either side of the banner, a pair of big-bosomed girls jiggled spastically in a parody of enticement. A green and red logo bounced into the centre of the screen: *Hot Targets*. 'I know it doesn't look very sophisticated, but I heard it's a very cool idea.'

The office was almost empty because it was mid-August, and most employees had kids. Steve was marking time until six o'clock. Staff at Penning-Karshall weren't supposed to go online for any other purpose than business, but everyone did. Steve was temping because his own software game design business was quietly imploding and he needed some money quickly, even if it meant working for a company as deathly boring as this.

He had spent most of the week messing around on the net, but was careful enough not to download anything traceable or sticky. He loved to gamble online, and lately the pastime had turned into an addiction. Now he owed just over £3,650 and trying to win it back seemed like the only option left open to him. The odds of virtual dice and card games were rigged; he needed something where they could be balanced through the employment of skill.

Steve knew he must have looked bored to anyone passing, but Gabriel took boredom to a whole new level. The guy looked like he hadn't had a drink of water in years. He probably smelled bad; Steve was careful never to get that close. He treated Gabriel with total contempt, and the geek bounced back like a lonely puppy. He seemed to do no work at all. As soon as he found out that Steve designed games in his other life, he started bombarding him with jokes and funny jpegs and footage of dumb oblong-state students hitting each other on the head with planks. There seemed to be no way of stopping him, so Steve gave him a task: *find me a way to make fast money on the net*. And now Gabe reckoned he had actually come up with something.

Let's Have Some Fun! turned out to be a paintball-challenge website featuring the giggling bikini-clad girls of the home page running through a forest live online. You were the paintballer, and followed close behind them, chasing them between the trees until you could unleash a volley that splattered across their wiggling butts. Five shots for a pound, twenty back if you got three hits. *A good marksman should be able to hit a woodcock in flight through those trees,* thought Steve. Catching some top-heavy Essex girl thundering through ferns should be a piece of cake. 'Let's try it out,' he said, logging in.

'The company will be able to trace that,' Gabriel warned.

'Like I'm going to be here in a month's time,' said Steve, tapping in the credit card details he had borrowed from the unsuspecting idiot at the next desk who had a habit of leaving his wallet inside his jacket on the back of the chair.

'Let's Have Some Fun!' The banner scrolled down the page,

and suddenly he was standing at the edge of a wood, not a computer graphic but somewhere real, with a bored and rather cold-looking bikini blonde waiting to take instruction. In one corner of the screen a paint-bar appeared, while in another a clock began to tick down. Steve hit the direction keys and the screen moved forward. With a false-sounding giggle, the girl turned and ran, diving into the ferny undergrowth of the wood.

'I wonder how it works,' Gabriel wondered.

'It's just a webcam strapped on the helmet of a site technician,' said Steve. 'A pretty straightforward interface, but you're relying on a human being to react at the other end, and that means human error. Damn, she moves fast. They might have built in a time lag. I need a joystick.'

On the screen, the girl turned and teased him. He aimed and hit the space bar, firing. Yellow paint spattered the trunk of an oak tree as the girl laughed and darted away. He charged forward, aiming more carefully this time, but the blonde swerved at the last moment and his paintball went wide, landing in some ferns. A third shot also went astray.

'She must know every fucking tree in the forest,' said Steve, frustrated. A sign rolled across the screen: Want To Go Again? 'You bet your ass I do.'

Gabriel was trying to attract his attention. 'Can I have a go?' he asked pathetically. 'After all, I found the site.'

'Knock yourself out.' Steve pointed to another terminal. For the next hour they played and were defeated. The girls were regularly replaced with others stationed in different parts of the wood, so they never grew tired or got lost. After a while, Steve could discern different areas of the terrain, a fern-covered slope, a dense patch of beech trees, an area of elderberry bushes and scrub. 'This is real time,' he said. 'Look, it's getting dark outside, and the sun is setting behind those trees on the screen. It's a little lighter there, so I'd say the site is further south.'

Gabriel was growing bored, and started to pack away his paperwork. 'It looks easy but it's some kind of trick,' he moaned.

'Someone has thought this through very carefully,' Steve complained, but could not keep a tone of admiration from his voice. 'If we could find out where they're filming this I could grid it from a Google map and pin down the layout.' He had spent over fifty pounds already.

'The girls know what's going to happen in advance.' Gabriel closed his briefcase but hovered by the desk, peering over. The game was proving very addictive.

'How can they? This is live, look, I move forward, then left, the paintballer is being fed my movements, but I think she's getting my actions slightly ahead of her pursuer, so he makes sure that she has a head start. Not one – I bloody haven't hit one of them.'

'Yeah, well – goodnight.' Gabriel headed for the door. He could see he was being ignored, but was used to that particular sensation.

'But I can get this.' Steve hunched closer to the screen. 'Human error is the key. I have to deceive them into thinking I'm moving in a different direction, that's all. Then we'll see who starts losing money.'

It was almost dark now, and suddenly the bikini girls were running in torch-helmets, like deer scattering before hunters. It was almost impossible to see. After a few more minutes he gave up.

The next morning he called in sick, and started playing the *Hot Targets* from home. The real-time aspect of the game made it impossible to log notes, and now it looked as if they were playing in a different woodland area altogether. The designers were probably running the site without permission to use the land, and had to keep on the move. Steve wished he'd thought of this little money-spinner first.

During the second hour of the morning he got his first hit, a bright pink splatter of paint on a girl's thigh. She squealed with mock delight as a *HIT!* logo popped on, then pouted at him and giggled, running off-screen, to be replaced by a different girl. What made the damned thing so tricky was the sheer impossibility of making predictions. This was no platform game, where every character moved within the same instices; they were real people who could think for themselves, so he was directly pitting his wits and reactions against theirs.

After another half-hour he made a few more hits, and the satisfaction kept him going, even though he was still losing money. The weekend was approaching, and he knew that he would continue to play.

By the middle of Saturday afternoon he could identify quite a few of the girls, although fresh ones appeared all the time. He figured they would be easy enough to hire. There was no speaking involved in the job, so they were probably migrant workers. Now he was breaking even, and getting vicarious pleasure from spraying their thighs and buttocks with different coloured paints.

By early evening he was winning, and was able to carry his total points over to the next day's game. On Sunday, however, there was a new twist. He received an email from *The Team At Hot Targets!* offering a new game that, they said, was already proving popular in the US, the chance to hunt ducks and deer with the rifle of his choice. The thought of internet game-hunting was kind of repulsive, so he went back to paintballing, telling himself that he would just play until he was in credit.

Inevitably, it went on far beyond that. He played until they owed him over £760. When he hit £800 he received another email: *Congratulations – You are this month's top scorer.* At £1,000 he received another: *To collect your winnings, call this number.* He did so, and two days later was sent a cheque.

Realising that he could keep up the pressure and eventually clear his debts, Steve gave up his dull temping job and devoted the next few days to winning. He reached the point where many of the bikini-babes finger-waved at his screen when they realised who was playing. Suddenly it was no longer just about the money, but meeting girls. In fact, the closest he had come to dating in ages was through the game. Gabriel came around and watched in awestruck, hero-worshipping silence as he raised his score.

One day he received an email from the team, inviting him to attend the launch party of another new service. That windy Saturday night, the invitation brought him to a brick factory leased as a party venue, just beyond the end of the Dockland Light Railway line. The bouncers admitted him into the bare concrete foyer, and one of the bikini-babes handed him a protective vest and a plastic glass filled with champagne before sliding open the door to the main hall and closing it behind him.

Steve found himself in a maze of black-painted, ultraviolet-illuminated corridors that ran off in every direction. Above him, a familiar electronic voice boomed a countdown to zero, and then bellowed the phrase he had heard so many times before, 'Let's have some fun!'

Laser hunts went out in the nineties, he thought, disappointed, before realising that he hadn't been given a gun.

'It's a very impressive site, and he makes a lot of money on it,' said Gabriel, who was trying, unsuccessfully, to impress his new boss after work. When his contract at Penning-Karshall had ended, he had transferred to their sister office in Houston, Texas, although this sounded more exciting than it really was, because he handled their invoicing queries in a windowless office which he never left before dark.

'We had paintballing sites here a couple years back and they were nothing to get excited over,' said Tyler, tipping back his chair and attempting to regard the obsequious little Englishman with anything other than pity. 'I've seen these guys. I tried their deer-hunting site, but it was nothing like the real thing. Small beer.'

Thinking that showing an interest might encourage his employee to go away, the Texan clicked through to *Top Targets'* latest game.

'One thousand dollars for three shots?' Tyler whooped. 'Damn, this is more like it.' Punching in his password, he armed himself with the most powerful virtual hunting rifle on the rack and began to track down the panic-stricken guy who was pounding through the black corridors with a day-glow target on his back. It was only when Steve looked back in terror that Gabriel recognised his old colleague.

'Don't shoot him in the head,' said Gabriel. 'Go for the backs of his fucking legs and really make it last.'

forcibly bewitched

Magnus Peregrine had been expecting to discover the spell in the damp-fattened pages of an old leather-bound book, but was surprised to find it turning up on an appallingly misspelled website put together by some lonely loser student in a Louisiana suburb. The site – too gloriously tacky to be ironic – was peppered with library woodcuts of goats' heads and pentacles. It hosted a section on third-rate heavy metal bands and another created by the webmaster's mother, who was touting tarot readings, online fortune telling and candle art from some address that looked suspiciously like a trailer park. Under a section labelled *Merchandise*, one of the blogger's geeky blimp classmates was trying to sell bullfrogs for use in 'mistical rytes' (*sic*). To make matters worse, the entire site was written in red lettering on a slime-green background, making it all but illegible.

Magnus persevered because, against all expectations, the boy had listed an unusual keyword in his hotlinks. The English version of the term for which he had been searching, or at least its nearest equivalent, was *Kezxetliani*, and had apparently been formulated by Romanian gypsies to denote a form of Apocrypha rarely transcribed in print but often used in vocal incantations by village seniors, specifically to open paths between this world and a specific plane of dark magic.

Magnus Peregrine thought it would most likely lead nowhere, but was nevertheless worth a try. At this point, he was ready to try anything. His masculinity had been maligned, and he had to act fast to save his reputation, even if it involved casting a spell found on a website. As the longest-serving lecturer at The Institute of Alternative Expertise, he prided himself on his open mind, for he remained convinced that strange discoveries could still be made in the unlikeliest of places.

'The original Institute for Advanced Study at Princeton was founded in 1930,' Magnus told his students, 'and counted Albert Einstein among its earliest members. An intellectual hothouse for the world's most advanced brains, it was dedicated to the leisurely contemplation of anthropology, astronomy, philosophy, physics, history, politics, sociology and anything else that might throw some light on the order and interpretation of the world. Without classes or curriculum, it continues to allow its members free rein in their attempts to create a unified theory of everything.'

In other words, if they wished to spend thirty years of their lives studying string theory (which many of them did), so be it. If the glue that bound the universe together could be analysed and understood in just thirty years, it would be deemed a fantastic result, even more so if the government could use the findings to create new weapons.

However, few students knew that in 1946, a secondary establishment was founded just outside a small village called Canterley in Hertfordshire, England, in one of the area's country houses that had been used by army officers during the war, and subsequently sold to the government. The Institute of Alternative Expertise had seemed like a good idea in postwar years, having been created to augment the Princeton institute's orthodox think-tank with complementary studies in less respected fields, like folk medicine and unexplained phenomena. This secondary institute maintained a status comparable to the one a technical college holds against a university, and had now been disowned by its older sister for producing results that were unquantifiable and faintly ridiculous.

The problem was that it attracted students who had been kicked out of other colleges for being a disruptive influence, the ones who had drifted into arcane studies because they had not proven successful at anything else. The Thatcher government withdrew its funding of the college in 1982, and unsuccessfully tried to have the estate sold off. Since then the institute had been financed by student legacies and private means. So it remained in Canterley, unnoticed and unhindered, right up to the present day.

At about this time, the IAE had attracted Magnus Peregrine, who had heard about it from some friends he had made on a somewhat drug-addled camping trip to Machu Picchu.

In his early twenties, Magnus had wasted most of his father's trust fund financing attempts to locate and contact mystical communities. His parents had been hippies, which was why he'd been stuck with a name that sounded as if it belonged to a second-rate wizard, and as he had not known what to do with his life, he'd decided to follow the path of his nomenclature and become an expert in the satanic arts. However, this chosen career had proven somewhat tricky to pin down, and instead he'd wasted time and cash traipsing across the globe in search of something so elusive and indefinable that he'd all but given up hope of finding it.

He soon abandoned wizardry to become a serial Lothario, romancing young girls, promising fidelity for ever and blithely impaling them before moving on. This was to become his second favourite occupation (the first being the making of endless lists detailing slights and grudges, imaginary and real). He became adept at screening indignant calls, and retreating across streets with anxious female pleas in his ears. As he once admitted in his restaurant criticism column in the *Guardian*, he loved the preparation of the meal, but never stuck around for the washing-up. As his sense of self-preservation was more developed than his conscience, Magnus realised that when you no longer care about hurting the feelings of others you can do anything you want.

Magnus began writing for newspapers, and became a food critic, an art critic, a style critic. What he knew about each of these subjects could have been inscribed with a needle on the proboscis of a Red Admiral but that didn't stop him from having an indignant opinion about everything and anything. Besides, it was a wonderful way to meet attractive females who could be tricked to fall for a man with a glib tongue and a ponytail. After a few years of this hedonistic lifestyle, during which time he was fired by women he had bedded and who had now risen above him, he decided that there must be more to life than simply maximising his pleasure on a daily basis, and joined the IAE, where expertise from his earlier studies won him an internship (although, to be honest, becoming an intern at the institute was now fairly easy, where a lack of funds and the poor quality of the students had allowed it to become the St Trinian's of scholastic studies).

Still, Magnus had worked hard in his chosen field, English witchcraft, and had in the process abandoned the delights of sex and alcohol to become almost respectable.

Until the day he had fallen in love.

The whole thing was really rather absurd. Grazyna was a Polish waitress in the tiny village café he had once destroyed with a spiteful review. She had come to his office and pleaded with him to try another meal there. The chef had been off sick, and on the day he had visited, the replacement had not been able to cope. Would he not consider rewriting his mean-spirited article?

As it happened, Magnus would – for a price. But Grazyna had refused to go to bed with him, even to save the reputation of her father's restaurant. He had cajoled and begged and attempted to bribe her with offers of lavish dinners in London, and the more he had offered, the more she had politely but firmly refused him. He knew she needed money, and was working long hours to pay her brother's tuition fees, which made her vulnerable. And yet, for some unfathomable reason, she continued to resist his assaults.

One evening, working late in the institute's laboratory, he had seen her scurry past his rain-spattered office window with her arm linked to a handsome young waiter. So Magnus had written a second vitriolic piece ridiculing the café and its outmoded style of cooking, sneering at the decor, insulting the staff.

This time, Grazyna was ready for him. She posted the review in the window of the restaurant, where all could see. And above it she placed an extremely unflattering photograph of its author hanging out of a pair of sagged underpants, which she had taken on her mobile through his bathroom window.

Magnus decided to behave like a responsible adult and put his grievances behind him. He told himself that she was nothing, an invisible Eastern European who would spend her life working hard until her looks faded. He ignored the pangs of regret in his heart and forgot all about her.

He made himself a fresh list of goals:

1. *Get Grazyna's boyfriend fired from his job*
2. *Have café closed down on health grounds*
3. *Get its employees' work permits revoked and have them deported*
4. *Make Grazyna beg me for forgiveness*
5. *Get her to strip naked in public, then refuse to take her back*

It seemed that he would have to make do with mundane forms of revenge, until he discovered the website.

One look at the site told him that its creator had no idea of the power that had come within his grasp. The boy had scanned pages of spells lifted from God-knows-where, and had dropped them on to what was essentially a Goth site in an attempt to give it some *gravitas*. He clearly had no idea of the power that had come within his reach. The spells had been transcribed from a cycle of West Country oral maledictions as lost as spoken Cornish. Magnus copied the pages to his desktop, then prepared to perform a rite that would bring him revenge on the girl who had been uncultured enough to refuse his advances. His pride had been wounded, and he had been made a laughing stock. In order to restore his manhood, she would have to be totally, utterly humiliated.

There was just one problem. He could not translate the spell accurately into speech, so he took it to his local fishmonger, who was the Romany son of an old Cornishman, and swore he understood the ancient dialects of both his forefathers. Magnus had met Anthony Penrith on holiday in St Austell several years before, when he had been caught naked in Penrith's daughter's bedroom. The ensuing uproar had got him kicked out of his hotel (she was sixteen, after all) but Penrith had believed his story over his own daughter's, and the two of them had got blind drunk in the Green Man that night, remaining in contact when they returned to London.

'Ah yes, I think I understand,' said Penrith, who radiated little confidence that he did anything of the sort. He wiped halibut scales from his red hands, screwed up one thyroidal eye and scanned the pages. 'This is for opening a drain.'

'What on earth do you mean?' asked Magnus, already regretting his decision to involve a local tradesman.

'No, not a drain, how you say, a walve.'

'A valve? You mean it's a portal.'

'Not like one on side of boat.' The Romany-Cornish fishmonger shook his head sadly. 'It is the kind that must be opened *wery* carefully.' His peculiar accent and fearsome appearance suited someone who spent his days with guts in one fist and a sharp knife in the other, even though the accent was provided purely to annoy tourists.

'What kind of a portal?' snapped Magnus.

'Clearly, you still know very little about the dark ways,' Penrith complained, eyeing an anaemic squid with suspicion before slitting it open. 'To get what you want, it is sometimes necessary to cross this world with the next. There are certain forbidden rituals which open the doors.'

This was nothing new to Magnus; he had been hearing about such doorways for years, but had never uncovered specific instructions to make them open. Real black magic had remained as frustratingly elusive as ever. He was sure it had been invented by village elders to frighten, to control, and to make them appear interesting to others. It hadn't occurred to him that there were easier ways of taking revenge on Grazyna, ones that did not involve the invocation of ancient curses.

'This boy – this *child* – does not know what he has discovered,' said Penrith, re-examining the pages printed from the website.

'So, how do I perform this one?' Magnus asked with impatience, stabbing at the paper with a fat forefinger. *'Destroying The Sexual Appeal Of A Spurning Lover By Manner Of A Pronounced Curse.'*

'You will need my help, and it will be dangerous,' the fishmonger warned. 'That makes it expensive.'

Magnus was growing queasy at the sight of Penrith slicing fish guts on a blood-slick marble slab. 'Can you perform this for me?' he asked.

'I cannot risk being there when you invoke the curse, but I

can obtain everything you need to undertake the rite yourself, and if you follow the instructions *very* exactly, you will have great success, I think. It is a very cruel rite, for it prevents the victim from ever being able to bear children, and it can never be lifted once it is invoked.'

'What does it do, exactly?' asked Magnus, dreading the answer.

'Why, it creates a poisonous creature from the dark realm, and when this creature touches his victim he causes a burning sensation down here' – he thrust a fish-guts-covered hand down to his crotch and gave it a squeeze – 'quite unlike any pain you can imagine, and it never goes away you know, just *skritch skritch skritch* for ever—'

Magnus inwardly grimaced. That was the thing about these ancient local curses, they were always designed to make their victims suffer horribly. 'Cut to the chase, Penrith – how much do you want?'

The fishmonger named his price, Magnus snorted derisively, Penrith dropped to a more realistic figure, Magnus agreed to pay the second half of the fee only after proof of the spell's efficaciousness, and a deal was struck.

Two days later, a small white packet arrived at the institute with Magnus' name scrawled on it. Inside were instructions on how to incorporate the enclosed incantations with the phrases Magnus had discovered on the website. There was also a lock of what he presumed to be Grazyna's hair, a badly typed-out coda that read more like something from an old recipe book than a spell, and more oddly, a pair of fishmonger's shellfish clippers, steel-bladed and razor-sharp.

Magnus rolled up his sleeves and got to work. His ire had been freshly stoked the evening before, when he had once again seen the waitress walking home with her waiter, who was ridiculously young – her age, in fact – when it was obvious that what she needed was someone with worldly maturity, like himself. He wanted to hurt her very badly indeed.

Night rain had begun to drift against the tall windows of the institute's science laboratory as he flicked on the lights and made himself comfortable at a work-bench. The curse required the burning of some basic chemicals (magnesium sulphate, sodium dioxide, potassium carbonate, blood, flies, an earthworm) and sent an appalling stench through the room. Magnus scanned the written incantation into the speech-mode program on his laptop computer, recording it in a variety of intonations and accents, just to cover himself, then left it running.

Absolutely nothing happened.

After an hour of waiting, during which time he resolved to threaten Penrith with a punch in the face if he didn't return his money, he cleared up the burned mess, put his computer to sleep, turned out the lights and was about to shut the lab door when he saw a crescent of emerald light forming on the bench where he had mixed the ingredients of the spell. The room filled with the overpowering reek of rotting fish as the circle of sharp green light completed itself, folding back to reveal something within. It was a small upright homunculus about a foot high, rather like a hairless weasel with the silver-black skin of a long-dead mackerel, standing on spined hind legs. There was no hint of cuteness as its glittering beads looked about hungrily and its mouth opened and snapped like a dying fish, revealing rows of tiny needle-like teeth. After remaining motionless for about a minute, it climbed down the leg of the bench and disappeared from sight.

Magnus lowered himself to the floor and tried to see where it had gone, when another popped out of the fiery jade circle and dropped to the ground with a grunt. It skittered after the first, then slipped under the desk. Another flew from the hole and hit the floor, sliding around as it attempted to gain purchase on the linoleum tiles. Magnus was still on his knees looking for the first one when he heard a fourth and fifth arriving. He looked up at the bench and saw the silvery homunculi dropping, scrambling, dragging, tumbling and jettisoning themselves from the portal one after another, and suddenly knew he had a problem. The spell had been left to repeat on his computer, and was replicating the curse over and over. He dived over to the laptop and hit 'quit', closing the program and cutting off the spell in mid-incantation.

Magnus looked back at the portal. It was still wide open, and the spiny homunculi were now pouring through. It was as if he had wrenched open a mains pipe that could no longer be shut off. The portal was a running tap that would soon flood this room, then the next, and who knew – perhaps the entire world, unless some action was quickly taken. The floor of the laboratory was covered with the little beasts, climbing the walls, fighting each other, scampering all over the floor, slamming into the doors, squinting, skittering, snapping, scratching, sussurating.

Then quite suddenly, as if on a prearranged signal, they all turned to look up at him, awaiting orders. Magnus recalled that he still had the remaining parts of the operation, the parts involving the rest of the lock of hair and the clippers, but held no instructions for their use. He had been so filled with wonder that the magic had worked at all, he had forgotten that he needed to direct his acolytes to attack. Digging into his pocket for the twist of paper containing the hair lock, he unfolded it and raised the curl between his thumb and forefinger, so that all the creatures could see it.

He now realised how the curse would work. When Penrith had told him it would render the victim unable to have children, he'd actually meant that these foul-smelling creatures would attack with their needle-teeth and slashing claws. It seemed an extreme form of revenge to take on a penniless teenaged waitress, but after a moment of regret he determined to remain upon his course, and prepared to see it through.

'Tonight,' he cried, holding the lock aloft. 'You must attack tonight.'

The creatures gathered closer together for a better look. As they did so, they began to shrink down in the same way that rats do when flattening themselves to crawl under doors. The portal seemed to be shutting at last, and fewer homunculi were arriving, but now Magnus wondered how they were to go about taking revenge.

The creatures grew more slender still, all the while staring up at the curl of hair in Magnus' fingers. In gradual understanding, they collectively bared their teeth. Then, after a moment or two of absolute stillness, they shot up Magnus' trouser legs.

At this instant, Magnus, the great charlatan and seducer, understood the truth about several things at once. As the sea-reeking homunculi reached their destination, and began to slash open his scrotum and bite hard into the tender delicacy of his testicles, a final list of hitherto unregarded facts flashed through his agonised brain.

First, he realised that Penrith had not forgiven him for deflowering his daughter after all.

Second, he guessed that he had probably lost a lock of his hair after drunkenly passing out with her father in the Green Man.

And third, as the searing pain began to scratch away at the organ which had caused so much grief to so many others, he realised what the razor-sharp shears would be needed for.

all packed

Stuart stared in dismay at the open cupboard before him. 'Am I to take cardigans, Daniel?' he called back. 'It seems unnecessary.'

'You'll know it if the nights turn out to be cold,' his partner called back.

'But they won't, will they?'

'They might at this time of the year, you never know. Just take one or two. Take your favourite, the black Calvin Klein. The one Laura bought for you. It would be a gesture.'

'I know what gesture I'd like to give her,' Stuart muttered under his breath. 'The sleeves are half a foot too long. She buys the wrong sizes deliberately to show her disapproval of me.'

In the last few months, they had developed the habit of holding conversations through walls. They always seemed to be doing different things. Daniel working on his evaluations, listening to the kitchen radio, Stuart downloading his beloved music and river-watching from the small perfectly square window in the yellow bedroom. With a sigh, he pulled down the stack of musty-smelling sweaters and chose one.

The scuffed leather suitcase had belonged to his father and was heavy even when empty, but he did not care for nylon sacks with zips. Stuart liked structure and order, lists and hierarchies, elements that had all but disappeared from his life in the last few years, except for an unbreakable regimen of pills. It seemed that as a man matured, his ageing process lost step with the progression of events, until it was barely possible to keep up. Whole styles and fashions were now passing him by. Television shows were populated by loud, crude people he had never seen before and had little interest in acquainting himself with. He walked along Old Compton Street, passing unnoticed through the next generation of self-absorbed Soho boys, and the rituals of the young seemed as secretive and threatening as Masonic greetings. Even children had become alien, transforming from miniature versions of their parents to glaring, hooded homunculi.

Opening the lid of the suitcase, he felt the padded lining of tan satin, a touch of quality from a bygone age. He was thirty-eight years old, and an old thirty-eight at that – he had always been more mature than his partners, and felt sure that the desire for calm and continuity marked him down as a duffer.

He wasn't sure how he felt about the upcoming trip. It would be like going away to scout camp, he supposed, placing socks and pants carefully in the corners of the case.

He raised his large crop-haired head, lost in thought, absently staring at the Herb Ritts calendar above the bed. Over this year's date, 1987, was a monochrome photograph of an oil-streaked man carrying a pair of car tyres, an absurdly idealised vision of youth and health, as if this angular male model had ever lifted anything other than bench weights at a white-collar gym. The image of the manicured, fetishised workman was incongruous and absurd. 'How many shirts am I to take, then?' he called helplessly. Daniel had always made the decisions requiring common sense. In almost every relationship one partner would be more lost without the other.

'Enough to get by on. For God's sake, do you want me to do it for you?'

'I was just asking, that's all.'

Eighteen months ago, he had undergone radiotherapy for a growth in his throat. The scare had been unexpected, and had upturned their life together. If one good thing had come out of it, Stuart supposed it had been Daniel's newly learned ability to operate the microwave oven. Before that, he had always been relied upon to do the cooking. He buffed a pair of smart black Oxfords and put them inside a cotton shoe bag. Shirts, trousers – he didn't care for jeans – and a carefully folded jacket all went in. Shaving kit, a framed photograph of Christine, his sister, two plain ties – what had he missed? He glanced back at the photograph. How young and unformed she had been then, before her particular fall from innocence, a pregnancy and termination that had divided the family. How lacking in innocence were children now, sealed within carapaces of cynicism, always so ready to show injury from perceived lack of respect. His sister was still a kind, decent woman, but worked as though the world turned upon her efforts at the office. Their mother was frightened to ring in case she somehow impeded the wheels of industry by doing so. As a consequence, brother and sister had been left alone too much, to find their own way in the world.

A decent book – something he could reread if it turned out there was no decent library. He grazed the shelves and finally selected a sunbeaten copy of *Bleak House*. Into the suitcase it went. The danger lay in packing too much and not using any of it. He had always hated waste.

'It's hard to know what to take,' he said, half to himself. 'I mean, it's not like the holidays we used to take in America, before South Beach became unfashionable. You won't be with me, for a start.'

'I can't, you know that. You have to do this on your own.'

He hated the idea. In the six years of their relationship he had only been apart from Daniel three times, all business trips. Loyalty ran in the family, and against the grain of life around him. His grandfather had never left his wife's side, apart from his war service, and had died just a few weeks after her, from no particular cause the doctor could find.

He looked around the bright little room, and saw now how cluttered it had become. There was hardly an item in the place that did not conjure up some memory of the past. A little Ford Prefect made from glass and filled with coloured sand, a souvenir of a fossil-hunting school holiday in Ventnor, a studded onyx box bought with his first pay cheque, his silver christening ring, reworked by his father into part of an off-kilter letter-rack, a green and silver metal train purchased in Cologne on their first weekend away. They weren't particularly attractive objects, but they remained symbols of continuity, tentative marks of hope and faith. They still meant something.

He decided to pack a few of the ornaments, carefully wrapping each one in a sock. Outside, sharp winter sunshine filtered through oak leaves in the quadrangle below, patching the threadbare lawn in puzzle-pieces of light, showing up dust on the bedroom windows. The flat was ill-fitted and draughty, but they had bought it together, without help or influence from friends and family. It was something they had created, like the hand-covered lamp on the bedside table.

Stuart decided to pack that as well.

His grandfather had loved to carve. As a boy, Stuart had sat at the kitchen table watching the old man curl thin shavings of beechwood shaped like the slivers of caramel ice cream his mother had scraped from frozen cartons for him. The pair of them had always been packed off to the shed when his grandmother's threshold of mess had been breached. They stood at the lathe together, turning table legs in the hut that smelled of iron filings and fresh-cut wood. To this day, the scent of the mixture summoned his grandfather's creased thin face to him. Stuart had taught Daniel how to make the lamp, and they had filled the tiny flat with sawdust producing this wonky, amateurish object.

He opened the cupboard and reached on tiptoe. Old computer boxes filled with photographs – he could hardly leave them behind. After all, he didn't know how long they would be apart, and was bothered by the idea that he might forget Daniel's face. The wall montages of their friends were needed, too. He began to remove the framed pictures from the wall and insert them into the suitcase one by one. He had intended to take just one or two, but ended by packing all six. For good measure, he added the moulting teddy bear he had clutched through his early childhood.

'You're taking your time,' called Daniel. 'You're going to be late. What are you up to in there?'

'Nothing,' Stuart called back, checking to see if he had missed anything.

'Don't take too much. You've got to carry that case all the way by yourself, and you know how heavy it is.'

He realised he had spent the entire morning deciding which clothes and personal items to take with him, and was stricken with indecision. Looking at his watch, he realised that he was due to check out of the flat in just a few minutes. 'I'm trying to see if I've missed anything,' he said.

'You can't be late,' Daniel replied. 'The departure time can't be moved, you know that.'

'We have too much stuff,' he sighed. 'I have no idea what's important any more.'

'You don't have to take anything, you know, just the clothes you're standing in. It won't matter. You can probably get everything you need at the other end.'

'I know we've only had the flat a few years, but this room

feels like it contains a lifetime of memories.' He looked around again, rubbing at his eye. 'Every room in the flat does. I can't just leave it all behind. If I do, what was it all for?' The bottom shelf beneath the window contained his alphabetised collection of music magazines, lifestyle porn, Daniel called it. Seized with a sudden panic, he began to load them into the suitcase, twenty at a time.

'There's no need to get sentimental, they're only belongings,' Daniel called back, a hint of exasperation in his voice. 'You have to think of it as a holiday, which is exactly what it's going to be. You never took your ornaments to America.'

'I came back from America,' he countered. 'I'm leaving this place for good. Think on that. You're going to miss me, for a start.'

'It's not for ever, you daft sod. If I thought you were going to make this much fuss about such a short trip—' Daniel appeared in the doorway, leaning against the lintel in that pose of sexy insolence that had first caught Stuart's attention on the night they met. 'God, how much stuff are you cramming into that case?'

'It's not even full yet. Room for a bit more.'

'All right then, what's it to be? Some of the furniture? Your grandfather's folding snack table? Go on, knock yourself out. Let's see you pile it all in, you'll be like a hermit crab dragging its house around on its back wherever it goes.' He came closer, annoyance evaporating as he placed his hands on Stuart's shoulders. 'Sometimes you have to scrape a few barnacles from the boat in order to make the boat go faster. You're carrying way too much luggage. All this stuff, this isn't our life together, this is.' He touched his heart, then pressed his fingers on Stuart's chest, the kind of corny, sweet gesture he performed unthinkingly.

'All right,' Stuart finally decided, 'just one more pair of trainers, then I'm done.'

'Good man. I'll be by the front door, ready to wave you off. The taxi should be here by now.'

But the moment Daniel was gone, he saw the stack of books in the corner, and his nerve failed him. When Stuart had been thrown out of his old flat, they had slept in the twin children's beds in Daniel's old bedroom at home for two weeks, weathering the silent disapproval of Daniel's father until his forbearance had imploded in an indignant torrent of disgust. Walking the wet February streets, they had stayed in hostels for weeks before finding the damp little flat that needed fumigating and treating before it was habitable. But on the day they had finally lowered their paintbrushes and moved in together, they had sat on the floor of the empty apartment and culled their book and music libraries, reducing two collections into one. The process required sacrifice on both sides, but they matched each other item for item, removing Chaucer and Pepys, Handel and Stravinsky, while retaining guiltier pleasures, the Philip K. Dicks and X-Men comics, the boy bands and cheesy old soundtrack albums, the inexplicable personal choices that had hitherto been enjoyed alone. It was a measure of their commitment, a gesture of self-denial that paradoxically opened a wider path forward.

Now he wanted to take them all, every last thing that they had agreed could stay in their shared life together.

'You are really going to be late now,' Daniel called from the hall. 'You always do this. Come on, Stewie, zip it up and move it out.'

He checked his watch; 7:10 am, which meant that he was due to leave in just five minutes. Danny, their dishevelled blue and yellow budgie, started chirruping and dropping on to the floor of his cage, scattering seeds in an attempt to draw attention to himself. They had bought him at the Parkway Pet Store shortly after painting the bedroom canary yellow. Canaries were more expensive, so they had settled for a budgie. Daniel hadn't been keen on keeping him in the bedroom, not because it might be unhealthy, but because he didn't like the idea that the bird might watch them making love.

Stuart smiled to himself as he reached into the cage and gently closed his fingers around the budgerigar. He could feel the tiny warm heart beating against his palm. Carefully withdrawing it, he slipped it into a paper bag and nestled it, chirruping, inside the case.

'It's here, the car's here.'

'All right, I'm coming.'

Stuart reluctantly closed the suitcase and managed to zip it partly shut, but not even sitting on the lid could close it all the way around. Worse, it weighed so much that he couldn't move it from the bed, no matter how hard he pulled. The damned thing felt as if it was made of lead. He gripped the handle in both fists, and although he could feel sweat breaking in beads on his forehead, nothing would shift it. The more he pulled, the less it seemed to move. He dug his boots into the carpet and strained harder, but now his face was hot with pouring sweat, and rivulets broke down his back.

'Let go, Stewie. There's no more need to fight it. Just let go.'

And Daniel was there again.

He wiped his cheeks with a white paper cloth, and laid it down on the pillow, although it was supposed to be dropped in the yellow plastic biohazard bin. He gripped Stuart's hand with his own, but the icy sweat made his fingers slip.

'Come on, baby, just let it go.' He studied Stuart's strained face and stroked the side of his neck. The Septrim drip was nearly empty. The nurse would soon reappear to change the bag, but Stuart's lungs were filling faster than the drug could clear them. His skin was as yellow as the walls of their apartment. The previous evening, Daniel had helped the nurse transfer him to another bed, one with a mattress that would prevent the sores on his back from returning, and it seemed that Stuart had become weightless. His wrists were swollen and blackened from the endlessly changed drip-needles. Two other clear plastic tubes hung discreetly from the bed, one to administer Valium, the other to take away the contents of his bladder.

Dr Mallory had estimated that he would survive the night, but had warned them all to prepare for the worst. It was just coming up for 7:15 am. Stuart's parents were attempting to grab some sleep on the plastic chairs in the hall. Daniel's father did not want to know about any of it. He was at home, furiously clipping at his garden.

It was very quiet now, so calm and white that anything dramatic would have felt unseemly. He was finally alone with Stuart – they had moved him to a private room in the university hospital the night before, more from fear instilled in visitors by ominous newspaper headlines than from concern for the privacy of dying. Daniel knew that they all thought the disease unmentionable at best, disgusting at worst, in the same way that cancer and 'women's troubles' had been mentioned in hushed voices by his grandparents. They could burn in hell for all he cared. His concern was for Stuart alone; nobody else existed any more. Stuart had been hidden for most of his life; now there would at least be truth in his passing. He looked back at the skeletal figure sunk flatly into the high white bed, and held his hand a little more tightly, taking care not to cause him any further pain.

'Come on, baby,' he coaxed softly. 'Let it go.'

Stuart slowly opened his eyes and his fingers.

He was standing in the bedroom, beside the great leaden suitcase. He released the handle now, stepping back from it. The lid would never have closed completely, anyway. He reached down and pulled on the zip, allowing it to ride all the way back and release the contents. Unrestrained, all his belongings burst from within, spilling out on to the bed and the floor, floating out into the air. Now that the suitcase was easier to move, he upended it, completely tipping out the contents: the clothes, photographs, gifts, music, childhood toys, tokens of affection and their beloved books cascading outward like released emotions, freed from purpose and desirability. He watched the rainbow colours tumbling and folding together for a moment, rising and hovering in the still air until they completely filled the room.

'It's difficult. You'll see one day.' Walking away from it all, skirting the iridescent scraps of his life that turned and drifted past him, Stuart made his way slowly along the shadowed hall. Daniel was standing beside the open front door, smiling ruefully in the light, pleased for him, but heartbroken. He paused to embrace Stuart for a few moments. He felt the warmth of his back beneath his palms, a solid beating life from which you could draw strength like fire.

'You're right,' he said finally, studying Daniel's eyes. 'I shouldn't really take anything else. I have everything I need.'

Then he stepped out into the soft and silent winter sun, the glittering sea, the sky, the sky.

old friends

I was reading about the increasing likelihood of terrorist hacker assaults on Supervisory Control and Data Acquisition systems in power plants and financial institutions, when I looked up and saw Margaret Rutherford boarding my 134 bus. The geriatric doyenne of so many English film comedies made her way up the aisle in a short cape and tweed skirt, with a pheasant feather sticking out of her cap, and a bundle of ancient parchments wedged under one arm. As she passed, one of the parchments slid out and landed on the floor. I picked it up and handed it to her.

'Thank you so much, young man,' she said, her great chin wobbling as she spoke. 'These are most important, for they may reveal the history of the state of Burgundy.' And she passed on by to her seat. When I reached my stop and rose to leave, I turned around and she gave me a little wave before readjusting her half-moon spectacles and returning to her studies.

All very odd, as I was sure she'd died at some point in the early 1970s. The reference to Burgundy suggested that this was Margaret Rutherford as she appeared in *Passport To Pimlico*, a film in which part of London is discovered to belong to a French duke. To be honest, I thought I'd perhaps drifted off for a moment, and forgot about it moments later, because I had a lot on my mind. The British Telecom clients were coming in to demand another revision on their contract that morning, and everyone was in a state of high stress. They had threatened us with their legal team and we were being forced to back down, so now our profit predictions had to be revised to take account of the added costs.

Andy Miller sat in the meeting pouring sweat from his scarlet forehead, his lips and fingertips blue with lousy circulation, looking like he was about to have a heart attack. As we left the room, he turned to me and hissed, 'I thought we had solidarity on this, Paul. How could you let me down?'

'What was I supposed to do?' I asked. 'You know their tactics. They'll just keep throwing lawyers at us until we fold. You want us to go to court and keep fighting until the costs drag us down?'

To my surprise, Jenna, our shared PA, sided with Miller. As she headed back to her work station she gave me a look that suggested she'd just scraped me off her shoe. It wasn't fair. I was working without back-up, trying to save the company from another round of redundancies, and got no support from anyone.

On the way home, I was sure I saw a young Frankie Howerd on the bus, or someone who looked very like him. His face, already like that of a dyspeptic bloodhound, loomed through the window at me as I got off at my stop. I'm not in the habit of hallucinating old British comics and film stars into existence, and decided I was just overtired.

I worked late that night. Anne gave up waiting for me and went to bed alone, leaving the room with a series of little sniffs that was her way of saying I wasn't paying her enough attention. What was I supposed to do? She knew how important the next month was to us. Miller emailed me at 11:15 pm. He was still in the Holborn office, trying to make sense of the figures. His wife had left him after a mere eight months of marriage, saying that she would never be able to compete with his job. Anne worked in corporate PR and spent her day barking at underlings until she was hoarse, but at least she got home on time.

I couldn't sleep. My sinuses were blocked, so I got up and left Anne in bed. It was half past five. I cleared my emails for an hour, working in the dark lounge, then watched a programme about the Thames flood barrier, and how it would provide no protection in future emergencies caused by global warming. I caught a tube into town, only to realise that I had left the office keys in my other jacket. This meant waiting until the doors opened at eight, so I headed for the Starbucks near Chancery Lane.

I was surprised to be served by a sleepy-eyed blonde in a sculpted angora sweater who was the image of the fifties B-movie actress Liz Fraser.

'You want froth on that cappuccino?' she asked, her threatening breasts jutting out at me as though commanding me to keep my distance, and I was reminded of her role in Tony Hancock's *The Rebel*, in which she uttered almost the same line. When she saw that I was studying her, she headed back behind the counter to busy herself with muffins that looked like mutant toadstools. While I was finishing my coffee, abstractedly staring out through the rain-speckled window, Sid James and Sidney Tafler came into the shop, arguing about a hundred-to-one outsider that was due to race in the two-thirty at Kempton Park. Now, I began to suspect that I was on some kind of practical-joke TV show, because they looked exactly like their counterparts, except I knew that both of the actors were long dead. They always played wideboys and gamblers in the films of my childhood.

'What, that old nag?' Sid was saying. 'It would have more chance of placing if my missus was riding it.' Their vocal intonation was pure 1950s as Sid laughed his unique 'hyuk-hyuk' laugh.

I knew there was an acting school somewhere in Covent Garden, and wondered if these people were trying out these nostalgic characters in public, but Sid James looked like his counterpart, a grizzled, bristly walnut-faced fellow with a nose like a small grapefruit. Tafler was a classic spiv, in his pencil tie and too-sharp suit. He even wore a little homburg tilted back on his head. Oddest of all, nobody in the coffee shop seemed to notice them or think anything was unusual. Then I realised why: nobody here was old enough to remember these forgotten postwar stars. I was surrounded by workers in their twenties. At most, they might have seen a film on TV one Sunday afternoon, some faintly recalled black-and-white Rank comedy that now looked a hundred years old.

'Where the hell have you been?' said Miller as I walked through the door. 'Did you know that Sky are planning to pull out of the deal as well? If you thought the BT lawyers were bad, wait until you meet the ones Fox employs; they'll keep coming at us in waves until the entire pricing structure collapses, and Ofcom won't do a damned thing. We've got until tomorrow morning to re-evaluate our strategy. Where have you been?'

'Having coffee with Sid James and Liz Fraser,' I told him, heading for my desk to look for a fresh pack of antacid tablets, but if Miller heard me he said nothing. He and I had been partners ever since we started the company in 1974, and we were both tiring fast as the paranoia of communications technology paced up around us. I had always felt it was too risky bringing in younger staff to handle the deals; ambition drove them to cut out the middlemen and go behind our backs to clients. Two weeks ago, Miller had ushered in a sharp-featured young woman called Natalia, whom he had introduced as our new corporate finance manager. My first thought was that he had been impressed by her no-nonsense attitude, but as the days passed, I saw how she flirted mercilessly with him. What had all the feminist battles of the seventies been about, I wondered? Had equality been hard won just so that women like Natalia could turn back the clock? If she'd picked our company to sleep her way to the top, she couldn't be that bright after all, I decided.

At lunchtime, I ran out to get a sandwich and bumped into Arthur Mullard, who was digging up the road in a collarless shirt and braces. 'Oi,' he shouted, 'wachoo lookin' at, mate?' I would have recognised him anywhere; there was no mistaking his broad, flat nose and his fleshy tyre of a neck, but I was forced to move on before I could stare further. He was one of a battalion of character actors from films of the fifties and sixties, where performers always stuck to one type of role: landlady or bricklayer, politician or doctor.

The rest of the day was filled with screaming matches and tantrums as we tried to get the strategy document finished in time. While we were waiting for the whole thing to be transferred into a Powerpoint presentation, we went over to the Deveraux pub for a beer, but I couldn't take my eyes off the barman.

'Does he look like Michael Ripper to you?' I asked Miller, pointing covertly at the little round-faced man pulling the pints.

'Who the hell is Michael Ripper?' he asked, annoyed at being interrupted.

'He was a character actor in Hammer horror films, usually working behind the bar in taverns, and he played the liftman in the St Trinian's films, only he had a moustache in those,' I explained. 'There's one where he's in Rome, and taps the thermometer and says "If it gets any hotter I shall have to take my pullover off."' I looked at him uncertainly. 'It was a very sweet film, gentle and funny,' I explained.

'Are you going fucking insane?' His thyroidal eyes bulged wetly at me. 'Our business is falling down around our ears and all you can do is quote fucking movies at me? What the hell is wrong with you, Paul?'

'I don't know,' I admitted wearily. 'I've been working hard lately.'

'We're all working hard, that's what we do, and we'll keep working harder until we retire and die, so get used to it.'

'It never used to be like this,' I told him. 'Remember how much fun it was when we started? We weren't doing it because we had to. There was still a stupid idea that we could stop whenever we wanted. I thought we'd reach the top of our profession, instead of getting stuck somewhere in the middle.'

'When you talk like that, you sound like someone who deserves to get fucked over,' said Miller, thumping his empty glass on the counter.

The weekend was approaching, but we always worked on Saturday. I carried on through the day without a break, but by 7:00 pm I had a migraine and needed to stop. Across from the office was a little park that stayed open late, so I went over and sat on one of the benches, just to take in some sooty London air. While I was there, three men in bowler hats and black pinstriped suits walked past with furled umbrellas. They bore a remarkable resemblance to Richard Wattis, Eric Barker and Thorley Walters, who always played men from the ministry in old monochrome comedies. While I was watching them go, I sensed someone sitting down beside me. I had been joined on the park bench by Terry-Thomas, the archetypal cad in British films.

'Now look here,' he said in the persuasive, treacly voice I remembered so well, 'you can't go on like this, old chap. I mean, it's obvious to all of us that you're living on your nerves. You're forced to work with an absolute shower of the most ghastly people, your strumpet of a wife pushes you through the hoops, your frightful business partner treats you like a doormat. It's about time you jolly well taught them all a lesson.' I looked at his bared teeth with the famous centre gap, and felt sure this was the real Terry-Thomas, not an impersonator.

'What am I supposed to do?' I asked him.

'I say, I'm going to be late for dinner at my club. Toodle-oo, old chap.' He rose and sauntered away from the bench. *I'm going mad*, I thought, *or suffering from some kind of stress-related illness.*

I tried to ignore the *Evening Standard* posters that read 'Knife crime soars' as I headed for the tube. Anne was still furious with me for working late, and had recently taken to going out by herself. I wanted to discuss the problem with her, but she seemed uncomfortable with the idea of sitting down long enough to talk things over. On Sunday I went for a walk beside the river. On the south embankment I saw Kenneth Williams and Hugh Paddick mincing past in stereotypical sixties camp outfits, lime-coloured loon pants, broad woven belts, roll-neck sweaters and corduroy caps. They sounded much as they had in the sixties radio show *Round The Horne.*

'I would have been fantabulosa in *Hamlet*,' Williams was saying. 'I'd have taken my part lovely, I've got the legs for tights, you see. I've been held back, that's the trouble.'

It felt as if parts of time were rolling back around me, returning me to an earlier English world. But how was it possible? And why was it happening?

I was still pondering the question when I arrived home to find Anne's letter. Her wardrobe had been emptied out, and one of our suitcases was missing. She said she had gone to stay at her sister's house in Windsor, but when I rang, there was no answer. She had left me before, but this time felt different. The house had been thoroughly cleaned, as though Anne had scrubbed out her presence from it. Part of me hoped she was having an affair, because I wanted her to be happy. I knew it was too late for me to find peace with anyone else, or even alone. I was fifty-eight, with no sign of retirement in sight, and not much hope of keeping the company afloat for longer than two or three years. My rivals were young and rapacious, my clients were soulless number-crunchers, my life had become a painful, anachronistic embarrassment.

When I arrived at work on Monday morning, I poured a bitter coffee and ate three antacid tablets while I waited for Miller to appear. Instead, Jenna and Natalia appeared in my doorway. Jenna looked as if she had been crying.

'Mr Miller had a stroke late last night,' she explained. 'He was in the office at the time. We tried calling you at home, but there was no answer.' I remembered I had not taken my mobile out with me.

'Where is he now?' I asked.

'At St Thomas's,' said Jenna. 'He has suffered brain damage because nobody found him until the cleaners came in early this morning. They expect him to pull through, but don't think he'll be able to come back to work.'

'I'm sure you'd like to go and check on him.' Natalia sounded keen to dismiss her new boss's tragedy in order to move on to practicalities. 'Someone has to present our revised pricing structure to Fox this morning. I assume you want me to do it?' She clearly thought I wasn't up to the job.

'No, I can handle it,' I told her, happy to wipe the smug look from her face. 'I'll go and see Andy afterwards. When are they coming?'

'They're already here in the boardroom.' Imparting this information subtly changed her features: the delivery of harmful information clearly provided her with small triumphs. As I headed for the meeting room with my laptop, I looked down into the street and saw a voluptuously fat woman in a black dress pause on the pavement and look up at my window. Hattie Jacques gave me a saucy smile and a little wave with the tips of her fingers. I jumped back from the glass, alarmed.

What did these *Carry On* characters from the past all want with me?

The presentation was a nightmare of recrimination and intractability. It transpired that Fox had come to cancel their deal with us, not listen to our new proposals, and without them, I realised that we were pretty much doomed. At 1:00 pm, the lawyers made us take a fifteen-minute break to regain our composure, and I went outside for a cigarette.

Now that Miller had bowed out so suddenly, I was the last smoker and the oldest staff member left in the company. I stood under the eaves of the building, guiltily dragging on a cigarette. The silvered rain fell inches from my face as I tried to recompose myself. I was wondering why Terry-Thomas had harangued me about my life when a heavy-set blonde in a shiny red rain-mac stopped before me. By this time, I wasn't surprised to see that it was fifties British sex symbol Diana Dors. Her custard-yellow sideswept hair and kohl-rimmed eyes should have had commuters stopping to stare, but nobody seemed to notice her.

'Honey, let me give you some advice.' Her lasciviously wide smile was a protection against a life of hard experience. She took my cigarette and inserted it between her lips, taking a drag. 'I've had my share of bad men, and I can see these ones are no good for you. They treat you like dirt. You're no nearer saving the company, and now your wife has left you. You've got to pull yourself together, darling.'

'Are you really Diana Dors?' I asked.

'Sincerely yours,' she smiled, quoting her famous autograph.

'Why are you here?'

'We want you to come back with us. You're fighting it too hard,' she said, rebuttoning her mackintosh. 'Just remember, we'll be waiting for you.'

'Who's we?'

'Come on, don't play coy, darling. You know who we are.'

'No, I don't. You're all dead.'

'True, we're from a different time, a time when nothing ever seemed to change and you were very happy. But we never really went away. See?' She pointed back through the glass wall of the office, where the cleaning lady, who appeared to be played by character actress Irene Handl, was gesturing at me with her mop. 'Chucking fag ends on my clean flawer,' she complained through the open window. 'Flamin' cheek.'

When I looked back, Diana Dors had vanished into the rain. I checked my watch and realised that the meeting had restarted.

In the conference room, I faced a line of tight-collared, black-suited lawyers a third of my weight and half my age. They seemed to move in unison, as if controlled by a single central intelligence, and I knew they hated me. They hated the fact that I was over fifty, that I smoked, that I had grey hair, a grey face and a grey Marks & Spencers suit, that my body was not gym-toned and my shirt had not been starched by a Korean girl. They hated me because I looked desperate and took too long to react. They did not see a man who had fought moral battles in boardrooms so that they could have easier paths through life; they saw a loser, and so did Jenna and Natalia and Anne.

Did they honestly think I didn't realise this? What I saw when I looked at them was the smugness and condescension of wage slaves who thought they were reinventing the business world, when they were merely trudging over the bones of the million exhausted workers who had fallen in the same tracks before them.

'To be honest,' said one, cutting across my thoughts, 'I see nothing in your guesstimates to justify our attendance at a new round of talks. Without Mr Miller, I can only suggest that we recommence at a later date, and at a more favourable level of negotiation.' They began to pack up their laptops and leave the table, and I could do nothing but mutely watch them go.

I went home to an empty house, defrosted a chicken tikka and flicked on the TV, which was running an old Norman Wisdom film. In it, the comic was skidding along a hospital corridor dressed as a nurse. I carried the black plastic box containing the remains of my meal to the kitchen, and was putting it in the bin when I glanced up at the screen and found Wisdom watching me intently. With one hand on his hip, he wagged an admonitory finger. 'I'm disappointed in you, Paul,' he said, using the peculiar hooting voice he reserved for playing females. 'I thought you were going to sort this out instead of sitting around feeling sorry for yourself.'

Before I could reply, he had moved back into the script of the film and was batting mascara'ed eyelids at straight-man Jerry Desmond.

Of course I wanted a better life but I had no spare money, and these days freedom came with a hefty price tag. The next day, I went back to the office and took on Miller's workload as well as my own. I kept my head down, played hardball, under-promised, over-delivered and did more than was generally expected of me. And still, ladies' man Leslie Phillips passed me in the corridors with a cheery 'Hell-o-o'. Over the next few days I saw a host of British character actors I thought I had forgotten, vaudevillians who had once been more familiar to me than my own relatives, all going about their business on the streets of the city.

On Friday evening, lost in thought, I followed the route I had walked a hundred thousand times before, back through the rain to the tube station. Whether the young man bumped into me, or I into him, I have no idea. I just recall angry eyes beneath a baseball cap, a punch in the chest, an indignant complaint, something about where the fuck I thought I was going. As his hand disappeared slyly into his pocket, I turned on him. I told him why I hated his spite-filled face, and the face of everyone like him who wanted everything for themselves right now, this minute, everyone who expected the world to change in their favour without having to do anything for others.

I thought the blade missed me when I saw it slice the air, and only realised that it had nicked my neck after he'd walked away. I raised my hand to the spot and suddenly there was a phenomenal amount of blood on my shirt. I fell in surprise, my knees cracking on the pavement, my eyes losing focus. A high-pitched whistle faded from my ears and my neck began to sting.

When I was able to see clearly again, I recognised Peter Sellers, standing before me, leaning against a pillar box. He was wearing an elegant black suit and a narrow leather tie. 'Ah, there you are,' he said in some merriment. 'We were beginning to think you'd never get here. Look, do you remember when you were nine or ten, and you used to sit between your mother and father on the sofa, watching television on a rainy Sunday afternoon? Remember how safe and happy you felt? Well, it can be like that always, you know.'

'My world was never as happy as yours,' I said thickly, the blood pulsing unchecked over my fingers.

'Oh, but it can be,' said Sellers.

'You want me to kill myself.'

'Don't be so melodramatic, of course we don't, we want you to live. First of all, press your fingers to your neck and stop that blood from flowing. Then simply relax, let your mind go and we'll do the rest. You've resisted all your life. Now it's time to stop fighting the world. We're all here for you, and we can be here for ever.'

He spread his arms wide and I saw that they were indeed all there, standing right behind him, every performer who ever graced an old movie from my childhood: Dennis Price, Beryl Reed, Joan Sims, Dick Emery, Dandy Nicholls, Peggy Mount, Charles Hawtrey, Matt Monro, Raymond Huntley, Cecil Parker, John Slater, Rita Tushingham, Stanley Baker, Charlie Drake,

Felix Aylmer, Joyce Grenfell, Reg Varney, John Le Mesurier, Alfie Bass, Lionel Jeffries, Bernard Cribbins, Terence Alexander, Bernard Miles, Esma Cannon, Arthur Askey, all welcoming me with encouraging words and open smiles.

And I smiled back, because they were my oldest friends.

It's wonderful here. There are striped lawns and rose gardens and trellis windows and overstuffed sofas, and pots of tea and sandwiches at five. The doctor is Alastair Sim, and matron is played by Joan Hickson.

Last week, Anne came to visit me. She hasn't been so often lately, because she got promoted at the office and has to do a lot of travelling to European factories. She finds the job extremely stressful. I finally told her about my old friends, and how they taught me to stop resisting, and to my surprise she took me very seriously.

She said she thought it was strange I should have told her that, because lately she's been seeing Abba quite a bit in Sainsbury's, and bumped into the lead singer from Boney M on the train only this morning...

unnatural selection

Me and Shezree wuz bord, wot wiv the rane fallin all week, an now it wuz the weekend, so there wuz no wok, an wen the sun cum art I sed lez go to vat nu park, iz sposd to be buetful wot wiv orl the plantz an flowrz an vat, and she sed souns lik a chanj wy not? We can afford it now cuz we robed a bloke with lotza munni in his wollit and stabed him an that. So we wen to the park at the uver end of the tarn.

And there wuz thez grate big irn gatze an it sez 'this is the property of the crown estate' speld lik vat orl wrong. An we had to pai to get in cos the blok on the dor wont let us in for nuthn, even tho I offrd to let him fuk Shezree he dint want to, even wen I tol him he culd cum in her marf, so we payd up wich wuz xpenziv and wen in.

There wuz sum old ladiz there on the path an wen we went by they got art the way lik they thort we wuz gona stab them or sumthin, but I sed its orl rite we are gud peepl but they stil lukd scard of us an made roum.

An there wuz a big trea biga than any I seed befr and Shezree sed lez clime up it but this old gard bloke chasd us orf and sez litl cunz get art of it. So we just lukd up at the branjez an orl the leevs makin vis noys in the wind lik sumwun rubin bitz of paypa togevr anit wuz buetful lik nuffn I ever sore.

An Shezree sez luk ovr here, luk wot I farnd lodz of fuckin flarz I aint nevr sen nufn lik it, so I goz ovr an thez orl veze flarz grone art of the grand, just art of dirt an vat, orl difrent colerz yela blu wiv grin leevs an orl. An thez this werd smel lik my mumz owl perfum she wore wen she wen art to fuk blokz, only itz lik itz cumin from the flarz.

The smel wuz so strong it mad me fil sik so I went rand the corner an fund a farntane wiv stachus and worta sparkling art of the top and runin darn the sidz, an orl we culd here is berdz singin an it wuz totali wikid. Shezree sed therz nuthin lik vis darn mi street jus brikz an brokn glarz an kidz trine to stab yoo for no reezn an corlin yoo a cun orl the tym. An she sed this lot muz be worf a fukn fortoon we cud cum bak an dig it orl up at nite and sel it on the stret. An I thort yer it wood be a gud ideer but a shaim az wel coz it orl lukd so niz tergeva in wun plaze, orl the bunjes of flarz and the shiny grin graz an vat.

An it wen on for milz rand orl veze lital parves and Shezree sed ow cum we dint no abart vis plaze? My ole bitch nevr tole me it wuz here. So I sed lez arsk sumwun abart it, an we wen up to the old gard bloke an sed don be skard we juz wont to kno wot is vis plaze? An he sed it is the qweenz park wuns corld Regenz Park, an wuns the hole of Lundun wuz lik vis wiv flarz an parkz an farntanes, an it wuz safe to wok abart wivart carryin a wepon, but vat wuz befr the war. I sed there wernt no war, an he sed nowun remembrs it now, he wuz probli wun of the larst suvivers, lotz of peepul got kild an orl the land got poysund, so they rebilt vis plaze so peepl cud cum here agane and remembr an enjoi fings az they wuz befor. It is a conservashun airya. An he showd uz a statew of sum soljer bloke an a rusti plak wich sed '*We must leave behind proof for a new generation that the horrors which befell our nation happened here*'.

I sed boloks I dint bileev him abart no war wiv peepl dyin an vat, still I wuz veri pleezd to cum here but I culdnt tell my frenz coz they wud cal me gai-boy and not bein hard an vat an they wud tri to stab me. So the old gard bloke sed Im glad yu are bofe brav enuff to cum an enjoy the park wivart been afrade of yore frenz yoo ar veri unooshal, moze yung peepl todai jus want to do there drugz and stab yoo an vat. He sed cum bak to the park anytime, but befor yoo go you muz see wun more fing the moz speshul bit of orl, and he sent us ovr to the treez on the uvva sid of the park and sed wate ten mor minitz an yoo will see.

So we wen over to the treez and just beyun them ther wuz a hole feeld of yella flarz, farzanz of them, with litl trumpit shapz an they wuz corld dafodilz. An I chekd my wotch an kep lukin at the flarz, and wen ten minitz wuz up vis music started up frum arta the graz, an it plade reeli lard. An it wuz a reeli gud band but I coont rememba the nam of the trak, an then orl the flarz started waving bakwod and forwod and spinin arand, an there petelz opend up and spraid culerd oylz evrywere and the leevz wuz buncin up and darn, cuz they wuz orl mad of plastik, and they started chanjin culer coz they wuz runin on elektrisiti. An the treaz turnd rand an they orl had fazes of telli selebritiz on them an they orl startd singin pop songz an that, cos they wuz made of plastik too an evrithin wuz plastik evn the graz.

An we wuz jus standin there wotchin wen anuver gard bloke cum ova an stuk a metl shuvvel rite in Shezree's fas and he nokkd her ova lik he wuz chopin darn a trea an blud cum out her noze, and he sed thatl teech yoo stupd litle cunz, evriwun knos there ant no flarz no plantz left any more ant bin for yeerz coza yoo lot, nuffin left but concrit an shit an killin out vere, so yoo got no rite to cum in ere this is a feme park for sofistikated rich peepl hoo wana see the dancing flarz an treaz so fuk rite orf, so we did, but not befor we cut him up bad an smashd evrithin up.

Wen we got art of the park an stopd runin I wipd the blud orf Shezree'z noz and saw she wuz cryin, and I sed wotza mata? An she sed I wontid the flarz to be reel that's orl, an I dint no wot to sai, so I put my arm aran her an we wen home.

invulnerable

I suppose I have always been out of step with popular taste. When my classmates went off to play netball after school, I went home with a stack of second-hand comics traded from the boys on my bus. Comics were always for boys. For proof, look at what we were stuck with, *Bunty* and *Girl* and *Jackie* and *School Friend*, articles on how to make a dainty purse and finding a boyfriend, while the boys got horror comics and monsters and superheroes.

When I got home, the ritual had to be carefully organised.

I would clear the small oak table in the kitchen, and place a cup of tea to my right, with a chocolate bar just below it, a Fry's Mint Cream or Cadbury's Fruit & Nut. I would square off the first comic before me and open it, solemnly reading from cover to cover (including all the advertisements for 100 magnets or an entire civil war army) so that its world entirely enveloped me, and I could no longer hear my parents fighting. Comics were my companions until I discovered books, and continued at my side long after. They provided solace and protection. Their panels were windows into a happier, safer, brighter place.

On the cover of the first issue of *Superman* I guiltily purchased, the Man of Steel had the head of a giant red ant. It was a 'Red Kryptonite' deal, and, as so often the case with DC, the cover was a dishonestly exaggerated version of the events depicted inside. Red Kryptonite was everyone's favourite chunk of Superman's home planet, because the results of exposure were always part of some unnecessarily convoluted and ludicrous hoax to teach Lois Lane not to be nosy. I loved Lois Lane because she was an argumentative, contrary woman with a job, like my mother. I tried all the comics, but always came back to Lois Lane and Superman.

I had trouble alighting from the bus that afternoon. Its design had changed since I last used one, and the doors trapped my raincoat. I looked about and tried to reconcile the road layout with my memory of it, but the old high street shops had gone – indeed, most of the street itself had disappeared. Where once the local shops had stood, there was now a vast shed-like building built of blue corrugated metal and glass, some kind of household superstore fed by a steady queue of fat families with oversized trolleys.

I wanted to superimpose the old layout over this view, to return the area to a state of elegant homogeneity. What had possessed them to carve away great sections of the terrace like slices of cake, leaving houses with bare brown sidewalls? The shoppers who waddled around me appeared to be functioning in a state of extreme medication. I had been a teacher for thirty years; what was the point of improving children's minds when their parents let their bodies fall apart?

Suddenly I was filled with doubt. Maybe I should never have returned to see this. I knew my old house had gone. The street had been diagonally chopped to make way for a slip road to the bypass that no one ever used. The remaining stub housed migrant workers who were happy to occupy the houses no one else wanted. Black traffic-dust settled over their front gardens from the bypass, killing the few hopeful blooms they had planted. I hadn't expected to see anything quite so melancholy as these sooty window boxes.

Superman and Batman had been the star titles of my comic book world, but they were expensive swaps. Beneath them were Green Lantern, Green Arrow, Wonder Woman, Aquaman and The Flash, whose villains, characters like the Mirror Master and Mr Freeze, were only invented because they made great cover art. When my pocket couldn't afford these, I bought comics that were doomed to unpopularity and failure, like *Metal Men*, *The Atom* and *Sea Devils*.

DC Comics also ran *Imaginary Tales* (although of course they were all imaginary), tales of what *might* happen in the Superman universe under different circumstances, the holy grail of this strand being 'Superman Red and Superman Blue', in which Superman split into two separately outfitted heroes, one red, one blue, and I loved this, but I now think it must have been about the sexy new costumes more than the plot. I didn't know any real boys, so drawn ones had to do. There was also a story called 'The Death of Superman' (the cover screamed 'Not a hoax, not a dream, but REAL!') that I was desperate to get my hands on but could not find anywhere. DC had got themselves into this 'Having-To-Explain-It's-Not-A-Hoax' situation because they had made their hero so invincible, his powers negated most of the more dramatic storylines, so the writers resorted to ever more elaborate ruses for their sensational covers. Superman was good, so he could do no wrong. He was invulnerable, so nothing would ever hurt him. And only the people with whom he surrounded himself, ordinary flawed human beings, could ever get hurt, which is why he refused to become intimately involved with anyone. He was the opposite to Jesus; everyone else had to suffer for him.

It was therefore possible to become fascinated by the

Superman comics for all the wrong reasons. Just once I wanted someone to not take his side merely because he was a good, strong man. Why should he be the only one who was impervious to pain? Lois Lane suffered, Lana Lang suffered, even Lori Lemaris suffered and she was a mermaid, for God's sake. Superman hid behind a cloak of righteousness, but actually he was a louse. I wanted to see how absurd his situation could get before something cracked. And I wanted that 'not a dream, not a hoax but REAL' issue in which Superman's vulnerability was finally exposed.

My disappointment faded when I made my way behind the main road. Here, things were much as I had remembered them. How could you explain the power these streets still held? On rainy nights, the wet pavements folded away the present to reveal houses trapped in the sulphurous lamplight that existed after the war, and conjured a thousand other residual memories: the smooth caramel-coloured paving stones perfect for roller-skating on, the water-carts that sprayed the dusty summer roads, the shunt and thud of steam trains above the railway embankment. The world had been larger then. Everything appears large to children, a reality of changing scale; when you're four feet tall, buildings have the power to overwhelm, and a rain-streaked alley can be as unsettling as a horror film.

On bad days, I thought of my life as just something to keep darkness at bay. But darkness, I knew, could always find a way in. It settled all around like the dust, stinging as it sifted into my throat, drifting into my eyes. Panic rose like bile, tightening my chest. Darkness always *fell*.

It had fallen through my life in clouds of night, dimming clear forms into vague, threatening shapes that stole my courage and crushed my few remaining hopes. Dr Murray said it was the pattern of the world, that civilisation was a cycle, like the death and renewal of forests, or crystals in a Petri dish, nothing more. It grew afresh and then crumbled into corruption, moving from what was right to what was left, and I would have to invent my own prescription for dealing with it. There were parts of my life, he warned, that would always be unknowable. But for how long?

After my thirteenth year I existed in the left phase of life, the sinister, left-handed life where nothing was safe, and civilisation was just a crust as thin as celebrity. The safety nets were whisked aside; anything could happen to people like me, and probably would. I remembered so little of the particular time that caused this. That was why I had come back here today.

Lois Lane and *Jimmy Olsen* were unfashionable comic book series dedicated to Superman's adoring sidekicks, and these were particularly instructive to me, because they took the hoax gambit to some kind of ultimate level. The Man of Steel played endless tricks on Jimmy Olsen to punish him for using his signal watch too often, although Superman's pal spent most of his time undergoing strange transformations like being turned into a human porcupine, Elastic Lad or a giant turtle boy. I had a weirdly erotic fixation with Superman because, unlike my father, he was clearly a stern Christian who hated anyone having fun and lived by lots of really strict rules. Nowhere in the DC universe were these rules stranger than in the Lois Lane comics. We were led to believe that Lois was an intelligent alpha-female who risked her life to win journalistic prizes, but she spent her whole time scheming to find a way to trick Superman into marrying her before she became an 'old maid', whatever that was.

In every issue, she would be humiliated, bullied, deceived and placed in danger by a man who was prepared to disguise himself under a rubber mask just to 'teach her a lesson'. Her spinster status was endlessly mocked. *Spinster* – what a damning word. Forever depicted in a pink pillbox hat, matching skirt and unflattering pudding-basin haircut, she would be duped by gold-digging monocled counts who turned out to be Superman, whisked back in time to meet 'suitors' whom she would regretfully turn down, or she'd get bashed on the head and have dreams in which she was married to the Man of Steel, only to find that her super-children made her feel hopelessly inadequate.

As an insight into the way men's minds worked, these stories were invaluable. Lois spent one story with her head in an iron box, too ashamed to go out because the Man of Steel had staged another cruel trick to teach her not to be vain. Sometimes all of Lois' friends were in on these ritual degradations, but were unable to warn her because they were being *watched from space*. I wondered if my father had played tricks on my mother like this, to get her to marry him. There had to be some kind of explanation. The wedding day, I realised, was always the last page of any story, not the start of it. I thought the idea was to meet your perfect partner and begin your life, not end it.

When you're a kid you only really read comics for about five years before real life intrudes upon your imagination, and your teenage years arrive. DC's storylines really began to flounder after the liberation of the sixties, and as our school went co-ed, so the comic-geek boys switched to Spiderman. But there were no real girl characters there, and the Lois Lane comic got discontinued, even though she continued to crop up in Superman comics, falling off piers or out of office windows, into his waiting arms. What was wrong with the woman? Did she have some kind of balance problem? Had she thought of removing her high heels before leaning over rooftops?

I had decided to come off my medication regime because it was making me sleep too much. Days, weeks, months had drifted past in a barely remembered haze. I was supposed to inform Dr Murray of such a decision, but knowing he would try to talk me out of the idea, I hadn't placed the call. Instead, I had come up with a way to exorcise my own demons that did not involve swallowing a daily drug cocktail to keep depression at bay.

Why not go back to the place where it had happened, I had reasoned, and see how shrunken and powerless the houses were now, in bright daylight? At least, that had been the plan, but the buses had run late, and I had arrived in East Greenwich an hour after I'd intended, when the faint winter sunlight was already fading in the sky, to be replaced by miasmic brown rainclouds.

I turned into Constance Avenue and studied the front gardens, the grey net curtains, the dripping box hedges, the terrace broken halfway along by a builder's yard. The Sunday school now sold pine furniture, but the houses looked much as they had when I was a child. Our family had moved here shortly after my brother's death, two days after my tenth birthday. We had been happy enough, although the house was small and my father had kept his motorbike in the back room, much to my mother's disgust. She waged a lifelong battle against germs, and eventually lost when they got inside her.

Kids are pretty resilient. The sound of my parents bickering on a Sunday morning was part of the background, like *Two-Way Family Favourites*. I still loved the house where I grew up, and cried when they demolished it. The most vivid day of my adolescence didn't occur in the house, but behind, in the row of shops. I could remember the high street quite clearly. Lynch's corner store, a butcher, a bakery and a chemist. On the other side, a toy shop with a model railway in the window, a dingy furniture store and a newsagent's, run by Mr Purbrick. He was thirty-five, and when you're thirteen that's as old as Tutankhamun. He hardly ever went out, and lived in the house above his shop, where the alley ran behind in permanent shadow...

He stocked other comics, too, shoddily reprinted monochrome boys-stuff that usually featured twist endings and cover art from Jack Kirby. The lead stories were always about giant creatures called Koomba or Zatuu, who were usually defeated by an insignificant bloke in a hat. Theres was something slightly sleazy and unsavoury about these one-shilling collections. My favourite British comics were *Dandy*, *Buster* and *Topper*. The best were the oddest, like 'The Jellymen', aliens who sealed people in unbreakable pink bubbles, 'Maxwell Hawke, Ghost Investigator', who uncovered ruses to scare people away from gothic mansions, 'Kelly's Eye', an amulet that protected whoever wore it, and 'The Steel Claw', which featured a man with a metal hand who turned invisible (except for the hand) whenever he was electrocuted. In order to have adventures, its hero had to walk into power cables as often as I crossed the road. I knew that merely liking these stories made me a tomboy in my mother's eyes, which was a secret code-word for 'lesbian'. More and more, I caught her looking at me with suspicion. The day I bought a pair of jeans, she nodded as if to say 'I knew it.'

A few months into my tomboy phase, my father finally walked out on us and my mother eased up on me, presumably because she regarded herself as no longer able to keep a man, and therefore a failure as a woman. We carried on living in the little house, and my mother cleaned out the motorbike room, turning it into a bedroom for me. For a while everything was fine. Then, seemingly overnight, she came to dislike me, and remained in a state of indifference until the day she died.

I was surprised to find the shop still there, a surviving remnant of an obliterated history, brought about by council vandals who had placed more value on an unused road than an entire neighbourhood community. The newsagent's was the only property still standing, a shabby brown-brick oasis in an acre of traffic-ruckus, tarmac and steel fences. When I managed to get across the road, I saw that it was boarded up and scheduled for demolition.

I had not been near the shop in all those intervening years, and although I was surprised to find it still standing, I was even more shocked to realise that it no longer held any resonance for me. Purbrick's was just another forgotten terraced storefront now, its windows shuttered, its door boarded, its past sealed away and abandoned like the Tressie dolls Mr Purbrick sold in tissue-filled cardboard cartons. This was not the cathartic experience I had been expecting. I actually think I was disappointed.

You always wonder about bad childhood memories: what would have happened if you had behaved differently? I know what I would have done on that rainy Saturday afternoon at the back of Mr Purbrick's shop; I would have left.

The attraction of Purbrick's, of course, was that he stocked the latest American comics in a squeaky wire turnaround rack at the rear, next to racks of Ellisdons' Jokes offering fake dog poo and dirty-hands soap. I hung around there after school, waiting for deliveries, annoying Mr Purbrick, who was trying to stock-take and didn't want to climb around a moping kid. From the money I now made buying and selling old comics, I could afford the new ones I wanted, but I still couldn't track down *The Death of Superman*, because I heard there had been such demand in America that it had sold out. By this time, I was thirteen, and according to my mother, going through a 'difficult' phase, which meant sticking up for myself and asking questions she didn't want to answer. It was pouring hard on the afternoon of the latest delivery. I ran to the shop in my plastic mackintosh, the water dripping from its hem on to my freezing legs, and waited in the store while Mr Purbrick signed for the cartons holding the American imports. I watched the wet world beyond the newsagent's awning while he opened the boxes and stacked the new comics into the rack.

'Does your Mum know where you are?' he asked.

'She's gone to the Co-op and Macfisheries, back at five,' I told him, swinging about on the stool beside his counter, beneath the ornate brass cash register.

He dropped a bundle on to the dusty floorboards and looked about for a Stanley knife to cut the plastic strap that held it together. 'You're waiting for *The Death of Superman*, are you?'

'Did it come in?'

'Doesn't look that way.' He carried on stacking.

'Oh.' I stopped swinging.

'Unless this is it.' He held the comic above his head, not bothering to turn around. The front cover of the fabled *Superman* No. 156 showed the Man of Steel in a glass box, warning his super-friends that he was dying from a rare virus that would require him to remain in isolation until the end. The story was called 'The Last Days of Superman'. My heart was pounding so hard I could hear it. I couldn't believe that this fabulous artefact was actually here, in the shop, ready to be sold just like any other ordinary old comic. I must have made some kind of noise that revealed my uncontained enthusiasm, because Mr Purbrick said casually, 'You'll get it ruined if you take it home in this weather. Why don't you read it here? I'm closing up now, so you won't be interrupted.'

I thought about the disruption of my personal reading ritual. 'No, it's OK,' I said. 'I'll keep it dry under my mac and read it at home.'

Then he said, 'I'll let you have it for nothing.'

There was a rusty padlock in place on the door to the boarded shop, but the window beside it was cracked. It was an easy matter to knock out a triangle of glass and feel inside for the door handle. I had assumed that kids would have wrecked the place, but as I shoved the door open, I was surprised to find it recognisably the shop I had frequented as a child. The counter and all the shelves had been torn out, but the layout was just as I had remembered it, and the wooden floor was untouched. With the windows whitewashed and partially boarded, it even had the same dingy light level I remembered, an effect caused by Mr Purbrick's habit of keeping the awning lowered and the lights off until he absolutely had to turn them on.

Standing in the shell of the old store, I began to wonder what I'd thought I would achieve by coming here. Memories good and bad were nothing more than memories. In an effort to recreate the feeling of being small again, I went to the back of the store where I had stayed to read the comic, and crouched in a corner. Feeling inside my jacket, I removed the comic from its plastic bag and, opening it, began to read. Back on that rainy day I had lain on my stomach beneath the racks, reading eagerly while Mr Purbrick prepared to close for the night, bolting the front door.

In the story, a Kryptonian coffin lands on Earth containing a rare virus fatal to everyone from the planet Krypton. Soon after, Superman falls sick, and the doctor tells him that in thirty days he will be dead. How far did I get on that rainy afternoon? To page five, where Lois Lane and Lana Lang are crying bitterly over Superman's diagnosis, or further down the page, where Superman ruefully bids farewell to his beloved Metropolis, in order to be alone and think through the process of his slow death?

How far had I got before Mr Purbrick placed his hand on my bare leg?

I thought it would be good to see how my hero coped with vulnerability. Everyone knew he had a problem with Kryptonite, but it was just a mineral, a piece of rock you could avoid.

Superman could bend railway tracks in his hands, but viruses were invisible. His mighty strength was useless to him now.

As Mr Purbrick's hand slid higher, his fingers probing beneath the hem of my skirt, I concentrated on the panelled page until the colours sang. I could feel his warm, ragged breath on the back of my neck, and knew that he was first crouching, then kneeling behind me. If I acknowledged what he was doing there would be a confrontation, and that was unthinkable, so I read on, falling deeper into the pixilated panels of the story as I felt him find the elastic of my knickers and start to tug them down.

As he lay in his glass isolation booth, strength ebbing slowly away, Superman grimaced in pain and gave orders for the final tasks that needed to be performed for the Earth, while Mr Purbrick gently parted my legs and positioned himself behind me. The gloomy store was silent but for the dripping of distant rain. I forced myself to continue reading, allowing nothing in from outside. There was only the fiercely coloured world of Superman and his friends.

I remember the final chapter of the story most vividly of all. Superman remembered all the women he ever loved, and burned a motto on to the moon with his heat-vision that read: DO GOOD TO OTHERS AND EVERY MAN CAN BE A SUPERMAN. Then he collapsed, and was just about to die when it was revealed that Jimmy Olsen, his best friend, was killing him. A piece of Kryptonite had become lodged in his camera, and as Jimmy had been with him all the time, Superman had been growing steadily weaker. With the Kryptonite removed he became invulnerable once more, and everything returned to normal.

I remained rigid, concentrating on the pixilated panels until I read the words: THE END. When I dared to look up from the comic, I found that droplets of Mr Purbrick's sweat had fallen on to my back like dots of ice. His arms were pressing into my sides, and something hot and sluglike was sliding between my thighs. A shadow passed the store window.

I examined the crumpled, sun-discoloured cover of *Superman* No. 156 with its rusted brown staples and creased corners, and read it just as I had done that day, lying on the filthy floor in approximately the same position I had all those years ago. When I reached the last panel, I closed it and looked up.

This time I saw what I had not been able to remember since that distant afternoon. Across the store, a woman was peering in at the plate-glass window with her hands cupped over her eyes. My mother had finished her shopping and had come here to buy cigarettes. She was trying to see why Purbrick's had shut so early. Suddenly she was yelling and hammering on the glass so hard I thought she would smash right through it. Mr Purbrick jumped up and virtually ran to the door, unbolting it for her.

When my mother pulled me outside, the first thing she did was slap me across the face. She refused to let go of my hand on the way home, and as I ran by her side in the pelting rain she told me that I was no daughter of hers, that I disgusted her. She knew what I had been trying to do and it made her sick. Her shame rubbed off on me. I was Lois Lane, tricking men into showing an interest, just so I wouldn't become a spinster. But that's exactly what I did become.

The day before my mother died of emphysema in the Whittington Hospital, I sat beside her bed, and she told me that I had once broken her heart. But by then, I could no longer remember how or why.

I rose to my feet and dusted myself down, then dropped the comic on to the floor. It seemed appropriate to leave it behind. Perhaps Superman could stop the building from being torn down, but I doubted it. His powers had waned now. Climbing through the gap in the boarded door, into the dying red afternoon, I turned to look back at the storefront. The building seemed to shimmer in the traffic fumes, then faded into flat colours and dots, nothing more than a series of bright panels separated by blinks of my eye.

The scene became the pages of my childhood, all dynamic angles and clenched fists, muscled heroes and adoring women, superheroes in dazzling costumes racing across the universe to perform nick-of-time rescues, making selfless sacrifices as they breasted meteorites and forcefields, caused planet-splitting explosions, confronted villains and lovers, full of grand emotions, bravery, innocence and hope for the future, because they were not just comics, they were us, they were me, always had been and always would be.

I smiled to myself and slowly walked away, knowing that I would never need to come back again. Knowing that things, even at this late stage of my life, could still be different.

There are so many ways to become invulnerable.

that's undertainment!

Undertainment
n. Film which is intended to provide entertainment and pleasure, but which does the exact opposite, to the point of boredom, then horror.

Utopia Destruction (Rated 18)
Starring Ben Affleck, Angelina Jolie
A crack troop of Hollywood film-makers travel to the most unspoiled sacred temples on earth to saw down trees and make deafening catering demands on their Nokias before leaving mounds of empty McDonalds cartons and Coke cans behind. The film is a gun-totin' action flick with an impassioned plea for global understanding and a covert Christian message tucked in it to appeal to Middle America. Affleck's hair receives a full-screen credit, its own trailer and theme song.

Unbelievable (Rated 18)
Jack Nicholson, Nicholas Cage
A small boy sees dead people, but they turn out to be movie

stars whose acting styles have become so coarse that they can now only play werewolves, supervillains or the mentally ill.

Death of a Director (Rated 18)
M. Night Shamalyan's fantasy tale of an egotistical pool janitor who thinks he sees a mythic godlike career as a director rising from a steaming pool of old 'Twilight Zone' shows. The twist ending reveals it was all in his mind.

Frat Smut (Rated 18)
Ashton Kutcher, Scarlett Johannson
The most unruly campus in California gets into trouble when the Dean discovers the mass graves of tortured Muslims under their frat house. High jinks ensue!

Antiques Roadshow – The 3-D Movie (Rated PG)
Keira Knightley, Hugh Grant
In the increasingly desperate search for a successful franchise based on a family TV show, Working Title casts Hugh Grant as an expert in nineteenth-century desk knick-knacks who discovers his latent superpowers after stumbling on a global plot to dominate the novelty ceramics market with cheap Korean imports. High jinks ensue!

Albert Barmy and the Warlock's Monocle (Rated PG)
Maggie Smith, Daniel Radcliffe and the entire Anna Sher graduating class of 2010.
The ninth in the series concerning a British schoolboy who enchants his classmates with dextrous use of his fairy wand had Albert magicking himself to the real Britain of the twenty-first century, where he had the living shit kicked out of him by unimpressed classmates. In this new episode, Albert traumatises

a generation of teddy-clutching schoolgirls by revealing his densely sprouting pubes.

Hats (Rated G)
Pixar's latest tells of a lonely trilby who goes in search of his lost love, a David Shilling Ascot hat, and gets set upon by a bunch of Nike baseball caps. Uma Thurman voices the hat rack.

Jurassic Park 5 (Rated 18)
Sir Richard Attenborough, Vin Diesel
A third island, Islar Esta, is discovered off the coast of Costa Rica, where John Hammond taught his more evolved dinosaurs deportment, table manners and the correct form to use when addressing a bishop. Hammond's dreams are shattered when the T. Rexes refuse to carry clean hankies and several raptors are caught downloading Dutch porn and Killers bootlegs after lights out. Hammond switches to human experiments after Diesel is mistaken for a stegosaurus.

Committed Concerns (Rated 12)
Susan Sarandon, Tim Robbins, Robin Williams
Susan and Tim are idealistic Californian activists who track down wise old guru Williams and discuss how best to help Gaia restore her earthly balance after the rape of the Madagascan rainforests, before inexplicably choosing to beat Williams to death with planks.

Jackalhead Goes Gonk (Rated G)
Orlando Bloom, Annette Funicello, Fabian
Having exhausted the permutations of comic-book characters duking it out in long-haul locations, desperate studio execs cobble together a time-travel plot that transports Anubis back

to beach-blanket-era Santa Monica. In the first of the franchise, perky Egyptologists battle pagan hordes of darkness by mocking their upper torso definition, and the Jackal God attempts to enslave mankind by dancing the Frug in a bikini.

Thing Man 3 (Rated 12a)
Starring: No one real
Thing Man, the popular comic-book hero, returns to fight arch-nemesis Man Thing, while his love interest spends her limited screen-time screaming to be rescued, despite having told interviewers that she is a feminist role model. During the troubled production, the original cast was fired and computer-generated to save on junket bills. During the publicity tour, Love Interest tells reporters that there's more to her than just a body, that she can't imagine anyone finding her sexy, and that she wants to end global warming by giving hair-care tips to Africans.

Who Are You Calling a Tosser? (Rated 18)
Ray Winstone, Jason Statham, Jade Goody
In this sequel to the flop *Did You Call My Pint a Poof?* Guy Ritchie directs retro-gangland Britporn set in the dog-eat-dog world of bar-snack sales. Six drunk men in Costa del Crime tans and Cecil Gee suits bellow 'Tosser' at each other over and over until they wet themselves with rage and pass out. Filmed entirely on location in the Gents' toilets of The Dog And Radiator, Bethnal Green. Rhys Ifans' credential-shredding comic turn as 'Darkie the Crack Dealer' will be praised by Richard Littlejohn and anyone who reads Andy McNab books on holiday. Jade Goody's role as a jumboid lap dancer who leads East End singalongs while crushing men's groins is a jaw-floorer. Already a cult favourite with shaven-headed fat men who drink tins of Special Brew in Leicester Square at eight o'clock in the morning and mockney directors desperately seeking street credentials.

The Angry Scent of Whooping Cranes (Part 1) (NR)
Tch-Hi Min, Tsui Hark
An elderly Ming Dynasty warlord makes a long and arduous journey across the great plain of China to discover the meaning of existence, but before he can reach his goal, everyone in the cinema has died.

Pearl Bailey (Rated 12)
Josh Hartnett, Jake Gyllenhaal, Keira Knightley
War drama in which the legendary black chanteuse is bombed by disgruntled Japanese fighter pilots, after the US makes her popularise a racist ballad mocking their difficulty pronouncing the letter 'L'. Rock's performance as Pearl requires him to raise his already squeaky voice into a range that only Patagonian bats can hear. European prints tone down racial slurs and redub Japanese High Command with funny voices from Bert Kwouk. The highly praised CGI effects take the audience all the way from the bomb-bay doors down into the soiled underpants of screaming sailors.

Rhubarb Fool (Rated G)
Jean Reno, Judy Dench
Crusty loveless schoolmistress discovers that her secret rhubarb recipe can help troubled villagers with their lives, only to realise too late that it also brings the dead back to life. Mayhem ensues. Miramax attempts to gain Oscar nominations for the film by burying dissenting academy members alive in hospital waste.

Flood-Plan (Rated PG)
Oliver Reed, Val Kilmer
Although dead, Oliver Reed attempts a return to film as a grizzled Republican fire officer who blames black people for being too fat and lazy to get out of New Orleans before a twister

hits. His strangled rendition of 'The Star-Spangled Banner' has caused critics to suggest that the future of film might not lie in Hollywood. Now available as a DVD with commentary divided into incomprehensible sections by phone calls, the arrival of a Chinese meal and seventeen bathroom breaks.

The Whisky and the Barley Water (Rated R)
Cillian Murphy, Liam Cunningham
Ken Loach's partisan look at the rebels leading the infamous early twentieth-century civil war in Ireland, or possibly Scotland, or Wales, filmed in incomprehensible dialect and designed to deepen liberal guilt about things that happened years before any of us were born. Subtitled to appeal to festival organisers and reduce audience enjoyment even further.

The Embarrasser (Rated G)
Adam Sandler, Courtney Love
Family fun as a young veterinarian discovers he has the ability to tell what his patients have been eating just by sniffing their intestinal gas. High jinks ensue. William Shatner guest-stars as a proctologist who doesn't wash his hands before noisily eating ring doughnuts and sucking his fingers. Also available as a bootleg Chinese DVD featuring a teenager obscuring the screen with big frizzy hair.

Eastern European Hostel of the Body Snatchers 4 (Rated 18)
Seth Green, Jake Gyllenhaal
Dopehead Californian teenagers head off on a fun-packed tour of Europe, only to discover to their horror that people smoke, drink and behave like individuals with opinions. Further shocks follow the revelation that not many people like American Republicans. The situation is resolved when

Glenda the Good Witch tells the boys 'there's no place like home' before gunning down a bus full of Lithuanians to make them feel better.

Rage: Penultimate Adventure (Rated 12)
Voice talents: Hank Azaria, Renee Zellwegger
Computer-generated space larks as Zwargs attack Barls in a distant universe that resembles the West coast of America, made obvious by the fact that everyone has big hair, ugly morals and talks new age rubbish. Realistic CGI first: Szwarlx has bowel problems after eating a stale planet.

SingalongaSeventhSeal (Rated 12)
Come along in fancy dress as your favourite character from Ingmar Bergman's biggest hit! Will you be the Knight, Death or the Chessboard? From the people who brought you 'Singalonga300' and 'SingalongaIrreversible'.

My Mom's a Darwinist (Rated PG-13)
Hilary Swank, Jude Law, Dakota Fanning
Little Dakota (eleven going on thirty-five) and her Mom have been looking after each other ever since Daddy was taken by the angels, but when Dakota overhears her schoolteacher-Mommy doubting that God created all the animals, she shops her to handsome Republican senator Law, who has her torn apart by stallions in the town square.

The Day the Entertainment World Ended (Rated R)
Everywhere, forever.
Ashton Kutcher, Scarlett Johannson, Diane Keaton, Nicholas Cage, Kevin Spacey, Hilary Swank, Jake Gyllenhaal etc. etc. etc.
Set five years in the future, this blockbuster disaster movie charts the horrifying implosion of major Hollywood studios

as their executives realise that the world's 'Audience Layer' has finally been depleted by their unscrupulous plundering of the world's entertainment resources. The movie's message, that doing things might be more fun than watching things, may be unsuitable for Republicans, Christians, the morbidly obese and the easily duped.

Poster tagline: That's Undertainment! The Shocking Secret They Tried To Ban!

afterword: Q&A with Christopher Fowler

Who are the writers you admire?

A partial hitlist would feature Charles Dickens, J. G. Ballard, Ray Bradbury, William Faulkner, H. H. Munro, E. M. Forster, Ira Levin, Virginia Woolf, Joyce Carol Oates, B. S. Johnson, Joe Haldeman, Peter Van Greenaway, G. K. Chesterton, Peter Barnes, Alan Sillitoe, Keith Waterhouse, Tennessee Williams, Franz Kafka, Daphne Du Maurier, Arthur Conan Doyle, Aldous Huxley, H. G. Wells, Graham Greene, Evelyn Waugh, P. G. Wodehouse, John Collier, M. R. James, Elizabeth Bowen, David Nobbs, Joe Orton and Alan Bennett.

You put a lot of black comedy in your books. Why is that?

It's an appropriate response to today's world. Black comedy, casual cruelties and embarrassments surround us. So-called 'weird tales' were something that every respectable author once turned a hand to, because it's a genre perfectly suited to short-form experimentation.

Do you think of yourself as a particularly English writer?

Not especially, although my love of language makes me one by default. I would like to be able to read stories from all parts of the world. After all, every country has its own lexicon of alarm: post-revolution French fantasy is filled with images of people losing their heads, and Czech stories feature slow death by suffocating bureaucracy.

What about dark fiction and the pulps of the past?

There's a certain amount of queasiness about early dark fiction because it extends from fear of the unknown, for which one might often read 'otherness'. Sax Rohmer's Fu Manchu tales are peppered with uncomfortable stereotypes, and Dennis Wheatley's once-ubiquitous witchcraft novels reflect the period's obsession with the idea that England might become enslaved by sinister foreign forces, although *The Haunting of Toby Jugg*, with its monstrous Nazi-empowered spider tapping the bedroom windows at night, still holds eerie resonance.

So do you advocate seeking out older works?

I think it's essential to read what's gone before, because each era creates the taboos most appropriate for it. William Hope Hodgson's *The House on the Borderland*, first published in 1908, unfolds like the surfacing fear of wars yet to be fought. Shirley Jackson's *The Haunting of Hill House* appeared in 1959, and unlaces the straitjacket of American conformity by bringing psychological depth to the traditional haunted house story. Ira Levin's *Rosemary's Baby* achieved breakthrough bestseller status by repackaging a pertinent moral dilemma – what are you prepared to surrender for status? Although most unknown fears have since been brought to light and dissected for us, individual stories like Jackson's 'The Lottery' lodge in the brain like hot pins. Writers like R. Austen Freeman and Peter Van Greenaway do not deserve to be forgotten.

So what's your favourite?

I would argue that Peake's *Gormenghast* is the greatest dark novel of them all. Death stalks the pages, the death of tradition and the melancholy end of all things. More recently, Susanna Clarke sprang a fully realised haunted epic on us in *Jonathan Strange & Mr Norrell*, a trilogy filled with shadows and portents. But the world is changing fast, and dark fiction can't always keep pace with it. With violence and poverty remaining, only the divertissements of the wealthy have improved.

You've said you like fiction to reflect life. What do you think life is about now?

Life is a moment between two eternities, or the reverse if you've ever queued in a post office. The pleasure comes from writing about the causeway that keeps us balancing between exhilaration and despair. But at least life is better than having your corpse hurled into a skip. This is what I concluded at the end of my one hundredth published story, 'Cairo 6.1', although it's precisely what happens to the protagonist. Despite everything, you hold out hope because you have to, not because it makes sense to continue doing so.

Your work is hard to classify. How would you describe it?

I've been erroneously segregated as a horror author, but I always saw myself as just a writer. My first novel, *Roofworld*, was arguably SF. Subsequent books were mostly satirical fables about urban life. I do continue to write short-form horror stories, though. The most upsetting story I ever wrote was 'Personal Space', about a pensioner being imprisoned in her own home by drug addicts, but the piece came from a newspaper article with a far more horrific outcome than the one I provided. I'm certainly no fan of kitchen-sink drama – I like stories that slip into strangeness rather than ones that faithfully replicate the ordinariness of life.

Are there still heroes and villains?
Yes, but they're also changing. In my childhood, heroes were sea captains and explorers separated from me by class and background. Now heroes can be anyone, from emergency medics to teachers. The villains work in morally unacceptable jobs and pretend life is not their problem, like people at arms fairs who argue that if they don't do the job someone else will. Likewise, TV executives will find arguments to justify themselves instead of admitting their opportunistic bottom-feeder status.

What do you like and dislike about genre writing?
I love the stomach-drop you get from truly emotional books and films, but they need an intelligence behind them to provide a kick. I don't enjoy the porno-dumb violence of *Kill Bill* and *Sin City*, films aimed at fourteen-year-olds discovering erections, and I abhor the misanthropic streak of much post-modernist writing, but I love stories that create fatally flawed humans. I don't appreciate the ghettoisation of the genre, and many of the stories I consider to be horrific do not fit into easy categories. Horror, like SF, has passed through its experimental golden period. I don't enjoy 'comfortable' mainstream dark fiction populated by vampires in black leather coats and aimed at Goth girls who buy cute scar-dolls.

What's your most biographical book?
Psychoville is the most overtly biographical, but elements of my life are present in *Soho Black*, which was written as catharsis, and *Calabash*, which offended my mother. My biggest problem arises in the choice of subject matter, and how to balance real life with Grand Guignol. I've written a more biographical book called *Paperboy* to explore this.

Have you noticed you often write stories in pairs or trios?
It's to do with not getting all your ideas into one story, and being drawn to particular styles that are worth exploring further. So I've produced pairs of bleak fairy tales like the Britannica Castle stories, and exotica like 'The Scorpion Jacket' and 'The Man Who Wound A Thousand Clocks', and dark comedies like 'Looking For Bolivar' and 'Something For Your Monkey'. If you look for recurrent themes in my fiction you'll find pairs and opposites, usually two characters complementing or cancelling each other's personalities. I tend to create warring forces within single characters and then split them into duos, probably because I worked with my best friend Jim for so many years in my day job.

What's your advice for first-time writers?
Fiction means you can make stuff up, you only have to write from emotional experience. You should never be ashamed of embarrassing yourself in print. And be prepared to think the unthinkable.

Would you like to see more film versions of your stories?
Of course. Who wouldn't want to see their work circumcised by a Hollywood director with strange hair, a really high voice and a world view based around himself?

Is writing hard work?
Yes, because it involves small acts of bravery. Authors might hide behind the patina of the page, but all prose requires a certain degree of honesty and the voicing of an opinion. Obviously, this places you at risk and potentially reduces your audience, although it never hurt any of the authors I've listed as an influence. Readers are intuitive; any of mine looking for a *roman-à-clef* should be able to spot that I'm an urban democrat who believes

in change and optimism and embracing difference, and has no interest in the Little-Middle-England mentality. That doesn't stop me from loving my home and writing about the English. You can analyse fears without spreading them, even though the *Daily Mail* will hate you for ever. And writing truthfully means you never have to apologise for yourself.

Christopher Fowler was interviewed in King's Cross, London